"ARE WE THAT IMPORTANT TO THE RACE?" she asked.

"I think you are," replied the general, seriously. "What happened to Earth—and you—has become a test. Will man end by killing himself off, or by surviving his tendency to kill himself off? That's what the race wants to know—and why the peoples on twenty different worlds pitched in immediately to raise the tremendous amount of money needed to find and furnish this world for those of you that were spared. The race has been challenged. The question has been raised. Can the will to survive be killed in a people? None of us dares face the possibility of an answer of YES to that question."

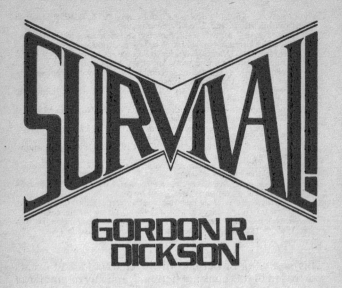

SURVIVAL!

GORDON R. DICKSON

**With Preface and interstitial material by
Sandra Miesel**

A BAEN BOOK

ACKNOWLEDGEMENTS:

"The Question," *Amazing Science Fiction*, May 1958, © 1958 Street & Smith Publications, Inc. Used by permission.
"Our First Death," *Magazine of Fantasy and Science Fiction*, August 1955, © 1955 Fantasy House, Inc. Used by permission.
"No Shield from the Dead," *If, Worlds of Science Fiction*, January 1953, © 1952 Quinn Publishing Company, Inc. Used by permission.
"The Underground," *Imagination*, December 1955, © 1955 Greenleaf Publishing Company. Used by permission.
"After the Funeral," *Fantastic*, April 1959, © 1959 Ziff-Davis Publishing Company. Used by permission.
"The General and the Axe," *Infinity Science Fiction*, November 1957, © 1957 Royal Publications, Inc. Used by permission.
"Button, Button," *The Magazine of Fantasy and Science Fiction*, September 1960, © 1960 Mercury Press, Inc. Used by permission.
"Rescue," *Future Science Fiction*, June 1954, © 1954 Columbia Publications, Inc. Used by permission.
"Friend for Life," *Venture Science Fiction*, March, 1957, © 1956 Fantasy House, Inc. Used by permission.
"Carry Me Home," *If, Worlds of Science Fiction*, November 1954, © 1954 Quinn Publishing Company, Inc. Used by permission.
"Jean Dupres," *Nova One*, ed. Harry Harrison, Dell Publishing Co. (Delacorte), 1970, © Harry Harrison 1970. Used by permission.
"Breakthrough Gang," *Magazine of Fantasy and Science Fiction*, December 1965, © 1965 Mercury Press, Inc. Used by permission.

SURVIVAL!

This is a work of fiction. All the characters and events portrayed in this book are fictional, and any resemblance to real people or incidents is purely coincidental.

A Baen Book
Baen Enterprises
8-10 W. 36th Street
New York, N.Y. 10018

First printing, December 1984

ISBN: 0-671-55927-3

Cover art by Alan Gutierrez

Printed in the United States of America

Distributed by
SIMON & SCHUSTER
MASS MERCHANDISE SALES COMPANY
1230 Avenue of the Americas
New York, N.Y. 10020

CONTENTS

PREFACE by Sandra Miesel

Where are the drifts of yesteryear's snow?

What force drives the flower's roots to cleave the stubborn rock?

How can feigned maiming of a wing ward naked nestlings?

What do starving prisoners share mouldy crusts of bread?

Who bids the standard-bearer perish that the banner should prevail?

When shall we conquer fears that we may cease to be?

Each living thing's survival is a miracle of tenacity. From the bacteria that dwells in boiling springs to the whales that frolic in arctic waves, this instinct glows in all that lives. Consciousness can only fan the flame to brighter blaze. Then concern expands beyond simple preservation and propagation to encompass the fate of cultures, artifacts, beliefs, and causes. Altruism may be the ultimate survival mechanism: we must literally "love one another or die."

Behaviorist B.F. Skinner claimed that "we do not choose survival as a value; it chooses us." Nevertheless, human beings do exercise a fundamental option—to cling to life or lay it down. Nor is this the perogative of a masterful elite alone. The will—and skill—to live can be fostered in almost everyone. But if choice is possible, how is it to be made and at what cost?

Mere existence cannot be a rich enough reward. We humans hunger for something beyond familiar reality. We long to see ourselves existing for some lofty purpose, pursuing some grand destiny. Can it be that we are here to know truth, love goodness, and create beauty so that through us the universe may contemplate the wonder of itself? Then, over us, "Death shall have no dominion."

In an age of starships and planet-searing weapons, an old Anglo-Saxon warrior's boast will still resound as bravely under fire: "Will shall be the sterner, heart the bolder, spirit the greater as our strength lessens."

THE QUESTION

The alien official entered the office of his superior with a film case under his arm.

"Well?" asked the superior.

"I'm sorry," said the official setting his film case down on what passed for a desk among those of that race. "Professionally, I have to report failure."

"Failure?" echoed the superior, coming upright suddenly behind the desk. He was a pale, smooth-skinned creature, very humanoid as far as shape went, but, of course, completely hairless and possessing one extra joint in each leg. "What kind of failure?"

"May I demonstrate?" asked the official, gesturing toward the film case.

"Of course."

The official opened his case, extracted the film

1

and fed it into a projector built into the superior's desk.

"These films," he said, as he worked, "were made by concealed perceptors inside a human redoubt that had been especially prepared with them. The men you will see pictured on them were deliberately driven toward this refuge and the films have been edited down to relevant moments and whenever possible built up by interpretive material by our psychology department. They represent absolutely the best we can do in this direction and they demonstrate our problem."

He touched a switch. One wall of the office seemed to dissolve. The two aliens found themselves apparently looking into the interior of a concrete-walled cave. It was furnished with human-style bunks, a table and some plain metal chairs. A wrecked cupboard sagged against a far wall, and a sink next to it had its water tap dangling and apparently useless. The image shifted point of view slightly and they looked out through one of the square ports in the front wall of the redoubt onto a bouldered slope falling away down into a little gully and rising beyond into a sharp, unscalable cliff at a distance of some three hundred meters. In the bed of the gully the boulders were enormous.

"This redoubt," said the official, "was on the far west wing of the original human line of defense, on Otraca IV, where we and they had both established colonies and where we both came into contact and conflict originally. The redoubt was abandoned early, in the first human retreat. By the way, I might mention that for all practical purposes, Otraca IV is ours, the only humans left there now being such as you are about to see. The perceptors were installed and the men driven toward it for the purpose of making this particular film and answering a specific question—now you see them approaching . . ."

*   *   *

The point of view in the projector was suddenly stepped up by magnification. Framed on the screen there appeared four men as they emerged from among the enormous boulders of the gully and approached the small stream running down the gully at a distance of some sixty meters from the redoubt.

The men were obviously in the last stages of exhaustion. The best part of them seemed to be their clothing—jackets and trousers and boots of some nearly indestructible plastic. All of them were almost ridiculously overarmed with weapons of various kinds, all were bearded and gaunt-faced, and one—who leaned heavily on the shoulder of another—seemed wounded in the leg.

The leading man fell belly-down at the edge of the stream and began to drink from the running water in long gulps like a tired horse. He was a big man with light red, curly hair and the freckled face of a boy. The dark, bright barrel of his gun glinted in the afternoon sunlight. The other three came up and fell down at the stream alongside him. The second man to reach the water was lean and dark as a strip of meat hung and dried in the sun. He seemed too frail for the weight of the weapons he was strapped about with, but he moved with a quick nervous energy. The third and fourth were, respectively, a tall, slim blond young man and the oldest of the four, a large-boned lanky individual of middle age with thinning hair and a face prematurely cut into deep lines of character. It was this oldest and last that dragged his left leg as if it was of little use to him.

The large redhead, having been the first to reach the water and drink, was the first to raise his head. He got to his feet with the sun at his shoulder, throwing his long distorted shadow off to his right over the bouldered ground; and, shading his eyes with one hand, gazed up to the redoubt. He was still looking as, one by one, the other three rose to join him. Their voices came distantly to the ears of the perceptors in the redoubt.

"What about it?" This was the lean, youthful blond who had been helping the injured man.

"One of ours," replied the redhead. "No doubt of that. And looks empty. Could be booby-trapped, though."

They stood for a second.

"Want to try it?" asked the redhead.

"Why not?" said the lean, dark one standing beside him—and without waiting to discuss it further, he waded out into the stream toward the redoubt. The others followed him.

They approached the cave in a staggered line. The dark one led, the redhead behind him, and the remaining pair coming together, the one assisting the other as they had to the creek. The dark one came up within a dozen feet of the entrance and stopped. He waited for the redhead to come up and join him. They stood framed by the half-open door.

"What about it?" the dark one asked. The redhead shrugged, and, reaching to the holster that dragged down his belt on the right side, drew out a heavy-handled, four-hundred-shot magazine automatic. He fired and the door slammed back to the impact of the explosive slug, revealing the redoubt's abandoned interior. Dust, disturbed by the explosion and the door's action, fumed out through the entrance like light smoke.

"Good enough, Tyler?" asked the redhead, grinning down a little lopsidedly at the dark man, and reholstering his sidearm.

"It'll do," said Tyler, dryly. He went forward cautiously, however, slinging his rifle around to a ready position before him as he stepped through the entrance. The redhead turned to wait for the other two.

"Can we ... go in?" gasped the wounded man, as he came up.

"Enoch's about done up, Win," said the other.

"It's all right," said Win, running a big hand wearily through his red mop of hair. "I could tell it when we came up. You get a feeling after a while." He stood aside and let the wounded Enoch be supported through the entrance by the blond man. They went straight for the nearest bunk and Enoch collapsed upon its dust blankets.

Bringing up the rear, Win stopped for a second before closing the door to examine the spot where the slug from his automatic had exploded against it. Only a small bright spot marked the metal at that point. Win grunted with satisfaction, closing the heavy door behind him. He turned about.

"Where's Tyler?" he asked. "Where'd he go, Paul?"

The blond answered, jerking his head in the direction of a dark entrance at the rear of the redoubt. He was bent over, straightening out Enoch's wounded leg upon the bunk.

"He went back up the rathole." He looked back down at the man on the bunk. "How's that now, Enoch?"

"Let me rest for a while," sighed Enoch. "Just let me lie still for a bit."

Win turned back to check the inner bar-locks of the door. Then he went up and down the front wall of concrete, checking the ports and the metal shutters that could be slid across them. All worked well. Finished with this, he made a tour of the redoubt's interior, sniffing as if to smell something past the damp-dustiness of its atmosphere. He stopped at the sink and played with the broken faucet. No stream of water came forth."

He turned to the cupboard, and rummaging

around in it came down with a couple of empty plastic bottles and a large five-gallon tin that had evidently by its label once contained food concentrates.

"Canteens," he said, carrying these items over to the two men at the bunk. Without a word, Paul unhooked his own canteen and gently detached the one on Enoch's belt. He handed both over to Win.

There was a scraping noise from the dark aperture and Tyler emerged back into the dim light of the redoubt.

"Canteen," said Win. Tyler took his off and came across the room to hand it over.

"Rathole's blocked," he said. "Rockfall—maybe an explosion, maybe natural. But blocked."

"I figured as much," said Win. He took his load of containers and went out the door. Tyler drifted across to one of the ports and watched the big man as he made his way down to the creek, filled with water all the motley assortments of objects he was burdened with, and brought them back. Before he returned, Win drank again.

"That's good water," he said, coming back into the redoubt and setting down his full containers on the table. He wiped his mouth as Tyler closed the door and locked it behind him. After he snicked the last bolt home, the dark man drifted across to the nearest port and took up a post there, his rifle at rest upon the thick ledge of the concrete sill.

"We can't go on," said Paul from the bunkside, "Enoch can't make it any farther the way he is."

"Sure," said Win. He sat down on one of the chairs and it squeaked to his weight.

"You can leave me," Enoch spoke from the shadow of the corner where his bunk stood. "I can go on on my own after a bit."

"I'll stay with you," said Paul.

"Be a damn fool," said Tyler, without turning his gaze from the gully beyond the open port. "Outside, we can still run. Here, we're trapped."

"I won't leave Enoch," said Paul. He turned toward Win. "How close behind us do you think they are?"

"Two hours, according to your watch," replied the redhead with his eyes half-closed. "Give or take an hour."

"I think we ought to bug out," said Tyler, without turning.

"Go if you want," said Paul, calmly.

"No," said Enoch. "I don't think—"

"Listen," said Win, speaking up suddenly. "What's the difference? We all got to rest. Maybe," he grinned, "tomorrow's our lucky day. Maybe they won't catch up with us tonight. Also maybe they're a small enough group so we can stand them off from here. They can't get at us in this place as long as we stay buttoned up."

"Artillery," said Tyler from the port.

"On that rockpile?" asked Win. "Don't make me laugh. You can hardly stand a body up straight, let alone a launcher. Also—you notice the armor on the front of this? Collapsed steel over three feet of concerete. It'd take atomics to get us out of here."

"I still don't like it," said Tyler. "If only that rathole was still open for a way out."

"So we've got one place less to watch." The redhead's voice was amused. "That's the trouble with you civilians. You're always trying to figure the situation. When you been fighting as long as I have you'll know—you can't ever figure it. You take a guess and hope for a happier deal tomorrow. That's life, buddies."

There was a momentary silence in the redoubt after he finished talking. Then Tyler spoke again, without moving, without changing the inflection of his voice.

"I'll take first watch."

"Second," said Paul.

"And Enoch's out of it," said Win. "I'll take third." He walked across to an empty bunk, unbuckling his weapon's belt as he went. Drawing the hand-gun from its holster, he lay down with it in his hand. He was almost instantly asleep.

Three hours later, or thereabouts, Tyler turned his head slightly from the port and said in a quiet voice—"Win!" The big man woke up instantly. He was walking across the floor toward the port, auto-matic in hand before his eyes were fully open. On another of the bunks, Paul, also awakened, raised himself on one elbow. Only Enoch slept on, breath-ing the deep ragged breaths of exhaustion. Win reached the port, being careful not to get in line with it, and glanced out over Tyler's shoulder.

"Where?" he asked.

"In the gully," said Tyler. "Coming up from downstream."

"A squad? A platoon? How many?"

"I can't tell," said Tyler. "I've marked fourteen of them—at least a platoon." He tensed a little suddenly. "See there—at one o'clock, the big black boulder with the gray streak running slantwise up and down on it."

Framed in the port a small segment of some-thing palely white moved for a second past the gap between the boulder Tyler had pointed out and the one next to it.

"Half-armor troops," breathed Win. "They wouldn't be sending them up for a walk over those pebbles in full armor. Maybe it's only a skirmish patrol—maybe."

"Think they'll go by?" asked Tyler. "That is, if there aren't more than a few of them."

"Depends on their officer—and whether they're actually on our trail or not."

Paul had joined them at the port. His close breath stirred the light, curling red hairs on the nape of Win's neck.

"Should we button up the ports?" he asked.

"Not yet," said Win. "Wait a bit. Wait and see."

They waited. The long shadows of afternoon lay still across the tumbled stones and seemed to creep imperceptibly with the passing minutes.

"An hour of daylight left," whispered Win. "Maybe a little less in this gully. If they don't move before dark, maybe we can sneak—"

He broke off. A figure had emerged into full view just beyond the creek. It was one of the aliens, his head helmeted and his upper body carapaced in some stiff, black material. Win hissed.

"Second-year armor. The rifles'll go through it at thirty meters and the handguns at six. That means he's safe where he is right now unless you hit him in the face. Think either of you could do it?"

Tyler lifted his rifle. Win put his hand swiftly upon it.

"I didn't mean now. We want more of them than that. And we want them closer. They'll come. It's that closed door that's making them suspicious."

The alien soldier, after standing still for several minutes, suddenly began to move. He sloshed across the creek, holding his rifle ready before him and stopped on the near side at about fifty meters distance from the redoubt.

"I could nail him now," said Tyler.

"I think I could, too," said Paul.

"Fine." Win spoke between them. "We'll still wait. Paul, you and I'll take another port apiece. And wait. Don't either of you fire until I do. I'm going to let them get right on top of us."

*   *   *

They waited. Slowly another alien soldier emerged from the boulders some ten meters to the right of the first. And then another came out an equal distance to the left. The first soldier had meanwhile slowly begun to plod up the rubbled slope toward the redoubt; and gradually, as he came ten more aliens showed themselves, five to a side in echelon behind him so that he was like the point of a living arrow pointed at the front door of the redoubt.

On the bunk, Enoch groaned in his sleep.

The men at the ports did not stir, standing well back at an angle and in the shadows, holding their rifles low so as to let no stray beam of sunlight reflect from barrel or sight. The aliens toiled upward in silence. It seemed to take them an exaggeratedly long time to mount the slope.

"A point of ten," murmured Win. "That means there's at least forty of them out there. At least a short platoon, maybe a full one. Pick your targets. I'll take the point man, himself, and the two on both sides of him. Lay on the right flank, Paul; on the left, Tyler. Lay dead on one man ready for my signal and then get as many more as you can."

"Quit calling them men," muttered Tyler between tight lips.

"Shut up. Lay steady. Hold your fire until I shoot. Hold it now—"

The aliens were already more than half the way to the redoubt. Still the big man waited. He was watching the point alien and in particular the rifle in the point alien's hands. The aliens came on. Suddenly, the rifle in the point's hands flashed up overhead in a signal. A harsh, high cry burst from his lips and he broke into a run.

Win squeezed the trigger of his rifle and the alien face in his sights exploded, the helmet flying high into the air like a tin can when a firecracker has been lit underneath it.

On either side, Paul and Tyler were firing steadily and methodically. The alien ten, caught in the moment in which they had started their charge forward, were checked for the moment in which it took them to reverse direction. In that moment the thousand-slug magazine rifles in the three men's hands, set on semiautomatic, did wicked damage. Six of the ten were cut down before they could turn to retreat. Three more died before they had covered half the distance back to the safety of the boulders; and the last was dropped by a pelvis shot just short of the creek. He lay thrashing on the ground. Paul raised his rifle.

Reaching over, Win knocked it out of aim.

"Save your ammunition!" he snapped. Paul looked at him for a calm moment; and then, turning back to the port laid his rifle on the ledge, waited for the moment when the wounded alien's face jerked into view, and blew it off. The last alien lay still.

"Damn you," said Tyler from the other port. "Do you think they'd be that kind to you?"

Paul shrugged.

"Shut those shutters!" roared Win. "You can talk later!"

They slammed the metal shutters home across the ports, leaving only the tiny rifle holes open. It was no more than just in time. A steady fire from the rest of the aliens hidden amongst the boulders was drumming like some giant's tattoo all along the face of the redoubt.

"Let them shoot," said Win, stepping back. "There's nothing we can do until they slack off or show themselves again."

He walked back and laid his rifle down on the table. The battle had at last wakened Enoch. He turned his gaunted face to Win.

"What happened?" he asked.

"We're pinned," said the big man. "By at least a

short platoon. And that's the way that works." He
reached absently for a canteen, then took his hand
away from it. He turned to Tyler and Paul as the
other two men came up and sat down at the table
with him.

"Now what?" asked Tyler.

"Just like I said." Win drummed his big fingers
on the table top. "All we can do is sit and wait—at
least until dark."

"And after dark?" Paul said.

Win shrugged. He turned to the wounded man.

"How's the leg, Enoch?" he asked. "Very painful?"

"Not so painful," Enoch answered.

"Think you can move along all right on it now,
if we help you?"

"I can try," said Enoch.

"No," said Paul. "I don't think he can. If you're
thinking of making a break for it, after dark—"

"Leave me behind," said Enoch.

"No," said Paul. Win said nothing. Tyler said
nothing. "I'll stay here with him," said Paul.

"No," it was Enoch. "You've been a good friend,
Paul, but I can't take that sort of sacrifice from
you. Death means nothing to me anyway. And
maybe I can delay these animals outside until the
rest of you get away."

"They aren't animals," said Paul, softly.

"Well, we'll see," said Win. "We'll wait until it
gets dark and then have a look outside—"

He broke off suddenly. All the sound of firing
outside had ceased. The abrupt silence hung heavy
on the air. Win rose quickly and walked to the
nearest gun port. He peered through the small
rifle hole in it. Paul and Tyler went to the holes in
the shutters alongside.

Outside the slope lay marked by light and shadow
in the later afternoon sunlight. The strip of darkness from the far cliff face was half the distance to

the creek on its other side. There was no sign of
any of the alien riflemen; and then, suddenly, there
stepped into view just beyond the creek a single
soldier without armor or weapons. He lifted his
arms briefly above his head and showed his hands,
and then began stolidly to cross the creek and
approach the creek and mount the slope toward
the redoubt. There was the soft scraping noise of
metal on concrete as the three men lifted their
rifles up into position.

"What is it?" asked Tyler.

"Parley," said Win, without turning his head.
The alien halted at a distance of some twenty
meters from the redoubt and held up his empty
hands again. He shouted to them in a high-pitched,
curiously accented travesty of the human words.

"You in there! You hear me?"

None of the men answered. After a moment the
alien went on.

"You listen! What is the use of more pain? We
are a full company—look where I point—" He
turned about suddenly and flung out his arm. As if
suddenly materializing upon the field of battle,
more than a hundred alien soldiers suddenly
stepped up into full view and as quickly dropped
back out of sight again. "You cannot escape us. We
know there is no food or water in there. At last you
will die. What is the use of pain? If certain death
comes, will it not be better to come fast?"

He paused again, momentarily. Tyler opened his
mouth as if to answer.

"Shut up!" said Win, in a tense, low voice.

"You in there!" cried the alien. "You have nowhere to go. Even if we were to let you go now, we
would hunt you down at last. You are alone on
this world. The end is certain. Come out now and
we will shoot you quickly."

Win grunted, a low, satisfied sound. The rifle in
his hands moved and fired. Outside the alien was

hurled back by the force of the explosion and lay
still.

"I wanted to hear him say it," said Win. "I knew
that was his offer, but it didn't hurt to make sure."

"Did you have to shoot him?" said Paul.

"No, but that makes one less," said Win. "Might
as well. Also, it's a better way of answering than
by voice."

"The great white heart here thinks you ought to
have let it live," said Tyler. Paul did not answer.
He turned to Win.

"Now what?" he asked.

"Whose watch?" countered Win.

"Mine," said Paul.

"Button up all the rifle slits but one, and keep
your eye sharp out of it. I don't think they'll try
anything tonight—they'd rather wait until we've
been worn down a bit. Don't bother watching the
slope before us—watch the creek. Anything that
comes has to cross the water and if the night's
clear and we get the little moon, you'll be able to
see them against the shine of the stream."

Paul nodded. He went down the line of shutters,
sealing them up, all but one to the right of the
door, where he took up his post. Win and Tyler
returned to their bunks and lay down.

"Drink now?" asked Tyler, rolling over on one
elbow, to stare through the thickening gloom of
the redoubt in Win's direction.

"Wait until midnight," said the big man. "It'll
be worse later." He rolled over on his back and
closed his eyes. A second later, Tyler followed suit.
Paul leaned still and watchful against his rifle
hole.

The night hours slipped by. Outside there was
silence. The little moon—one of the planet's two—
bathed slope and stream and nearer boulders
beyond the stream. There was no sound from out-

side and no sign of movement. Occasionally, Paul blinked his eyes and shook his head, as if to jar his attention to a fuller wakefulness.

Inside the redoubt, for a long time there was also silence, as if the three men on the bunks were all asleep and dreaming. And then an almost inaudible murmuring crept into the vacuum of sound. For a long time it rose and fell, and gradually words among it became distinguishable, and then sentences. It was the voice of Enoch.

". . . And therefore, O Lord, in this hour of our trial, alone and separate from our own people, and in the hands of the enemies, be with us in mind and body and in spirit. Strengthen our hearts with the knowledge that we are in your hands alone . . ."

There was a sudden rush and scramble in the darkness and the ugly sound of a fist striking against flesh and bone.

"You! You're not going to pray for me . . ." cried Tyler's voice wildly. Paul and Win turned and flung themselves upon the dimly struggling figures rolling back and forth over Enoch's cot. It took this combined strength to pry Tyler loose from the wounded man.

"Let me go!" shouted Tyler frenziedly. "He can't put his God on me! I don't want his God . . ."

"Atheist!" cried Enoch. And Tyler, struggling against the combined grasp of the two other men, spat back at him.

"Yes, I'm an atheist. I'm a man—that's all I need. I'll show you—"

A sudden thunderous explosion sounded, echoed and re-echoed between the rock and concrete walls of the bunker. Tyler was torn from the grasp of Win and Paul, as if by a giant's hand. An alien rifle was projecting through the rifle hole through which Paul had been observing. It fired again.

With one quick bound, Win reached the wall beside the port, and shooting out both his big hands, grabbed the barrel, jerked it inward, then thrust it back with all his strength. There was a thudding sound and the rifle dropped out of his hands and fell backward through the hole.

"I'll show you! I'll show you all!" screamed Tyler. He had snatched up his own rifle and as Paul and Win started toward him, he swung the muzzle of it menacingly toward them. A dark stain was spreading over his jacket. He jumped to the door, staggering a little, and with one hand shot the bolts back. "I'm a man!" he cried again—and jerking open the door, reeled through it out into the night.

Win leaped to the entrance behind him, slamming and shutting the door again. His face white, Paul had already jerked back one of the shutters. Both men gazed through it as Tyler yelled wildly and harshly.

An alien flare burst suddenly in the air high over the gully. Tyler was revealed in its actinic light, running, staggering down the slope, firing wildly on full automatic.

Alien guns opened up on him. The slope about him was peopled with at least a platoon of alien soldiers caught in all positions from that of crawling to full upright position, in advance upon the redoubt. Tyler swept his rifle about like a garden hose. He went down on one knee. He fell over sideways and lay still. Above, the alien flare was sinking to the ground, its light fading. From the redoubt, Win and Paul opened up on the few remaining aliens in the open on their side of the creek.

Then it was dark again. They slammed the shutter home; and alien guns beat upon the armor of the redoubt, fading gradually into silence.

The redoubt was locked up tight. Even the rifle holes in the shutters were sealed. The two men wearily leaned their rifles against the wall and had time to turn their attention to Enoch. He lay ominously silent upon his bunk.

Paul bent over him. A little flame sparked and burst into illumination as Paul fired the lighter in his fingers.

"Unconscious," he said. "He's been hit again. That second shot, probably."

Win let out a deep sigh and dropped in a sitting position on the cot alongside.

"Leave him alone, why don't you?" he said. "He's not feeling anything now." Paul shook his head. He had opened Enoch's jacket and was occupied in binding and powdering the new wound.

"Solid slug," said Paul, as if to himself. He turned to Win. "Got any morphine left?"

Win fumbled at his belt and passed over a small green cylinder. Paul turned Enoch's flaccid arm, put the cylinder against it and pushed the trigger. He threw the empty syringe away.

"It's no good," said Win, heavily from the couch. "You know that."

"I know," said Paul.

"Then why not just let him go?"

"I don't know," said Paul. "Instinct, I suppose." He sat down on the bunk on the other side of Enoch and looked across the unconscious man's body at Win. "Got a cigarette?"

Win passed one across.

"I didn't know you smoked," he said.

"I used to," said Paul. "I think one would help, now." He inhaled slowly, and for a moment the glow of the cigarette lit up his face. Outside the alien guns had fallen silent. "And now?"

"How's the water holding out?"

"Water?"

Both men turned instinctively to look at the table where the canteens and water containers had stood. It lay overturned by the struggle with Tyler, its four legs poking ridiculously in the air. All the containers were scattered and spilled.

They looked back at each other. Paul very carefully put out his cigarette; and Win licked lips that were not yet dry.

"I think I'll get some sleep," he said. "You might as well, too. They can't get in except by mining the door, and I don't think they'll try that for the rest of tonight, after what happened." He lay back on the bunk. Paul, after leaning over to check on Enoch, followed suit.

They were roused at an indeterminate time later by Enoch's voice. In the little light that filtered in through the buttoned-up rifle holes in the shutters, he loomed as a dark mass, sitting suddenly upright in the bunk.

"Mary," he called in a clear voice. "Mary! Turn the lights on!"

Suddenly, he started to sag sideways, and before the two other men could reach him he had fallen over on his shoulder on the bunk. Paul bent over him, putting his fingers on the limp wrist. After a moment, he straightened up.

"He's gone," Paul said. Win peered across the bunk at him in the darkness.

"Who was Mary?" he asked.

"His wife—she was caught in the first months of the attack."

"Killed?"

"Yes," said Paul. He sat back down on his own bunk. The dimness in the redoubt was too pronounced for either man's face to show expression. In the silence Win made an odd, thoughtful little sound, as if he had just thought of something.

"Half an hour to daylight by my watch," he said. "We'll see then."

"See what?" Paul asked.

"Well," said Win, "I'd like to put him outside. If

it warms up during the day—it's going to be rough enough on us in here without water." He leaned forward a little through the darkness toward Paul. "You wouldn't mind?"

"No," said Paul.

"I didn't think so," said Win's voice, sounding quiet and almost separate from the black shadow of his body.

"You've been a professional soldier all of your life, haven't you?" Paul leaned forward slightly on his bunk.

"Since I was sixteen. My folks didn't survive the trip out."

"What happened?"

"Contamination of the drinking water. Waste from the garbage system. Everybody got sick. They were two of the ones who didn't get better."

"You're not bitter about it?" Paul said.

"Don't see why I should be. It wouldn't make any difference."

"Tell me," Paul asked, "what does make a difference?"

"Damned if I know."

"Yes." Paul's voice sounded thoughtful. "That's the thing."

"Different for you, huh?"

"There's a lot of things I'd like to find out about," said Paul, softly. "I'd even like to talk to those people outside; and see if I couldn't understand them a little better."

"For a man who shoots as well as you do," said Win, "that's a funny statement."

"I suppose so," Paul sighed. "I don't understand myself any better than I understand anything else. Wonder if any of this would make sense to all of those people back on Earth?"

"Nah," said Win. "The only one who thinks he makes sense out of something like this is the guy

writing up a history on it five hundred years after—
and he's wrong."

"Yes." Paul turned toward the line of shutters.
"Light's picking up a bit. It must be almost dawn.
Got any suggestions?"

"Clean your gun."

"I did," said Paul.

"Then, that's it."

Win got up from his bunk, crossed the redoubt
and carefully cracked a rifle hole on one of the
shutters. A slim needle of pale light came through
and laid its sharp line across his cheek and shoulder.
He opened the rifle hole wider.

"Look," he said.

Paul moved swiftly to another shutter and opened
the rifle hole. Outside, halfway up the slope, a
small bastion of rocks had been piled up during
the dark hours; and now, as he watched, there
shot into the air from behind this protection, a jet
of brown liquid that spattered softly against the
outside of the redoubt's locked door, to his right.

"What . . . ?" Paul said.

"Jel . . ." answered Win. He brought his rifle up
quickly and fired at the rockpile. Stone chips flew
at the explosion of his pellet against the top of the
stacked boulders. The jet paused momentarily.
"Liquid explosive. If they can get enough of it
piled up against the door and soaked into the crack
between the door and the jamb, they can blow us
open." He fired again. "Make them keep their heads
down."

Paul brought his own rifle into action. The jet
started up again. But its aim was bad and the
brown stream angled off to one side and fell short,
where it trickled greasily among the stony rubble
before the redoubt. The jet stopped again. After a
while new boulders began to be pushed into position on top of those already erected.

Win and Paul fired alternately, keeping up a slow but steady fire. The jet continued to work at intermittent intervals.

"They're getting it," said Win, a couple of hours later. He turned to look across the inside of the front wall at Paul, wiping his sweaty forehead with the palm of his left hand. "They're building up enough to blow us open. If we only had a grenade or two—"

"Toss out a wad of pellets with a fuse?" suggested Paul.

"We can try it," answered Win.

They drew back from the shutters and set about cutting up one of the blankets. The result was a wadded mass holding a couple of dozen rounds of their rifle's ammunition and some inflammable stuffing from one of the mattresses. A twisted wick of stuffing trailed from it.

"You open the shutter when I count *three*," said Win, hefting the ball-like contraption in one hand. "Ready? One . . . two . . . *three!*"

Paul slammed back the shutter. Win threw. The homemade bomb tumbled through the air and dropped behind the rock bastion. There was a moment's absolute silence, and then a sudden, gouting explosion from behind the bastion, that flung pieces of metal and brown stuff and alien bodies skyward.

"We did it! We did it!" cried Win. "Look at that, Paul! That stopped them—"

"You're telling me?" shouted Paul. His eyes were glittering with a new light and his mouth was newly savage. "One more like that and . . . *Look out behind you, Win!*"

They swung around together in a single movement. From the mouth of the rathole—that escape passage that Tyler had earlier found choked with fallen rock—alien soldiers were erupting. The guns in the two men's hands exploded on full automatic fire, but still the soldiers poured out. And at that same moment there was a thunderous explosion at their backs. The front door to the redoubt blew inward and twisted wide, and close behind the sound of its smashing, came more leaping, alien bodies through this new opening.

The redoubt disintegrated into a mass of swirling action revolving around two separate foci, one of which was Paul and the other Win. Dust rose in clouds. For a second Win's face and wide shoulders could be seen in violent motion above the shorter alien heads, and then the butt of an alien rifle, appearing as if by magic from the ruck, swung full into his features, crushing them.

And the dust rose, obscuring all the screen.

The alien official shut off the desk projector. The lights in the office, which had dimmed imperceptibly as the film started, came up again.

"They were all killed, of course?" asked the superior.

"Of course," said the official. The superior tapped a little impatiently with the end of one digit on his desk top.

"Well?" he demanded.

"Well," said the official. "You see why it's failure." He looked at the superior. "You understand that while we have, for all practical purposes, cleaned them off this one world, our problem remains, and our question stays unanswered. There is no doubt, I think, that we could—if we wished to devote our entire race's energies and lives to it—manage to exterminate these humans, even on their home planet. But you understand the foolishness of such a project. We would be buying a sterile planet with the flower of our own youth."

"There's no need to labor the obvious," the superior said. "Will you come to the point?"

"I am," said the official. "We need to dominate,

not eradicate races like these if we wish to expand our own culture. This test was set up to demonstrate and perhaps answer the question we must have answered if we are to advance further against this race without paying a prohibitive price for our gains. What you have just seen illustrates a basic trait of human character that baffles us. Perhaps you saw or heard something that gave you a clue. We have none."

"What trait?"

"You heard these men talk," said the official. "You perhaps noticed that they all had individual differing philosophies. We have found this true of all humans. Each, unlike us in our race, has his own personal philosophy. They all produce the same result. Each one has a different answer to our question, which leaves us with no answer at all."

"Official," said the superior, addressing the other directly by his title for the first time, "are you deliberately trying to withhold the nature of this question from me?"

"Not at all, sir," said the other. "I merely wanted you to have all the background, as I have had, before being faced with it. It is as terrible and frustrating as all simple questions. It is, merely, in the case of these humans—what is it makes them fight?"

"You mean, don't you," said the superior, at last, "what makes them keep on fighting?"

Fear not the dying of the flesh, only the slaying of the soul.

OUR FIRST DEATH

Juny Vewlan died about 400 hours of the morning and we buried her that same day before noon at 1100 hours, because we had no means of keeping the body. She had not wanted to be cremated; and because she was our first and because some of her young horror at the thought of being done away with entirely had seeped into the rest of us during her illness (if you could call it illness—at any rate, as she lay dying), an exception was made in her case and we decided in full assembly to bury her.

As for the subsidiary reasons for this decision of ours, they were not actually clear to us at the time, nor yet indeed for a long time afterward. Certainly the fatherless, motherless girl had touched our hearts toward the end. Certainly the old man— her grandfather Gothrud Vewlan, who with his wife, Van Meyer and Kurt Meklin made up our four Leaders—caught us all up in the heartache of his own sorrow, as he stood feebly forth on the platform to ask of us this last favor for his dead grandchild. And certainly Kurt Meklin murmured against it, which was enough to dispose some of the more stiff-necked of us in its favor.

However—we buried her. It was a cold hard day, for winter had already set in on Our Planet. We carried her out over the unyielding ground, under the white and different sky, and lowered her down into the grave some of our men had dug for her. Beneath the transparent lid of her coffin, she looked younger than sixteen years—younger, in fact, than she had looked in a long time, with her dark hair combed back from around the small pointed face and her eyes closed. Her hands were folded in front of her. She had, Gothrud told us, also wished some flowers to hold in them; and none of us could imagine where she had got such an idea until one of the younger children came forward with an illustration from our library's *Snow White and the Seven Dwarfs*, showing Snow White in *her* coffin with a bunch of flowers that never faded clasped in her hands. It was clear then, to some of us at least, that Juny had not been free from the dream of herself as a sort of captive—now sleeping—princess, merely putting in her time until the Prince her lover should arrive and carry her off.

But we had, of course, no flowers.

After she had been lowered into the grave and all of us had come up to look at her, Lydia Vewlan, Gothrud's wife and colony doctor as well as one of the Leaders, read some sort of service over her. Then, when all was finished, a cloth was laid over the transparent face of the plastic coffin and the earth was shoveled back. It had been dug out in chunks—a chunk to a spadeful; and the chunks had frozen in the bitter air, so that it was like piling angular rocks back upon the coffin, heavy purple rocks with the marblings of white shapes that were the embryos of strange plants frozen in hibernation. Because of their hard awkward shapes, they made quite a pile above the grave when they were all put back; and in fact it was not until the following summer was completely gone that the top of the grave was level again with the surrounding earth. By that time we had a small fence of white plastic pickets all around it; and it was part of the duty of the children in the colony to keep them scrubbed clean and free of the gray mold.

After the burial we all went back to the mess building for our noon meal. Outside, as we took our places at the tables, the midday wind sprang up and whistled around our metal huts and the stripped skeleton of the ship, standing apart at its distance on the landing spot and looking lonely and neglected in the bleak light from the white sky.

The Leaders of our colony sat at the head of the file of tables that stretched the length of the mess hut. Their table was just large enough for the four of them and was set a little apart from the rest so that they could discuss important matters in relative privacy. The other, large tables stretched away in order, with the ones at the far end with the small chairs and the low tops for the very young children—those who were just barely able to eat by themselves without supervision. These, the children, had as a group been unusually silent and solemn during the burial procedures, impressed by the emotions of their elders. But now, as they started to eat, their natural energy and exuberance began to break free of this restraint and show itself all the more noticeably for having been held down this long. In fact they began to pose quite a small disciplinary problem, and this necessitating the attentions of their elders, a diversion was created, which together with the warmth and the good effect of the hot food, bred a lightening of spirits among us adults as well. Our natural mood of optimism, which the Colonial Office had required in selecting us for a place on the immigration rosters, pressed down before by the awareness of death in our midst, began to rise again. And it continued to rise, like a warm tide throughout the length of the hut, until finally it reached the four who sat at the head table. But here it lapped unavailingly against the occupied minds of those who, twenty-four hours a day, breathed the constant atmosphere of responsibility for us all.

To talk and not be heard, they must lower their voices and lean their heads together. And this, while a perfectly natural action, had a tendency to impart an air of tenseness to their discussions. So they sat now, following the burial, in such an atmosphere of tenseness; and although the rest of us did not discover what they were then saying until long afterward—indeed until Maria Warna told us about it months later—there were those among us at the long tables who, glancing upward, noticed something perhaps graver than usual about their talking at that meal.

In particular, it had been Kurt Meklin—Kurt, with his old lined face thrust forward above his plate like some gray guardian of ancient privilege, who had been urging some point upon the other three all through the meal. But what it was, he had avoided stating openly, talking instead in half-hints, and obscure ambiguities, his black hard eyes sliding over to glance at Lydia, and then away again, and then back again. Until, finally, when the last plates had been removed and the coffee served, Lydia rose at last to the challenge and spoke out unequivocally.

"All right, Kurt!" she said—she, the strong old woman, meeting the clever old man eye to eye. "You've been hinting and hawing around ever since we got back from the burying. Now, what's wrong with it?"

"Well, now that you ask me, Lydia," said Kurt. "It's a question—a question of what she died of."

Gothrud, who had sat the whole meal with his head hanging and eating almost nothing, now suddenly raised his eyes and looked across at Kurt.

"What kind of a question's that?" demanded Lydia. "You saw me enter it on the records—death from natural causes."

"I'll tell you what she really died of," said Gothrud, suddenly.

"Well now," said Kurt, interrupting Gothrud, and with another of his side-glances at Lydia. "Do you think that's sufficient?"

"Sufficient? Why shouldn't it be sufficient?"

"Well now, of course, Lydia . . ." said Kurt. "I know nothing of doctoring myself, and we all know that the Colonial Office experts gave Our Planet a clean bill of health before they shipped our little colony out here. But I should think—just for the record, if nothing else—you'd have wanted to make an examination to determine the cause of death."

"I did."

"Naturally—but just a surface examination. Of course with the colony in a sentimental mood about the girl—eh, Van?"

Van Meyer, the youngest of them all, was turning his coffee cup around and around between his thick fingers and staring at it. His heavy cheeks were slablike on either side of his mouth.

"Leave me out of it," he said, without looking up.

Lydia sniffed at him, and turned back to Kurt.

"Stop talking gibberish!" she commanded.

"Gibberish . . . sorry, Lydia," said Kurt. "I don't have the advantages of your medical education. A pharmacist really knows so little. But—it's just that I think you've left the record rather vague.

Natural causes really doesn't tell us exactly what she died of."

"What she died of!" broke in Gothrud with sudden, low-voiced violence. "She died of a broken heart."

"Don't be a fool, Gothrud," said his wife, without looking at him. "And keep your voice down, you, Kurt. Do you want the whole colony to hear? Now, out with it. You sat with us and agreed to bury her. If you had any questions, you should have come out with them then."

"But I had to bend to the sentimentality of the colony," said Kurt. "It was best to let it go then. Later, I thought, later we can ..." He fell silent, making a small, expressive gesture with his hand.

"Later we can do *what?*" grated Lydia.

"Why, I should think that naturally—as a matter of record—that in a case like this you'd want to do an autopsy on her."

"Autopsy!" The word jolted a little from Lydia's lips.

"Why, certainly," said Kurt, spreading his hands. "This way is much simpler than insisting on it in open Assembly. After curfew tonight, when everybody is in barracks—"

A low strangled cry from Gothrud interrupted him. From the moment in which the word *autopsy* had left Kurt's lips, he had been sitting in frozen horror. Now, it seemed, he managed at last to draw breath into his lungs to speak with.

"Autopsy!" he cried, in a thin, tearing, half-strangled whisper. "*Autopsy!* She didn't want to be touched! We agreed not to burn her; and now you'd— No—"

"Why, Gothrud—" said Kurt.

"Don't *why Gothrud* me!" said Gothrud, his deep sunk eyes at last flaming into violence. "A decision's been made by the colony. And none of you are going to set it aside."

"We are the Leaders," said Kurt.

"Leaders!" Gothrud laughed bitterly. "The ex-druggist—you, Kurt. The ex-nurse and—" he glanced at Van Meyer—"the ex-caterer's son, the ex-nothing."

Van Meyer held his cup and stared at it.

"And the ex-high school teacher," said Kurt, softly.

"Exactly!" said Gothrud, lifting his head to meet him stare for stare. "The ex-high school teacher. Me. As little an ex as the rest of you, Kurt, and as big a Leader right now. And a Leader that says you've got no right to touch my Juny to settle your two-bit intriguing and feed your egos—" He choked.

"Gothrud—" said Kurt. "Gothrud, you're over-wrought. You—"

Gothrud coughed raspingly and went on. "I tell you—" He choked again, and had to stop.

Lydia spoke swiftly to him, in low, furious German. "Shut up! Will you kill yourself, old man?"

"That's being done for me," Gothrud answered her in English, and faced up to Kurt again. "You hear me!" he said. "We're nothings. Leaders, Great executives. Only none of us has been five miles from the landing spot. Only none of us organized this colony. None of us flew the ship, or assigned the work, or built the huts, or planned the plantings. All we did was sign the roster back on Earth, and polite young experts with twice our brains did it all for us. By what right are we Leaders?"

"We were elected!" snapped Kurt.

"Fools elected by fools!" Gothrud's head was beginning to swim from the violence of his effort in the argument. Through a gathering mist, he seemed to see Kurt's face ripple as if it were under water, and rippling, sneer at him. With a great effort, he gripped the edge of the table and went on.

"I tell you," he rasped, "that people have rights. That you won't—that you can't—that—"

His tongue had suddenly gone stubborn and refused to obey him. It rattled unintelligibly in his mouth and around him the room was being obscured by the white mist. Gothrud felt a sudden constriction in his throat; and, gasping abruptly for breath, he pushed back his chair and tried to stand up, clawing at his collar to loosen it.

Through the black specks that swarmed suddenly before his eyes, he was conscious of Van Meyer rising beside him and of Lydia's voice ordering the younger man to catch him before he fell.

"Come on, Gothrud," said the voice of Van Meyer, close to his ear. "You've been under too much of a strain. You better lie down. Come on, I'll help you."

Through the haze he was conscious of being half-assisted, half-carried from the dining room. There was a short space of confusion, and then things cleared for him, to allow him to find himself lying on his bunk in the room he shared with Lydia. Van Meyer, alone with him, stood over the washstand, filling a hypodermic syringe from a small frosted bottle of minimal, his gross bulk hunched over concentratedly with a sort of awkward and pathetic kindness.

"Feeling better?" he asked Gothrud.

"I'm all right," Gothrud answered. But the words came out thick and unnaturally. "What are you doing?"

"I'm going to give you a shot to make you sleep," said Van.

"Van—" said Gothrud. "Van—" Talking was really a tremendous effort. He swallowed desperately and went on. "*You* understand about Juny—don't you?"

"Why, yes, Gothrud."

"She shouldn't have come, you see. We made

her—because she had no other family, Lydia and I. She never wanted to come. We talked her into it. She was just coming out of being a child—"

"Don't talk, Gothrud," said Van, struggling with the delicate plunger of the hypodermic. "You need to rest."

"—She was the only one that age. All the rest of us, adults or young children; and her in between, all alone. A whole lost generation, Van, in one lonely little girl."

"Now, Gothrud—"

"I tell you," cried Gothrud, struggling up onto one elbow, "we robbed her of every reason to live. She should have had love and fun and the company of young people her own age back on Earth. And we brought her here—to this desolate outpost of a world—"

Van Meyer had finally got the syringe properly filled. He came over to the bed with it and reached for Gothrud's arm when the older man sank back.

"That's why we owe it to her to leave her untouched the way she wanted," said Gothrud, in a low, feverish voice, as the needle went in. "But it's not that so much, Van. If it were for some good purpose, I wouldn't object. But it isn't. It's for Lydia—and Kurt. Van—" he grasped the younger man's arm as he started to turn away from the bunk, and held him, compelling Van Meyer to turn back.

"Van—" he said. "Things are going wrong here. You know that. It's Lydia. Married all those years back on Earth, and I never let myself see it. I watched her drive our son and daughter from our house. I watched her bend Juny to her way and bring her here with us. And Van"—his voice sunk to a whisper—"I never let myself see it until I got here, that awful hunger in her. It's power, she wants, Van, power. That's what she's always wanted, and now she sees a chance of getting it.

Listen to me, Van, watch out for her. She did for Juny. It'll be me next, and then Kurt, and then—"

"Now, Gothrud—now just relax—" said Van, pulling his arm at last free from the older man's grasp, which now began to weaken as the drug took hold.

"Promise me you'll watch . . ." whispered Gothrud. "You must. I trust you, Van. You're weak, but there's nothing rotten in you. Kurt's no good. He's another like Lydia. Watch them. Promise—promise. . . ."

"I—I promise," said Van, and the minimal came in on Gothrud with a rush, like a great black wave that swept in and over him, burying him far beneath it, deep, and deep.

When Gothrud awoke, the room he shared with Lydia was in darkness; and through the single small, high window in the outer wall, with its reinforcing wire mesh patterning the glass, he saw the night sky—for a wonder momentarily free of clouds—and the bright stars of the Cluster. Van Meyer's shot of minimal must have been a light one, for he had awakened clear-headed and, he felt quite sure, long before it had been planned for him to awaken. He felt positive in his own mind that they would have planned for him to sleep until morning; and only the unpredictable clock of his old body, ticking erratically, now fast and now slowing, running down toward final silence, had tricked them.

The illuminated clock-face on his bedside table read 21:20 and curfew was at 2100 hours. He fumbled into his clothes, got up, went over to the window and peered out, craning his neck. Yes, the colony was now completely lost in darkness, except for the small, yellow-gleaming windows of the Office Hut. Feverishly he turned and began to climb into his weather suit, struggling hastily into the bulky, overall-like outfit, zipping it tight and pulling the hood over his head. At the last minute, as he was going out the door, he remembered the diary; and, going back, dug through the contents of his locker until his fingers closed over the cylindrical thickness of it. He lifted it out, a faint hint of clean, light, young-girl's perfume reaching him from it momentarily. Then he stuffed it through the slit of his weather suit to an inside pocket; and went out the door.

The most direct route to the Office Hut led across the open compound. But as he started across this, leaning against the wind, an obscure fear made his feet turn away from the direct bulk of his destination and veer in the direction of the new grave. He went, chiding himself for his foolishness all the way, for although he knew now that the other three Leaders had held him in secret contempt for a long time, he was equally sure that they would not dare go directly against his wishes in this matter without consulting him.

So it was that when he came finally to Juny's grave and saw it gaping black and open under the stars, he could not at first bring himself to believe it. But when he did, all the strength went out of him and he fell on his knees beside the open trench. For a wild moment as he knelt there, he felt that, like a figure out of the Old Testament, he should pray—for guidance, or for a divine vengeance upon the desecrators of the grave of his grandchild. But all that came out of him were the crying reproaches of an old man: "Oh, God, why didn't you make me stronger? Why didn't you make me young again when this whole business of immigration was started? I could take a gun and—"

But he knew he would not take a gun; and if he did, the others would simply walk up and take it away from him. Because he could not shoot anybody. Not even for Juny could he shoot anybody. And after a while he wiped his eyes and got to his feet and went on toward the Office Hut, hugging one arm to his side, so that he could feel the round shape of the diary through all his heavy suit insulation.

When he came to the Office Hut, the door was locked. But he had his key in his pocket as always. His heart pounded and the entryway of the Hut seemed full of a soft mist lurking just at the edge of his vision. He leaned against the wall for a moment to rest, then painfully struggled out of his weather suit. When he had hung it up beside the others on the wall hooks, he opened the inner door of the Hut and went in.

The three were clustered around the long conference table at the far end of the office, Lydia with her dark old face looking darker and older even than usual above the white gown and gloves of surgery. They looked up at the sound of the opening door; and Van Meyer moved swiftly to block off Gothrud's vision of the table and came toward him.

"Gothrud!" he said. "What are you doing here?" And he put his hands on Gothrud's arms.

Gothrud struggled feebly to release himself and go around the younger man to the table, but was not strong enough.

"Let me go. Let me go!" he cried. "What have you done to her? Have you—"

"No, no," soothed Van Meyer. Still holding Gothrud's arms, he steered the older man over to a chair at one of the desks and sat him down in it. All the way across the room, he stayed between Gothrud and the conference table and when he had Gothrud in the chair, he pulled up another for himself and sat down opposite, so that the table was still hidden. Kurt and Lydia came over to stand behind him. All three looked at Gothrud.

Lydia's face was hard and bitter as jagged ice. The absorbent face mask around her neck, unfast-

ened on one side and hanging by a single thread,
somehow made her look, to Gothrud's eyes, not
like a member of the profession of healing, but like
some executioner, interrupted in the course of her
duty.

"You!" she said.

Gothrud stared up at her, feeling a helpless
fascination.

"You—you mustn't—" he gasped.

"*Du!*" she broke out at him suddenly, in low
voiced, furious German. "You old fool! Couldn't
you stay in bed and keep out of trouble? Don't I
have enough trouble on my hands with this one-
time pill-peddler trying to undermine my authority,
but I must suffer with you as well?"

"Lydia," he answered hoarsely, in the same
language. "You can't do this thing. You mustn't
let Kurt push you into it. It's a crime before
God and man that you should even consider
it."

"I consider—I consider the colony."

"No. You do not. You do not!" cried Gothrud in
agony. "You think only of yourself. What harm
will it do you if you tell the truth? It can't alter the
facts. The colony will be upset for a little while,
but then they will get over it. Isn't that better than
living a lie and backing it up with an act of
abomination?"

"Be silent!" snapped Lydia. "What I am doing, I
am doing for the best of all concerned."

"I won't let you!" he cried. Changing swiftly
into English, he swung away from her and ap-
pealed to the two men.

"Listen," he said. "Listen: you know there's no
need for this—this autopsy. Colonial Office experts,
men who *know*, certified this planet as clean. So it
can't be any disease. And what would it benefit
you to discover some physical frailty?"

"Ah? She was frail?" asked Kurt. "Something in the family?"

"No, she was not!" Lydia almost shouted. "Stop playing the goose, Kurt." Suddenly regaining control of herself, she dropped her voice all at once to normal level again. "I'm surprised at you, Kurt, letting yourself be misled by a sick old man who never was able to look on the girl dispassionately."

"Dipassionately!" cried Gothrud, straining forward against Van Meyer's prisoning hands. "Did you look at Juny dispassionately? Did you bring her along to die out here, dispassionately, taking her away from everything that she longed for? I tell you—*I* tell you, she died of a broken heart! God—" He choked suddenly. "God forgive me for being so soft, so weak and flabby-soft that I let you have your way about her coming. Better an orphanage back on Earth, for her. Better the worst possible life, alive, back there, than this—to have her dead, so young, and wasted—wasted—"

He sobbed suddenly.

"Van," commanded Lydia, evenly, "take him back to Quarters."

"No!" shouted Gothrud, coming suddenly to his feet and with surprising strength pushing the younger man aside, so that he half-toppled in his chair and caught at a desk to keep from falling. Gothrud took two quick strides across to a recorder that perched on a nearby desk. Pulling the diary from his pocket, he snapped it onto the spindle and turned the playback on.

"She died of a broken heart—for all she wanted and couldn't have," cried Gothrud. "And here's your proof. Listen!"

"What are you doing?" snapped Kurt.

Gothrud turned blazing eyes upon him.

"This was her diary," he said. "Listen. . . ."

The speaker had begun to murmur words in the voice of a young girl. Gothrud reached out and turned up the volume. The sweet clear tones grew into words in the still air of the grim rectangular office, all plastic and metal about the four who listened.

"... *and after that we flew out over Lake Michigan. The lake was all dark, but you could see the moon lighting a path on the water, all white and wonderful. And the lights went up the shore for miles. I just put my head on Davy's shoulder ...*"

"Shut it off!" snapped Kurt, suddenly. "What are you trying to do, Gothrud?"

"Listen to her heart breaking," said Gothrud, his head a little on one side, attentively. "Listen and try to think of her dispassionately."

"You're out of your head, Gothrud!" said Lydia. "What odds is it, what the girl recorded back on Earth?"

"On Earth? On Earth?" echoed Gothrud. "She recorded it here, night by night, in her own room."

Before them the diary fell silent for a second and then took up with a new entry.

"... *Month eight, fourth day: Today Walter took me to the Embassy ball. I wore my new formal all made out of yards of real night-mist lace. It was like walking in the center of a pink cloud. Walter has the high emotional index typical of such intense characters; and he was very jealous of me. He was afraid that I might take it into my head to turn around and go back to Our Planet and the colony. I let him worry for a little while, before I explained that I can never, never go back because of a clause the studio put in my contract that says I am not allowed to leave the Earth without studio permission which they will never give. And since I'm signed up with them for years and years ...*"

* * *

Lydia's hand came down like a chopping knife on the cutoff, killing Juny's voice in mid-sentence.

"That's enough of that," she said. "Van, take him out."

"You heard," said Gothrud, staring at the two men. Van hesitated.

"Go on, Van!" snapped Lydia. Reluctantly, Van moved forward.

"Kurt—" cried Gothrud.

"It's up to Lydia," replied the druggist, tonelessly.

"Then we'll go ahead," said Lydia decisively, turning away.

"No, by heaven, you won't!" shouted Gothrud, fending off Van and taking a step forward. At the motion, the sudden familiar wave of dizziness swept over him, so that he staggered and was forced to cling to a nearby chair for support.

"All right," he said, fighting to clear his head. "If you won't stop—if you really won't stop—then I'll tell you. Lydia has no right. Lydia—"

"Be silent!" shouted Lydia in German, suddenly halting and wheeling about, her face deadly.

"No," said Gothrud in English. "No. Not any more. Listen, Kurt—and you too, Van. You know what kind of doctor Lydia is. A fourteen-day wonder. She was a registered nurse and the Colonial Office sent her to school for two weeks and gave her a medical diploma." He looked straight at Lydia, who stood frozen, her mouth half-open in an angry gape and her hands fisted by her side. "What you don't know, and what I've kept to myself all this time is that the diploma means nothing. Nothing."

"What's this?" said Kurt.

Gothrud laughed, chokingly.

"As if you haven't suspected, Kurt. Don't think I don't know why you suggested this autopsy. But all you had were suspicions. I know. I was at the school with her."

"I suspected nothing—"

Gothrud laughed, hoarsely.

"Then you're a fool, Kurt. Who believes that a doctor can be made in two weeks when it takes eight years back on Earth? A two-week doctor would be prosecuted on Earth. But we little people who go out to colonize take what we can bring along with us. Us with our nurse-doctors, our druggist-Leaders, our handyman-engineers. Yes. Do you know what they taught us in those two weeks, Kurt—except that I didn't get a diploma for my part in it? Lydia learned how to attempt a forceps delivery, an appendectomy, and a tonsillectomy. They taught her the rudiments of setting broken bones and the proper methods for prescribing some two hundred common drugs."

He was still looking at Lydia as he spoke. She still had not moved, and her hands were still clenched, but her face had taken on an expression of complete serenity.

"This," said Gothrud, staring at her. "This woman who has never held a scalpel in her hand in her life before is the trained specialist that you are expecting to make a professional examination of Juny's body."

Kurt turned to face Lydia.

"Lydia," he said. "Lydia, is this true?"

"Don't be ridiculous, Kurt," replied Lydia, calmly. "He's lying of course."

"How do we know it's not you who are lying?"

"Because I'm in complete control of my faculties. Gothrud's senile."

"Senile?" said Van.

"Of course. The first signs showed up in him some time back. I was hoping it would come on more slowly; but you've all noticed these fainting fits of his, and how he gets wrought up over every little thing. Poor Gothrud," she said, looking at him.

He stared back at her, so aghast at the depths of her perfidy that he could not even bring himself to speak.

"He's made this all up, of course," she went on. "The method by which I was trained was naturally top secret. I've been sworn to silence, of course, but I can tell you that the required information is fed directly to the brain. It's such a new and revolutionary method that it's being restricted to highly important Government Service, such as training key colonists like myself. That explains why the ordinary medical colleges don't know about it yet."

"Lydia," said Kurt. "You say this is true? You swear it's true? How can you prove it?"

"Proof?" she said airly. "Watch me do the autopsy."

Kurt's old eyelids closed down over his eyes until he seemed to look out through a narrow slit.

"All right, Lydia," he said. "That's just what we'll do."

A wordless cry broke from the lips of Gothrud. He snatched up a chair and took one step toward Lydia. Instantly Van Meyer jumped forward and caught him. Frantically, the old man struggled, his breath coming in short terrible gasps.

"Hold him, Van, while I give him a sedative!" cried Lydia—but before she could reach the hypodermic kit on the table across the room, Gothrud suddenly stopped struggling and stiffened. His eyes rolled upward until only the whites showed, for just a second before the lids dropped down over them. He sagged bonelessly. And Van Meyer, lowering him into a chair, snatched back his hands in horror, as if they had suddenly become covered with blood. But Lydia brusquely came across the room, pushed him aside, and bent over the motionless figure.

She took its pulse and rolled one eyelid back momentarily.

"That's all right," she said, stepping back. "Leave him alone. It's easier this way. Come on back to the table with me, both of you, I'll need your assistance."

But for a second, yet, she herself did not move; instead, standing, she stared down at the man she had lived with for more than 50 years. There was a particular glitter in her eye.

"Poor Gothrud," she said softly.

She turned away crisply and led the way back to the conference table, re-tying her face mask as she went.

"Stand over there, Kurt," she said. "You, Van, hand me that scalpel. That one, there." Her eyes jumped at him, as he hesitated. "Move, man! It's only a body."

They went to work. When Lydia was about half through, Gothrud came to himself a little in the chair and called out in a dazed voice to ask what they were doing.

"Don't answer," muttered Lydia, bent above her work. "Pay no attention to him."

They did not answer Gothrud. After a little while he called out again. And when they did not answer this time, either, he subsided in his chair and sat talking to himself and crying a little.

It was an unpleasant job. Van Meyer felt sick; but Kurt went about his duties without emotion, and Lydia was industriously and almost cheerfully busy about her part of it.

"Well," she said, at last. "Just as I suspected— nothing."

She untied her mask and frankly wiped a face upon which perspiration gleamed.

"Wrap her up," she said. "And then you can take her back out again." She glanced over to where her husband was. He had stopped talking to himself and was sitting up, staring at them with bright eyes. "Well, how are you, Gothrud?"

Gothrud did not answer, although he looked directly at her; and Van Meyer, standing beside her, stirred uncomfortably. Kurt sat down on a desk opposite her and mopped his face with a tissue. He produced one of the colony's few remaining cigarets and lighted it.

"And you didn't find anything?" he said sharply to Lydia.

She transferred her gaze from Gothrud to him.

"Not a thing," she said.

Kurt blinked his eyes and turned his head away. But Van Meyer continued to stare at her, uneasily and curiously.

"Lydia," he asked.

"What, Van?"

"What was it, then?"

"What was what?"

"I mean," he said. "Now that you've ... seen her, what was it that made her die?"

"Nothing made her die," replied Lydia. "She just died. If I'm to write a more extensive report, I'll put down that death was due to heart failure—with general debility as a contributing factor."

In the silence that fell between them, the single word came sharp and clear from the old man seated across the room.

"Heart," said Gothrud.

"Yes," said Lydia, turning once more to face him. "If it makes you feel any better, Gothrud, it was her heart that killed her."

"Yes," repeated Gothrud. "Yes, her poor heart. Her heart that none of you understood. Lydia—"

"What?" she demanded sharply.

He stretched out his arms to her, his wrinkled fingers cupped and trembling.

"Her heart," he said. "Lydia. Give me the broken pieces."

*   *   *

The next day Gothrud was very weak and could not leave his bed. For three days Lydia looked after him alone; but it turned out to take too much of her time from the duties required of her by her colony positions, and on the fourth day they brought in Maria Warna from the unmarried women's barracks to stay with him and take care of him. And during the next few weeks he rambled a good deal in his talk, so that, one way or another, he told Maria everything. And eventually, later, she told it to the rest of us. But that was a long time after when things were different.

Gothrud lingered for a few days more than three weeks and finally died. He was cremated, as was everyone else who died after that. That was the same week that the last of the tobacco and cigarets were used up; and those of us who smoked had a hard time getting used to doing without them.

*A burnt-out tower may stand awhile ere it topples
into final ruin.*

NO SHIELD FROM
THE DEAD

It was a nice little party, but a bit obvious. Terri
Mac saw through it before he had taken half a
dozen steps into the apartment. A light flush stain-
ing his high cheekbones. "This is ridiculous," he
said.

The light chatter ceased. Cocktail glasses were
set down on various handy tables and ledges; and
all faces in the room turned toward a man in his
late fifties who sat propped up invalid-wise on
pillows in a chair in a corner of the room.

"The Comptroller is perspicacious," said the old
man, agreeably, waving one hand in a casual
manner. "On your way, children."

And the people present smiled and nodded. Quite
as if it were an ordinary leave-taking, they pushed
past Terri Mac and filed out the door. Even the
blonde, Terri had picked up at the embassy ball
and who had brought him here, strolled off casually,

but in a decidedly less drunken fashion than she had exhibited earlier in the evening.

"Sit down," said the old man. Terri Mac did so, gazing searchingly at the skinny frame and white eyebrows in an unsuccessful effort to connect him with something in memory. "This is ridiculous," he repeated.

"Really?" The old man smiled benignly. "And why so?"

"Why—" the situation was so obvious that Terri fumbled—a little at a loss for words. "Obviously you intend some form of coercion, or else you would have come to me along recognized channels. And any thought of coercion is obviously—well, ridiculous."

"Why?"

"Why? You senile old fool, don't you know that I'm shielded? Don't you know all government officials from the fifth class up wear complete personal shields that are not only crack-proof but contain all the necessary elements to support life independently within the shield for more than twenty hours? Don't you know that I'll be missed in two hours at the most and tracked down in less than sixty minutes more? Are you crazy?"

The old man chuckled, rubbing dry hands together. He said. "I'm shielded too. You can't get at me. And now the room's shielded. You can't get out of it."

Terri stared at him. The initial shock was passing. His own statements anent the completeness of his protection had brought back confidence, and his natural coolness was returning. "What do you want?" he asked, eyeing the other narrowly.

"Pleasure of your company," said the old man. "There are some very strong connections between us. Yes, very strong. We must get to know each other personally."

* * *

It occurred to Terri that he had misinterpreted the situation. Relief came, mixed with a certain amount of chagrin at the way in which he allowed himself to show alarm. He had looked ridiculous. He leaned back in the chair and allowed a note of official hauteur and annoyance to creep into his voice. "I see," he said. "You want something?"

The old man nodded energetically.

"I do. Indeed I do."

"And you think you have some kind of a bargaining tool that is useful but might not be so if it became known to official channels."

"Well—" said the old man cautiously.

"Don't waste my time," interrupted Terri, harshly. "I'm not an ordinary politician. No man who works his way up to the fifth level of the government is. I didn't get to where I am today by pussyfooting around and I haven't the leisure to spend on people who do. Now *what* do you want?"

The other cackled. "Now, what do you think?" he said, putting one finger to his nose cunningly.

"You are old," Terri said. "And therefore cautious. Consequently you would not risk trying to force something from me, but are almost certainly trying to sell me something. Now what do I want? Not the usual things, certainly. Within my position I have all the material things a man could want; and within my shield I enjoy complete immunity. No one but the Central Bureau, itself, can crack this shield. And no one but they can prevent the conditioned reflex that stops my heart if for some reason the shield should be broached. I have a hold on every man beneath me that prevents him from knifing me in the back. There could be only one thing that I want that you could give me—" he leaned forward, staring into the deep-pouched eyes— "and that is a means of getting at the man above me. Am I right?"

"No," said the old man.

Terri stiffened.

"No?" he echoed in angry incredulity.

Their eyes locked. For a long time they held, and at last Terri looked away.

The old man sighed—sipped noisily from a drink on the table beside his chair.

"Wait!" said Terri. To his own surprise, his voice was eager, even a little timorous in its hopefulness. "Wait. I've got it. There will be a test. There always is a test every time a man moves up. His superiors watch him when he doesn't suspect it. It will be that way for me when I am ready for the fourth level. And you have some kind of advance information. You know what the test will be. Maybe you know the man who will administer it. You want to sell me this information."

The other said nothing.

"Well," Terri spread his hands openly. "I am interested. I'll buy. What do you want. Money? A favor? Protection?"

"No."

"No?" Terri shouted, starting up from his chair. "What do you mean by no? Can't you say anything but 'no'?" A rage possessed him. He flung himself forward two furious steps to stand threateningly over the aged figure. "You doddering idiot! Say what you want, and quickly! My two hours are nearly up. I'll be missed. They'll be here in a few minutes—the Bureau Guards. They'll crack the room shield. They'll rescue me. And they'll take you into custody. To be questioned. To be executed. At my order. Do you understand? Your life depends on me."

After a little, the old man chuckled again. "Yes," he muttered, in a high-pitched old voice. "That's the way it'll be."

Terri stared at him. "You don't seem to understand. You're going to die."

"Oh yes," said the old man, nodding his head indulgently. "I'll die. But I'm an old man. I'd die anyway in a year or so—maybe in a day or so. But for you—for a young man like you—the up and coming young governmental with everything to lose—" he leered slyly at Terri. "Your death won't be so easy for you to take."

"I die?" echoed Terri, stupefied. "But I'm not going to die. They're coming to *rescue* me."

"Oh, are they?" said the old man, ironically.

"Of course!" said Terri. "Of course, why shouldn't they?"

The old man winked one faded eye portentously.

"Fine young man," he said. "Up and coming young man. Brilliant. Never a thought for the people he trampled on the way up the ladder. Dear me, no."

"What do you mean?" said Terri.

The old eyes, looking up suddenly, pierced him.

"Do you remember Kilaren?"

"K-Kilaren?"

"Kilaren," recited the old man as if quoting from a newspaper. "The beautiful young secretary of a provincial governor whose lecherous and unnatural pursuit drove her to suicide. So that one day to escape the governor, she jumped or fell from a high window. And the people of the province, who had for a long time heard ugly stories and rumors, finally mobbed the office and lynched the governor, hanging him from the same window from which the girl had jumped. They said that even the fall had not spoiled her beauty, but that was probably false." The old man's words dwindled away into silence.

"I—what of it?" said Terri. "What's that to do with me?"

"Why, you were there. You were the governor's aide, and when the mob had gone home and feeling had slackened off, you stepped into the gap and seized up the reins of government, handling matters so skillfully that you were immediately promoted to an under-post at Government City."

"What of it?"

"Why it was all your doing," replied the other, in a mildly reproving voice, "the rumors, the stories, the mob, even the suicide. Poor Kilaren—a pitiful pawn in your ruthless game to eliminate the governor in your mad dash up the ladder."

"I never touched her!" cried Terri, his voice cracking. "I swear it."

"Who said you did? The type of mind that stoops to murder would never have gotten you this far. But you were the one who hired her, knowing the governor's tendencies. You were the one that gave her work that kept her, night after night, alone with the man. You preyed upon her fear of losing her job. You threw the sin in her face after she had committed it. You told her what she might have been, and what she was, and what she would be. You broke her, day after day. In the sterile privacy of the office you reviled her, scorned her, brought her to believe that she was what she was not, a creature of filth and dishonor. You blocked off all avenues of escape but the one that led through one high window. *You killed her!*"

"No!"

"Yes!"

Terri brought his quivering hands together and clenched them in his lap. He stared at the old man. "Who are you?"

"I was a friend of hers. We lived in the same hotel-apartment. She had no family. I believe you knew that when you hired her."

"I see," said Terri. He drew a long, deep, shuddering breath, and leaned back in the chair. "So

that's the story," he said, his voice strengthening.
"I might have known it. Blackmail. There are always fools that want to try blackmail."

"No," said the old man. "Not Blackmail, Comptroller. I want your life."

Terri laughed shortly, contemptuously. "No knowledge that you have can threaten my life."

"They will come," said the old man, leaning wearily back against his cushions. "As you said, the Bureau Guards will come; and I think I shall kill myself when I hear them starting to crack the shield around this room. They will come in and find you with a dead man. What will you tell them, Terri?"

"Tell them? Anything I choose. They won't question *me*."

"No. The guards won't. But the Bureau will. How can they raise a man to the fourth level when there is a two-hour mystery in his background? They will want to know what you were doing here."

"I was kidnapped," said Terri.

"By whom? Can you prove it? And why?"

"I've been held a prisoner here."

"By a dead man? No, no, Terri. The circumstances are suspicious. You walk away from the embassy under your own power. You disappear and are found in a shielded room with a man who has committed suicide. This must be explained and in the end you will have to tell them the truth."

"And what if I do?" said Terri, truculently.

"But the truth is so fantastic, Terri. So uncheckable. I am dead, and I am the only one who could have supported your story. These people who were here when you came in are common actors. They have no idea why I wanted you decoyed here. These are my rooms. And there is no obvious connection between me and the dead Kilaren. And perhaps I will decide to live just long enough to denounce you as a traitor when they enter."

Ashen-faced, Terri stared.

"The Bureau will have to question you. They will clamp a block on your mind so that you can't operate the reflex that stops your heart. And they will question you over and over again, because the Bureau cannot afford to take chances. You will go into a private hell of your own, Terri Mac. You will tell the story of your own evil to that girl over and over again, pleading to be believed. And they will not believe you. And in the end they will kill you, just to be on the safe side. Because, you see, you *might* have been doing something traitorous in these two shielded hours."

Terri's head bobbed limply, like a drunken man's. He made one last effort. "Why?" he said. "Why do you do this? Your life. For a girl who was no connection to you?"

The old man folded his hands.

"I was a little like your governor," he said. "We all have our sins. I loved Kilaren and the shock of her death wrecked my health." He cocked his head suddenly on one side. "Listen," he said.

From beyond the closed door of the room, a high-pitched humming was barely audible. It grew in volume, going up the scale. Terri leaped to his feet; and for the space of a couple of seconds, he lunged first this way than that, like a wild animal beating against its trap. Then, as if all will had at last gone out of him, he stopped in the middle of the room and closed his eyes. For a fraction of a moment he stood there, before a faint convulsion seized him and he fell.

With a faint smile on his face, the old man reached out to a hidden switch and cut the shield about the room. Uniformed guards tumbled through the door, to pull up in dismay at the sight of the body on the floor.

"I'm sorry," said the old man, "I must have turned the shield on by mistake. I was trying to signal someone. The Comptroller seems to have had a heart attack."

When a believer outlasts his belief, life becomes a fate worse than death.

THE UNDERGROUND

They would fight on!

Yes, the fight would not slacken. For the Leaders were not surrendering to the enemy—instead they were going underground; and the little captain thrilled to the news that he was to head their escort. The war had gone badly, *this* war had gone badly, but the conflict would never cease until right triumphed and the Leaders were once more victorious. The little captain had always known this; but this final proof of it swelled his heart with pride.

He was the little captain to them all; just as they were numbers and not names to him. Not even in the privacy of his own mind did he refer to the Leaders by names. To their faces they were— "Sir!" and if reference to one must be made while respectfully addressing another, it was—"Sir! The official Number Three, sir—" or "Sir! The honorable Number Five, sir—". For this was Headquart-

54

er's Code. Only the Doctor, did the little captain refer to by title; and even then he uttered the word with a capital initial letter for the Doctor was not just any doctor, but the private doctor of Number One, himself.

And, just as he capitalized them, so they lower-cased him. He was the "little captain" to all the Leaders. So did great authority look down from lofty heights upon his insignificant rank. For he was not really small in a physical sense. A little short yes. A little young, perhaps, even for a "little captain." But it was a question of rank, not size or age, in the final essential.

The little captain was undoubtedly brave, although he had only seen action once. That had been right after he was graduated from the State Military School for officers' sons. He had been sent forth into the front lines as a lieutenant; and there they had given him a platoon of men and told him to follow a route marked out on a map, taking careful note of everything he saw and then returning. He had started out with his men; but at the first hill some big guns of the enemy had opened up and when the dust had cleared, there was no one left of the platoon, except the little captain. He was then still only a short distance from his own lines; but his orders had been to follow the route on the map; and so he went on, taking careful note of everything he saw until he reached the end of his route and came back to the lines once more.

When he got back to the lines, he learned that Number One, himself, the First Leader, had been inspecting this portion of the front. And this great man had seen, by remote control television, all that the little captain had done (though, of course, he was still only a lieutenant at this time); and he had given orders that the young man must approach him to be commended.

How the little captain's knees trembled as he

went up to Division Headquarters! But Number One was very kind. He put the young man at his ease and praised him, which made the little captain faint with joy, but also forced him to protest that he had really done nothing worthy.

"But the order was to follow the map, Sir!" he had said. "It is our duty to follow orders, Sir!"

And Number One had laughed and asked him questions about duty and loyalty and combat, to which the little captain had replied quite truthfully that they were all great and glorious things, as everybody knew because they were told that in school. And Number One had drawn back after a while and looked at him oddly; and asked him if he would want to join the Headquarter's Guard, which had the special duty of protecting the Leaders, the Numbers One through Twelve, at all times. And the little captain, hardly knowing where he found the strength to respond—so great was the honor— had answered yes.

So it happened that he had joined the Headquarter's Guard; and here fortune had continued to smile on him. For, though it was apparent to him at a glance that nearly all the men in it were much older and wiser and more experienced than he, he had been promoted to captain in charge of Number One's particular security. And he had from then on been closer than anyone—except the Doctor—to the life and actions of the twelve great men who were the Leaders of the People.

His devotion to them had never wavered. His trust in them had never faltered. He had listened to them; and found that he could not understand them; but for that very reason he had implicit faith in their omnipotence. They would lead and he should follow and everything would come out all right.

*   *   *

Therefore, the little captain, alone among the Leaders, their families with a few secretaries or close friends, and the soldiers of his escort, was neither disheartened nor dismayed as they traveled to the Underground. The war might be lost, but the fight would go on. Number One, himself, had announced this in his last broadcast to the people, his black eye flashing, his powerful jaw outthrust upon the television screen. So what did it matter if for a short time the enemy set their heel upon the people? Deliverance would come.

—And now, as he stood waiting by the tunnel entrance in the mountains—the tunnel entrance down which the Numbers One through Twelve and their wives, secretaries and friends, were disappearing, the feeling swelled within him that this was a great moment, and he was almost not surprised when Number One, the Supreme Leader, approached him.

"Captain—" said Number One.

"Sir!"

Number One took him by the elbow—the little captain's elbow small and frail in that large, capable hand; and drew him aside. The other hand passed something round and hard—like a grenade, only larger—to the little captain.

"The escort," said Number One, in a low voice, gesturing toward the Headquarter's troop which had accompanied them under the little captain's command. "We can take no chances. You will dispose of them."

"Yes sir!"

"But wait until all of us are safely in the tunnel."

"Yes sir!"

"This weapon should do the job," said Number One, pressing the round, hard thing into the little captain's hand. "If not, you have your gun. Do not attempt to join us until you have disposed of the escort. Is that clear? Now you pull the pin on this and then let it go. You understand?"

"Yes sir!" said the little captain. And he stood correctly at attention, holding the round thing hidden in his hand, waiting until all of the people in the Underground had disappeared down the tunnel and were safely out of danger.

After the last person had passed from sight and a few minutes had gone by, he turned to the escort.

"Aten—shun!" he ordered. "About face!"

—And when they about faced, he pulled the pin on the round hard thing that was like a grenade; and rolled it along the ground toward the line of men, stepping back into the mouth of the tunnel himself, to be out of the way of the explosion.

Then the world erupted. Much more violently than the little captain had ever expected it to do, the ground rose up and flung itself in his face. Rock rained upon him, battering him, and for a moment he thought he had been killed.

But after a while he managed to get to his feet. One of his arms was broken and he felt crushed and strange through the middle part of his body. But he drew his gun with his good hand and went out to make sure that his duty was fully discharged.

The grenade-thing had wrought havoc on the mountainside. Rubble and rock had been blown clear of a shallow depression in the undergranite of the mountain itself. The troop had disappeared completely except for a tattered thing which some freak chance had wedged between two boulders. The little captain, weak and dizzy, made his way to it and found it was barely recognizable as a man he had known and liked. He shuddered and closed his eyes.

But the thing was still alive. It looked up at him and spoke.

"You are a murderer," it said; and cured him.

The little captain felt his stomach turn over within him. But he said, very gently:—

"It is for the cause,"—and shot it swiftly and cleanly through the head. Then he turned and headed back toward the tunnel.

Rock crowded the entrance, which was broken down by the explosion; but after he had passed this, the little captain found the floor of the tunnel flat and easy to walk on. But dizziness kept overcoming him in waves; and he was forced to steady himself with one hand on the rocky wall, as he made his way down into the heart of the mountain.

It seemed to him that he walked for a long way in the dark, guiding himself by his hand along the wall. And then it occurred to him, finally, that something had gone badly wrong with him inside when the big grenade went off; and that he might not make it to Number One to report. He staggered a little from time to time and finally he fell.

For a while he lay where he had fallen; for the rock floor of the tunnel had turned wonderfully soft and sleep was tempting him. But then he reminded himself that he had not made his report and that Number One would be waiting to hear if all had gone well. So he struggled to his feet and pushed on; and gradually he moved into a dream world in which nothing was real but the rock beneath his fingers and a great tiredness within him and he moved through dark, milk-thick fog toward the inner end of the tunnel and the report he must give to Number One . . .

And finally there came a time when there were voices around him. But he could not see the people to whom the voices belonged and he could not understand them.

"It was for the cause," he told them. And he heard the Doctor's voice, near at hand, but with a strange and distant ring to it.

"I will take him."

—And then he remembered nothing for a long time.

When he awoke, he was in a narrow white bed in what looked like a hospital room. And the Doctor was standing over him.

"Where am I?" asked the little captain.

"Half a mile below the surface," answered the Doctor. "You're in the Underground." The little captain felt the prick of a needle in his arm. "Now sleep and regain your strength, my son."

The little captain closed his eyes obediently and sleep came swiftly, for he was still very weak.

After that, however, he began to mend. Day by day, as the calendar clock beside his bed measured time, the Doctor nursed him, his old bent-shouldered body, lame from a wound in a previous war, limping back and forth by the bed, his eyes deep and sad in his long face, under shaggy grey eyebrows. And the little captain questioned him ceaselessly about how the work of the Underground was going.

"Why are you so eager?" the Doctor asked him one day.

"There must also be work that I can do here," said the little captain. "I am anxious to get out of bed and begin it."

But the Doctor only shook his head when the little captain pressed him for an answer as to how soon he would be able to get up and go about whatever duties could be found for him.

"I am sure I will now," the little captain said. "I feel quite strong."

"Wait a while longer," said the Doctor.

Often the little captain, watching the Doctor as he moved about the room, was taken with wonder at the effort and attention that the older man devoted to him.

"—But I do not need so much of your time," the little captain protested one day. "Surely your duties must call you elsewhere. I am very grateful, but—"

"It is nothing," said the Doctor.

"I do not understand," the little captain told him, "why you go to so much trouble for me. In our fight for liberty, here in the Underground, I, as a person of lowest rank, can clearly be of no great importance."

The Doctor looked at him. "You would have died if I had not taken care of you," said the older man.

"True, but what of it?" said the little captain. "I was not important—"

"You reminded me of my sons," said the Doctor, turning away.

"Have you sons?" inquired the little captain, sitting up in the bed. "Are they here?"

"They died," replied the Doctor, harshly. "They were killed on the western front near the beginning of the war."

"Ah," said the little captain. "Now I understand. You must be very proud. You have gone to all this trouble for me in memory of your hero sons."

But the Doctor did not answer. He turned and went out the door.

Eventually, the day came when even the Doctor was forced to admit that the little captain was fit for duty. He came to the room to get the little captain and together they went to the rooms of Number One.

It was the first time the little captain had been outside his sickroom; and the Underground surprised him. For it was not full of offices and arsenals as he had expected; but instead seemed to be

split up into a number of apartments and rooms
dug out of the rock and branching off a large central tunnel. It was down this tunnel that he went
with the Doctor; and at the very end of it, they
came to the rooms of Number One.

The same butler that the little captain remembered from above ground, met them at the entrance and conducted them back through rich-
furnished rooms to one where Number One awaited
them, leaning back in a large overstuffed chair
and picking at a tray of food beside him. His big
frame was sprawled loosely in trousers and shirt
open at the neck. It was the first time the little
captain had seen the Leader of his people not in
uniform and it seemed somehow indecent that a
person of no importance like himself should view
the Supreme Commander in this state of undress.

It did not, however, seem to bother Number
One, himself. He looked up at the Doctor; and he
looked at the little captain, who came automatically to attention and saluted.

"Well," said Number One, looking at him, "so
here you are with me once again."

"Yes sir!" replied the little captain, stiff at
attention. "Thanks to the Doctor, sir!"

"Yes—" Number One glanced at the Doctor with
a look the little captain could not interpret. "Well
now, what are we going to do with you?"

This was clearly a rhetorical question. The little
Captain retained his stiff stance and said nothing.
Number One sighed.

"Well, put him to work in the broadcast section,
Doctor," he said. "He's your responsibility."

"He will be useful," said the Doctor. They exchanged glances once more and the Doctor took
the little captain out.

The broadcast section was a large, long room
filled with all sorts of radio equipment. Waiting
for them as they came in was Number Five, who

had been Minister of the Interior. He was a short, raw-boned man with stiff black hair springing up on a head too large for his body; and he rubbed his hands with pleasure as the little captain was brought in.

"Well, young man," he said. "Well!"

"Number One turned him over to you," the Doctor informed him.

"I asked for him. Yes, I asked for him," chuckled Number Five. "Yes," he went on to the little captain, "we've got a use for you here my boy."

"I am honored, sir!" said the little captain, saluting. The ex-Minister of the Interior did not look pleased.

"No military showing off here, now," he said. "I don't believe in it. Take off your coat and get to work."

Wincing internally, for he felt almost naked without it, the little captain took off his officer's jacket and hung it on a coatrack. The Doctor turned and went out the door, giving him one unreadable glance as he went. Then the little captain had no more time to think, for Number Five had him, almost literally, by the ear; and was teaching him how the broadcast section worked.

There was an immense amount of magnificent equipment, all of it automatic, or as near automatic as such stuff could be made. By some process that Number Five explained, but that the little captain did not understand, they could broadcast from the Underground here and yet not be traced by enemy monitors while their power was on. However, it was not really necessary to understand as long as he could execute; and a few hours later when Number Three came in to broadcast to the agricultural workers who had been his responsibility as Minister of Agriculture, the little captain pulled all the right switches and twisted all the right dials and was very happy. For the work he was doing was helping to win the country back from the enemy.

That night the Doctor came and took the little captain with him to the main lounge where everyone in the Underground gathered for recreation. It was a room as big as a ballroom, containing chairs, tables, a swimming pool, a dance floor and a bar, behind which stood Ki, a young man who had formerly been Number One's own private bartender but who here in the Underground served them all, even the little captain. Ki was the only one in the room that the little captain could consider being anywhere near his social equal, so, in spite of the Doctor's instructions to mingle with the others, he hung close to the bar and exchanged a remark from time to time with Ki.

These social evenings were really not to the little captain's taste. He preferred to read in his room. But since the Doctor had taken him there in the first place, the little captain made it a point to drop in every evening for a little while, before going off to his book, or back to the broadcast room to tinker with the equipment or listen to enemy broadcasts.

The little captain was the only one who listened regularly to enemy broadcasts—at least he was the only one who listened from the broadcast section. There undoubtedly were, he thought, other receiving sets in other parts of the Underground—or for all he knew, other broadcasting units. Indeed, he did not know what the others in the Underground did—which was quite right, of course, for their work would be top secret. Occasionally, passing down the central corridor, he would pass a door ajar and catch a glimpse of an apartment something like the rooms of Number One as far as

furnishings went. But undoubtedly the real work-
rooms were farther back.

After a good start, however, things did not go
too well with the broadcast section. Very soon
after he took up his duties there, Number Five
began to ignore him, and if the little captain wanted
to find him for anything, he would have to look him
up in the lounge, where the Ex-Minister of the
Interior would be hanging on the bar, and occupied in slow, steady drinking that ended with him
eventually falling off his stool and being helped to
his apartment by Ki.

It could not escape the notice of the little captain that Number Five was slowly disintegrating;
any more than it could escape him that the day of
their emergence from the Underground and the
defeat of the enemy seemed as far away as ever.
Part of the little captain's duty was to monitor
enemy broadcasts and digest the news in them for
delivery to Number One. As a result he was forced
to write down that all the Leaders had been tried
in absentia by the Enemy and condemned to death
for war crimes; and that a new, false government,
supposedly of the people, had been set up in their
place. But whether Number One ever actually read
these news accounts the little captain never knew.
Number One kept exclusively to his rooms and the
daily digest was taken from the little captain's
hands by the butler at the door.

But Number Five continued to go down. The
day came when he collapsed at the bar early in the
day and the Doctor was called to his apartment
after Ki had helped him back to his bed.

"He won't live," said Ki, to the little captain,
when he returned to the lounge.

"But who will take his place?" asked the little
captain. And Ki looked at him and laughed.

Possibly Ki knew that the little captain had taken
over all of Number Five's work a long time before.

And possibly others knew it too. For no one was appointed as new overseer to the little captain. Indeed, when he stopped to look around at the others, he could imagine none of them taking over the job. Possibly their own duties kept them occupied; but to the little captain's eyes they seemed to be always in the lounge, or otherwise occupied only in amusing themselves. Moreover, most of them drank too much; and were letting themselves go to pieces physically. How would they be in fit shape to assume their duties when they came back into the open again for all out battle with the enemy? Possibly this was all none of his business; but the fact that almost no one nowdays came to the broadcast section to speak to the people certainly was. The little captain had been forced to fill in his hours on the air with recordings of old speeches.

The little captain had been taught to obey without questioning. But the time came when he felt himself forced to ask the Doctor what he should do.

The Doctor looked across the dispensary desk at him. The old medical man had aged yet further and grown tireder looking in the months they had been Underground. He, together with Ki and the little captain, and possibly the servants in Number One's apartment were the only ones that seemed to have anything to do nowdays. And the Doctor seemed to be having too much. Everybody made demands upon his attention for some bodily disturbance or other. There were some, indeed, who seemed to make a hobby of being sick. And, in addition, the Doctor was liable to call by Number One at any time. And these summons came frequently and at any hour.

"What shall you do?" repeated the Doctor, after the little captain had asked him. "Why, nothing."

"Nothing?" echoed the little captain, wistfully.

"What can you do?" asked the Doctor, with a shrug.

"But the people—" in his agitation the little captain pointed straight up at the half mile of rock over their heads, as if the people were directly on top of them, "—they are counting on us. I mean they're counting on the Leader. If they hear nothing but the same old speeches how is the Resistance to stay alive?"

The Doctor looked down at the desk; he sighed.

"I did wrong," he said, finally, half to himself.

"Sir?" said the little captain, puzzled.

"I should have left you to die," said the Doctor. He raised his eyes to the little captain.

The little captain stared at him, not understanding. The Doctor leaned forward and his eyes were gentle.

"Try and take more advantage of your leisure hours here," he said. "Try and be less impatient. Do each day's work as it comes and make it a practice not to think beyond it. Will you try to do that? For me?"

"Whatever you say, sir," replied the little captain. "But—" A buzzer on the wall sounded, summoning the Doctor to the apartment of Number One; and cutting the little captain short.

"We must each live as we can," said the Doctor; and went out.

Conscientiously, the little captain tried to live up to the Doctor's advice. He closed his eyes to the drinking and the verbal fights that were becoming every day more common among the Leaders and the people they had brought with them. And he fed more and more old tapes into his daily broadcast until finally it was nearly all a rehash of something that had been done before.

One man, and one man only, still came occasion-

ally to speak to the people. And he was Number
Ten, the former Minister of Ports and Customs;
and a big, violent man who liked to mention his
own name in the broadcasts and was fond of em-
phasizing his past services to the country. Lately,
however he had been becoming more and more
wild, not only when speaking behind the micro-
phone, but among the others in the lounge. And
there came a night when he ranted and raved before
them all and finally went so far as to strike Number Two, with whom he was arguing.

Number Two was a wiry old man and he tumbled backward as if he had no bones at all; but
when he hit the floor, instead of lying still, he
rolled over on one side and a little gun appeared
in his hand. There was a sound like a stick breaking and the big Number Ten fell all at once, pulling at his chest with both hands. And lay still.

—And all the people in the room, except Ki and
the little captain, melted away through the entranc-
es; so that in a matter of seconds they two were
left alone with the dead man.

Ki came out from behind the bar and took hold
of the legs of Number Ten's dead body.

"Help me," he said. "He's heavy."

The little captain took the arms and together
they carried the dead man around behind the bar
and through a door there into a little room behind
where Ki washed glasses. But they did not stop
there, for in this room where the little captain had
never been before, there turned out to be a further
door. And Ki opened this and they went through it
and down a short flight of metal stairs into a big
echoing room filled with machinery of all sorts
that hummed and whirred.

"This way," said Ki; and led the way, still holding the dead man's feet, to a huge box-like affair
that was higher at the top than the little captain's

head. Ki opened a door set in the front of it and a blast of heat came out.

"What's this?" cried the little captain.

"What do you think it is?" grunted Ki. "Did you think our heat and our light and our air come from nowhere? Our Underground is as self-contained as a spaceship; and this machinery is what purifies the water and the air and keeps us alive."

"I never thought—" stammered the little captain.

"You're a fool," said Ki, shortly. "Take his legs and help me shove him into the incinerator."

After that, the little captain could never feel the same again. For some days he continued to go on with his work mechanically, but now it was all on tapes. The gatherings in the lounge were different. Now the Leaders and their people seemed to be wary of each other; and those who gathered there met in an atmosphere of brittle tenseness. The little captain saw this; he worried over it and thought very hard.

He did not want to go against the advice given him by the Doctor, who had always been so wise and helpful. But he began to think that the Doctor, immersed in his many duties, could not see the situation as clearly as he, himself, did. There was no doubt that the Leaders were failing in their duty to continue the fight against the enemy. At this rate they would never be ready to come forth and reconquer the country. The little captain thought of the millions of people under the false government set up by the enemy, sitting waiting for the Leaders to return and rescue them; and his heart turned within him. And so, finally, though it was a terrible step to take, the little captain determined that there was only one thing for him to do. And that was to inform Number One of the situation as it stood, for only Number One could repair the damage that had already been done the Resistance.

It was a big step to take; and the little captain quivered inside at the thought of it. But the fact that it was his duty stiffened his spine and he went in full uniform to the entrance of Number One's apartment and asked to speak to the Supreme Leader.

After a short wait, the butler returned and took him in.

At first, when for the second time he came through the door of that inner room, the little captain thought he must have been taken to the wrong place by a mistake on the butler's part. There was no one there but a fat, sagging man, sprawled in an overstuffed chair, nibbling at some pieces of cheese.

"Well, what is it?" snapped the fat man, throatily. And the little captain stared, for the voice coming from the creature before him was the voice of Number One.

Wondering, he approached the seated man; and when he got close he saw indeed that it was Number One; but with all his appearance of firmness and brute strength drowned and lost in an ocean of fat.

"What is it, I say!" repeated the Supreme Commander.

"I—I have a thing of duty to report—" stammered out the little captain; and stumbled through his report that the broadcasts were being ignored, the other Leaders were quarreling among themselves and that the work of the Resistance was being stifled by indifference.

When he had finished, the gross man—it was almost impossible for the little captain still to think of him as Number One—stared at him for a long time. Then he turned his head on its fat neck toward the butler.

"What kind of an idiot is this?" he demanded.

The butler raised his eyebrows, but said nothing.

The fat man turned back once more to the little captain.

"Did you ever stop to think," he said, "that you live only because I gave the Doctor permission to save your life?"

The little captain bowed his head.

"Well then," wheezed Number One. "If you haven't the brains to understand a situation when it stares you in the face, get back to your microphones and stick with them and don't come bothering me about it." He turned to the butler. "See that he isn't let in here again."

The butler nodded.

"Now get out," ordered the First Leader.

They went.

Stunned, the little captain wandered blindly down the main corridor. All his background, all his training, everything he had been taught to believe seemed tumbled in an inchoate mass which it was beyond the means of his poor brain to sort out. He caught himself drifting toward the main lounge; and checked himself and turned away. He did not want to face Ki, or anyone else who might be in there now, for a devil was pounding at his sanity.

Why?

Why had they given up? What straw had tipped the scales in the direction of defeat and indifference. What had happened? Why had they scrapped everything they believed in?

It was too big a question for the little captain. Something seemed to snap in his head and for quite a while he left the real world entirely and went down into hell where he wandered around as a soul in torment until he found a rope marked *duty;* and with the help of that pulled himself back to life and sanity.

He found that he had made up his mind. He went in search of the Doctor and found him in his dispensary. The medical man got up quickly from behind his desk at the sight of the little captain's face and came around to him.

"What happened?" he asked.

"I went to see Number One," said the little captain with a great effort. And, prompted by the Doctor, he told him the whole story of the situation as he had seen it; and his interview with the Supreme Commander.

When he had finished telling the story, the Doctor turned from him and took off his glasses and wiped them with hands that trembled.

"I should not have saved you," he said, brokenly. "No, I should not have saved you. But you reminded me of my own sons—" he broke off and looked back at the little captain. "My poor boy, what are you going to do now?"

"I am going to do my duty," said the little captain, squaring his shoulders. "Duty to what I believe is something that cannot be killed. If I cannot find it here I will find it elsewhere in the world. If I have to go to the ends of the world, I will find it."

"My poor boy—" whispered the Doctor.

"Neither poor nor a boy," said the little captain. "I am a man and a soldier. It is my duty to fight for the freedom of my people. If I cannot fight here, I will fight elsewhere. I want you to show me the way out of the Underground."

"No," said the Doctor. "No."

"Yes," replied the little captain. "If I can do nothing else, I can die as a soldier should, in combat with the enemy."

"But there is no army any more," protested the Doctor. "There are no troops, no central authority."

"I will find them, or make them, or be them," said the little captain, inflexibly. "The fight is never lost as long as one man will fight on."

"You can do nothing," cried the Doctor. "Here you can be the voice of millions, if nothing else."

"A false voice," said the little captain. "Once and for all will you show me the way out?"

The Doctor wrung his hands.

"Very well," said the little captain. "I will find somebody else and force the information from him." And he turned toward the door.

"No. Stop," said the Doctor. "I will show you. Don't ask anyone else." His voice was shaking.

"Thank you," said the little captain, turning back. "I had faith that you would."

The Doctor fumbled his glasses on to his nose and led the way out of the dispensary and down the corridor. They continued on until they came to the main lounge. It was deserted except for Ki behind the bar and he grinned at them sardonically as they came up.

"I need the captain's help downstairs," said the Doctor. Ki grinned and held up a glass and breathed on it.

"You know the way, Doctor," he said.

The Doctor and the little captain went behind the bar and into the little room and through the farther door and down the stairs. When the door was fairly shut behind them and the hum of the machines covered his voice, the little captain turned to the Doctor.

"I did not know the route went this way," he said. "You will have to come with me, now. They will blame you for showing me the way out, otherwise."

"I will not leave you," replied the Doctor, hurrying along with head down.

They went past the machines and past the

incinerator—the little captain shuddered when he saw it—and finally beyond to a door set in a wall. It was a heavy steel door like a fire door; and the Doctor strained at it to open it.

They passed through it into dampness and darkness. But the Doctor reached out and a switch clicked, throwing the place where they stood into brilliant illumination from the bulbs overhead. The little captain looked around him. They stood in a corridor rough-hewn out of the rock, more tunnel than corridor. Water glistened on the granite walls, the moisture of condensation; and the floor was rough and slippery underfoot.

The Doctor led the way. They went up the corridor for a short distance, around a bend to the right of it; and into a little room barely larger than the corridor, that ended in a blank wall in which was set a large, circular door like the door of a bank vault.

"Is this it?" asked the little captain.

"This is it," said the Doctor. He put his hands on the big metal bolt that secured it; but his strength seemed to fail him as he started to draw it. His hands fell limply and he turned to the little captain.

"For the last time," he said. "Will you stay? There is nothing you can do. Nothing!"

"I must go," said the little captain.

"To the end of the world?" choked the Doctor.

"To the end of the world."

The Doctor turned and laid his hands on the big bolt and pulled it back. On ponderous hinges the vault-like door swung open. Before him the little captain saw what had been the entrance to an upslanting tunnel; but which now was filled and packed with fallen rock.

"It is like that all the way to the surface," said the Doctor's dead voice in his ear. "And it has been like that since the day we all entered here; and they blew up the tunnel behind us on the orders of Number One. So look at it. Look at it. For you and me, this *is* the end of the world."

Clinging as well as parting may be all we need to know of hell.

AFTER
THE FUNERAL

As they left the cemetery gates behind them, he shoved the car's heater controls all the way up, but the blasting warmth merely nibbled at the shell of cold encasing him.

"Can't you drive a little faster?" his wife said. "I want to get home and have a drink."

"All right, Helen," he said, numbly. "It's the traffic, slowing us."

"Really, Henry!" She tucked the collar of her fur coat around her thinning neck. Above it, her sharp-boned face would now be turned to him with that look as if he had been one of her former pupils, back in the days before their marriage, who had failed again to learn some simple fact of word. "I think we could have left a little earlier than we did."

"No," he said.

"These graveside services! Louise *would* specify

a graveside service for her funeral. If that isn't just like her!"

"Little enough," he said. "After all these years." His words went out in a cloud of thin steam against the frosty windshield. He did not return Helen's gaze, which nonetheless he could feel, her eyes like two chill spots of pale gray shadow on his cheek. The street was frozen iron-hard, but the new coat of light snow upon it made it slippery; and the cars ahead of him moved creakily and with caution, as if their very joints and bearings were stiff with the cold. "She wanted us with her—to the end."

"Perhaps." He heard his wife sniff. "And maybe Louise just wanted us to suffer for it. You don't know women like I do. I wouldn't put it past her."

"She's dead," he said.

"Oh, stop it, Henry! You act as if she was one of your own family—or one of mine, for that matter. Instead of some little graduate student we've taken care of for nine years."

The cars ahead were beginning to turn off the direct route from the cemetery. He was able to speed up and he thought to himself that they would be back, in their own home, soon.

"Oh, I liked her, all right," his wife was saying. "—as well as anyone could. You have to admit yourself she was more than a little odd. Hardly a fit subject for your telepathy experiments and such, otherwise. Still, you never heard me complain about your bringing her into our house to live."

"No," he said, thickly, "you never complained."

"I understood from the first what an odd little piece she was. But I resigned myself to having all sorts of characters around when I married you. Though why you couldn't just teach psychology without going into research on mind-reading and psychokinesis and clairvoyance, and all the rest—

well, I resigned myself to associating with freaks. You turn here."

"I know," he said. "I know it."

"Of course," she went on. "I never expected to have you bring home one of them like a prize pig and install her under my own roof for nine full years."

"She was very gifted," he said. "She had no place else to go."

"For God's sake, Henry! The city takes care of people with no place to go, nowdays. Or the government, or someone. Besides, she wasn't so sick as all that. Just a bad heart."

"Bad enough to kill her—at the end."

"Well, goodness—home at last!" Helen leaned forward and he saw her nose, sharp in profile against the windshield. He swung in to the curb before their large old house. The snow was drifted high and frozen hard against the dull brown brick of the walls. "Henry! Aren't you going to put the car in the garage?"

"I want to get inside."

They got out; and the iciness of the gray afternoon wrapped itself around them, slipping in through the little crannies and gaps of their winter clothing, even in the short time it took to hurry up the front walk and up the three concrete steps through the big oak front door into the house.

"Whew!" cried Helen, taking off her scarf and shaking her dark hair out. "That's finally over! I'll light the fire in the living room. And you make us that drink, Henry. A couple of stiff ones."

He was slower removing his coat and hat. He hung them up mechanically and walked to the kitchen. Opening the refrigerator, he took out a tray of ice cubes. His chilled fingers shuddered away from its freezing metal as he set it down on the sterile white enamel of the kitchen table. He broke the cubes free into a glass bowl, filled a pitcher with water and carried them to the living room.

The fire was already beginning to crackle up. Helen stood before it, her tweed skirt stretched over the rather lean line of her hips, warming her hands.

"No ice for me," she said at the sound of its tinkle in the bowl. "I'm cold enough already, thank you. Just scotch and water."

He made two drinks without ice and carried one to his wife.

"Skoal!" she said, taking and lifting it. He turned away. The fire was no help to him. He turned and walked away from her, over to the window; and looked out at the car. A new little snow was beginning to dust down; and already its dark top and hood were powdered.

"What's the matter, darling?" she said behind him. "Can't you enjoy the wake?"

"The wake," he muttered.

He stood staring out the window. Behind him, Helen's voice took on a new note.

"You know the girl was in love with you, don't you?"

"She was?" He looked down at the glass in his hand. His fingers were curled around it so tightly they seemed frozen to it.

"Why, of course. I knew it from the first. The only reason I never objected or said anything to you about it was becuase you were so blind to it, yourself." She laughed. "And you were blind, weren't you, Henry? Nine years with your nose in your papers and she following you around with her sad sheep's eyes."

"You," he said between stiff jaws, clumsily, "are a sadist."

"No, just a woman. Tell me, Henry. Was she

really any good at telepathy—and all those things? Was she really enough of a success to justify to yourself having her around?"

"Yes," he said.

"No, I mean it. Did you really get into each other's minds? Really in? I know you said you did; but did you?"

"I told you so." The words were thick.

"Because, Henry, I'll tell you why I ask. I watched you too close for anything physical to happen between you. But if there was something else—something on this mental level—" she paused. "Turn around. I want to look at you."

He turned awkwardly and felt the weight of her eyes on his face although he would not look up to meet them.

"—there'd be a special hell for a man who'd cheat on his wife like that," he heard her voice, softly, "a man who'd live with his wife; and all the time—under the same roof—" her voice sharpened. "Well, don't just stand there! Answer me!"

"Answer—" his tongue stumbled, "what?"

"What I'm saying. Say it wasn't true."

"It—wasn't—true."

"That's my good Henry." She moved and he heard her going over to the table with the scotch, and the sounds of refilling her glass. "—and a little ice this time," her voice came gaily over the chink of cubes in the glass. A sound of stirring. "All right, love, it's all over now. Let's relax. Make small talk for me, Henry. Isn't the cold terrible?"

"Terrible," he said.

"—And that awful cemetery. I thought I'd freeze to death. Weren't you freezing too, pet?"

"Freezing too, pet," his numb voice said. "It's cold in the coffin."

"What?" her voice sharpened again. "Henry, are

you taking picks on me? I said, let's relax! What's that you said supposed to mean?"

He did not answer. She came furiously around to stand before him. He saw her face pale and two-dimensional, like a bobbing face on a movie screen.

"*Henry!*" she screamed. "What do you mean—cold in the coffin? Answer me!"

It was a great effort, but he obeyed.

"I'm cold," he said, between ice-glued jaws, "—cold. So cold. Here in the coffin."

The will to die can be as powerful in its perversity as the will to live.

THE GENERAL
AND
THE AXE

CHAPTER I

Gazing down through the observation window of the officer's walk and feeling his years, the general was aware of the settlement of New Earth floating up to him like a toy village on a circular tray of green cloth. It was marvelously complete, right down to small manufactories and automatic plants, all set aside from the landscaped living area and glistening with a certain air of highly-polished newness detectable even at this height. Even the concrete landing pad toward which the military transport was now settling reflected this newness, being possessed of a table-linen whiteness unscarred by years of takeoffs and landings on the part of deep-space craft.

There was the sound of a limping approach behind him.

"All ready to disembark, General," said a harsh,

baritone voice with the brisk ring of a professional soldier in it.

"Thanks, Charlie." The general turned to look aside and a little down at his equerry. Captain Radnik had come up beside him and stood at ease, swarthy in uniform slacks, tunic and boots. He, also, gazed down at the settlement.

"They say," Radnik said, "we're getting decadent."

"Philosophy?" replied the general, slightly astonished. "From you, Charlie?"

Radnik turned his dark, rather bitter face to grin briefly up at his commanding officer.

"Ever see anything like that yourself before, General?" he asked. And turning, he walked off, his shorter leg making a peculiar cadenced offbeat on the metal flooring of the walk as he went.

Of course, the general had not. But then, neither had anyone else until two years ago. He considered the chain of events that had gotten him this job. He should not, of course, have taken a punch at that reporter. But then, he had had forty years of service in the field, where you were trained to take direct action automatically from the start, and without thinking. And the reporter had known where to sink the needle.

Any reflection at all would have been enough to make him realize that the other was probably in the pay of one of his staff rivals at Arcturus Headquarters. However, he had done it, and after that there had been no hope of dodging this assignment. Not with the newsfax screaming in large headlines—

GENERAL TULLY PUNCHES
REPORTER; DENIES 'KALO'
METHODS REQUIRED
WITH EARTH SURVIVORS.

And, come to think of it, it was no less than his duty, after all. Earth *was* the world on which he had first seen the light of day, sixty-eight years ago.

The landing-warning bell rang throughout the ship. The general turned and made his way to the officer's lock anteroom, pausing there for a moment to make sure, with the habit of years, that his appearance was correct. The mirror gave him back his image, upright enough, but grayed and thinned from what it had been even sixteen years ago at the time of the uprising on Kalo. Most old men went to potbellies and rounded shoulders. He would go in the opposite direction, that of stringy flesh and spare bone. Well, one did the best with what one had.

The red light flashed over the outer lock. He hung on for the slight thump and jar of landing, and then, when the lock opened, went out, saluting the sideguards on the way. They gravely presented rifles in response. At the foot of the gangplank, a girl—no, a woman—was waiting for him.

"Sali Allson," she said, offering her hand. Her gray eyes looked into his own out of a face which owed its elusive beauty to that characterful maturity that comes to some women in their late twenties. "I'm the welcoming committee."

"All of it?" asked the general. Behind him, the off-beat thump of Captain Radnik's boots descended the gangplank. She looked that way. "Captain Radnik, my equerry."

She and the captain shook hands, measuring each other.

"Honor and a pleasure," said Radnik.

"Thank you, Captain." She turned back to the general. "All that would go to the trouble to come," she answered. "Want to look at the military section first—or would you like to come along with me and meet some of the people you're going to be responsible for?"

There was some slight challenge in her question. The general considered it.

"I'll come, of course," he said. But Captain Radnik was touching the braid on the sleeves of the general's tunic. "What is it, Captain?"

"Pardon me, sir—the C. O. of the installation's waiting over there, General."

The general looked and saw a short, square colonel with a look-it-up-in-the-files air about him, waiting unhappily with a brace of younger officers, alongside a staff car.

"I see. Wait a minute, Miss—Mrs.—"

"Miss," she said.

"Miss Allson—I'll go have a word with him and be back in a moment." The general turned and walked over to the colonel, who led the salute to him, punctiliously.

"Colonel—" the general searched his mind for the name. "Soiv?"

"Harvey Soiv, sir." They shook hands.

"I'm going to run along with this committee-woman here, right now, Colonel, unless there's something imperative in your department that needs me right away. I'll talk to you a little later. All right?"

"Yes, sir—but—"

"Well?"

"Well, General. It's just—" Colonel Soiv flushed a little more pinkly over his razor-clean cheeks. "Considering the situation here, don't you think it'd be better to talk to me, first? I mean, before you have anything to do with the civilians?"

"Why?" asked the general.

"To—to get the straight picture. You know I recommended martial law —"

"Did you, now?"

The colonel's face flushed even pinker and the general thought with a sort of despair that the years had whittled his tongue to too sharp an edge for him to risk using it in irony any more. He had promised himself to hide the contempt he felt for this pouter pigeon. "I'll see you after dinner, Colonel," he said.

"Yes, sir."

The general walked back to Radnik and Sali Allson. With the sun behind him, he was better prepared to appreciate why he had taken her, momentarily, for a girl at the foot of the gangplank. Her figure was as slight as a girl's, with the same sort of balance to it.

She and Radnik seemed to have come almost immediately to good terms. They were chatting like old friends as he came up.

"How do we go?" inquired the general.

"I've got a platform here." She gestured to the edge of the landing pad. "This way."

They set off.

"How many of you are there, Miss Allson?" asked the general, as the flying platform wheeled and dipped through the sky of New Earth.

"A little over five thousand—five thousand and thirteen, General," she answered. "The city here was set up to hold twice that number."

"All off ships and other systems where you were visiting?" asked the general. "None of you were in the Solar System when it—" A trifle too late, the general perceived he was drifting into what some people might consider tender territory.

"No." Her answer was perfectly calm. "None of us were near Earth when it blew up. And anyone on it, of course . . ."

"I understand," said the general.

There had been no perceptible emotion in her voice. Only something about the way the sentence ran down at the end. Funny I don't feel anything myself, the general mused. It was my home world, too, after all. But then, forty-odd years was a long time, and there was something almost too big to grasp about a tragedy that could wipe out the birthplace of your race and several billion people, all in the single flick of an eyelash. It left you feeling guilty at your lack of ability to react proportionally to it. Which was probably why the public subscription on the younger worlds had brought about this present mess. Everybody had felt they ought to do something, and collecting money was all they could think of to do. Foolish—you couldn't buy back the past. And the new puppy never quite filled the void left by old Rover's death.

"All of you with relatives on Earth at the time—" The general clamped his jaw shut in annoyance, realizing his woolgathering had led him right back into the restricted area again. The girl—the woman—blast it!—did not seem to mind, however.

"Almost everybody," she agreed, calmly. "Except one or two. Joachim Coby—the man I'm taking you to now—is one of the ones who didn't. Tell me, General." She turned to him and again her gray eyes seemed singularly penetrating. "Don't you know all this?"

"I've had reports on it," replied the general, with a touch of tenderness. "Reports don't always give you what you want, you know," he added. "I don't mean to distress you."

"I know you don't." Her voice was tired. "We've just had so many questions . . ."

"Maybe," he said, "I ought to just ask you to tell me what you want."

"Yes . . ." She seemed to think for a minute. "The main trouble is," she said, suddenly, "none of us asked for this."

He leaned a little toward her.

"I don't understand you."

"I mean—" she turned her gray eyes on him again—"we've been put in the position of accepting charity we don't want—for fear of hurting other people's feelings."

"Ah?" he said.

"All the younger worlds feel sorry for us," she said. "So they got together, collected all that money; and bought us this." She gestured out beyond the platform. "A new world, a new city. We're supposed to start Earth all over again. It's not that easy."

The general nodded. This was somewhat the same conclusion he had come to himself, but privately. None of which altered the facts. He had been sent here to do something about the situation; and something about the situation he would do.

The platform tilted and descended upon the parking pad of a living area set aside and a little way off from the city proper. The walls of the area were all on transparent; and in a sort of sunroom, or studio, a man was at work before an easel. He waved a brush at them briefly as they landed.

Sali Allson led the way inside.

"Joachim," she said. "Visitors. General Tully and Captain Radnik. Gentlemen, this is Joachim Coby. You may have heard of him."

Coby got up and shook hands with them. Under his short-trimmed crop of black hair, his thin, narrow face was vibrant with energy.

"Sit down, sit down," he said. "I'll join you. The light's shifted too much for me, already." He waved them to armchairs, and came over to sit down himself, wiping his hands on a cloth to remove the oil colors from his fingers.

"I'm afraid I've missed the honor of knowing about Mr. Coby," apologized the general. "My life's rather narrow and—Charlie?"

"As a matter of fact, I have," said Radnik, with

surprising enthusiasm. "Some of your Grand Banks fishing scenes—I used to try to imitate that bluish cast you got over everything."

"You, Charlie?" said the general, astonished. "I never knew you painted."

"I played with it once," Radnik gestured with one hand, a little awkward, embarrassed gesture. "Before I found out I didn't have what it takes."

"No such thing!" grunted Coby energetically. "The art in this's only the top froth on forty fathoms of trade skill. A man finds something to say— he'll find a way to paint it, somehow or another."

"Don't be offended," said Sali to Radnik. "He really doesn't know when he's being rude."

"Besides," said Radnik, quietly, "Mr. Coby's perfectly correct. I never did have anything to say. I'm not offended."

"Good for you," said Coby. "Most damn fools are. What can I do for you, General?"

"To be candid," said the general, "I don't quite know. It was Miss Allson's idea to bring us here."

"I thought he should hear our side of it first," she said.

"Waste of time." Coby looked up at her brusquely, and back to the general. "We haven't got a side. Just five thousand people who want to be left alone to die in peace."

The general considered him.

"That's a novel point of view, Mr. Coby," he said.

"Novel to you, perhaps," said Coby. "The Earth is dead. You can't lead a horse to water after his throat's cut, General." He threw himself back in his chair and dropped the cleaning cloth on a little table beside it. "It's no use trying to pretend these people want to start the Mother World all over again. They don't. Why should they? They all had useful lives on a world that's gone; but five years won't bring that world back, or fifty, or even five hundred. And the end result here won't be the old Earth over again, but something different—altogether different. So why should they struggle for something impossible? Just so other worlds can pat themselves on the back about the charity drives they put on to pay for all this?" He gestured about three-quarters of the surrounding compass and shook his head. "No, General. For most of us here, family, work and everything went when the Earth went. All we ask is to be left alone to die in peace."

"No will to live?" said the general. "How about you, Coby?"

Coby gestured at the easel.

"I've got a lifeline."

The general nodded.

"So what're you going to do, General?" asked Coby. "Declare martial law, lock us together in chain gangs and *make* us run this city for our own good?"

"It doesn't need much running," murmured the general. "The pile will furnish power for a thousand years—and the rest of the equipment's all but automatic."

"That's fine for machinery," said Coby. "But how about people? Radioactive isotopes won't keep them running a thousand years."

"Yes," said the general, with the inner sadness of a man who is, himself, beginning to feel the teeth of years. "What do you suggest, then?"

"I? How should I know?" demanded Coby. "I've found *my* answer—but you can't make five thousand people into painters overnight. Find them a reason to go on living, General—a reason to live for themselves and not just for some other planets' peace of mind."

The general sighed and stood up.

"I suppose so," he said. Captain Radnik and Sali had stood up also. Coby rose, and by common consent they walked together toward the landing pad and the waiting platform.

"I'll bet," said Coby, looking up at the general as the three of his visitors climbed aboard, "you're just old-fashioned enough to think there's something immoral in suicide, General."

The general looked down at him.

"Not immoral," he said. "But weak and wasteful—except as a last resort. Why do you ask that?"

"I was just thinking," said Coby. "That's probably why your staff headquarters picked you as the man for the job."

He stood at the edge of the pad and waved to them as they took off.

CHAPTER II

They flew quarteringly across the city to a suite of offices at the edge of a small, landscaped park. Landing, Sali led them in through a nearby door to a large room filled with drawing boards and piled with drawings. An oversize, shock-headed, square-faced young man, as tall as the general, met them with a shout.

"Here you are! Come in and find a chair. Sali said she'd be bringing you. Which is who, Sali?"

Sali made the introductions.

"Testoy Monahan, General," she said. "Captain Radnik."

Testoy Monahan's handshake was in keeping with his large self.

"Have a drink?" he demanded. They shook their heads. "Well, I'll have one on my own then, and the devil take it! Sit down. Tell me about yourself, General. What kind of man are you, and what kind of plans have you got for us?"

The general smiled. It was impossible not to.

"I'm an army man," he said. "And what kind of plans have *you* got to suggest?"

"Why, I'd suggest a large club," said Monahan. "And go around knocking on heads until you wake up whoever's sleeping inside them. Look here, General—" He flung out an arm at the piled draftings. "Plans, plans, plans; and I might as well be illustrating fairy stories for all the chance there seems to be of putting them to use."

"Testoy," explained Sali, "is a civic engineer by trade. The job of building up this new world attracts him."

"Think of it!" shouted Monahan. "A great, empty map of a planet, waiting to be written on. And these puling whimperers—yes, and your mother and our mayor's a pair of them, Sali; I'll temper my remarks for nobody—want nothing but to curl up and perish like autumn leaves!"

"We've seen Mr. Coby," said the general. "He seems to agree with you. How many others are there who feel this way?"

"None!" cried Monahan. "Five thousand and thirteen of us and the three of us you've met, General, have the only guts to look forward to a future. Oh, they'll listen when you talk. And say that's very nice and they wish you luck. But for themselves—" He leaned forward. "Listen to me, General. I had a mother, a sister and two brothers. I had a girl I loved, God rest her soul. And when the news about Earth came to me, there on Arcturus Five, they had to lock me up like a crazy man. I was for taking a ship and flying myself home and head on into that poor burning world that was once my home and was now the grave of all I cared for. For three months I would have killed a man to get at the means of killing myself in that fashion. But it goes, General—after a time it passes. You don't believe it, but it does. And then, if you've anything of a man inside you, you come around to face it, finally."

He broke off abruptly, walked across to a table

in the center of the room, poured himself a drink and drank it all in one huge swallow.

"What would you do in my place?" asked the general, quietly.

"I know what I wouldn't do," said Monahan. "I'd not let them get away with it—this lying down to die. I'd not let them get away with it. No, I wouldn't!"

And he stared at the general with a fierce and almost desperate challenge in his eyes.

After they had left Monahan and brought the platform down at last at the quarters that had been assigned to the general, they found that there was someone waiting for them there, also. This was a tall, gray-haired, upright woman, with a striking resemblance to Sali. They hardly needed the introduction to recognize her as Sali's mother.

"This is our living area," explained Sali. "It's just about the center of town. The mayor thought it would be most convenient for you if you wanted a place to stay, away from the camp. And of course," she added, "I wanted you."

"You're most kind," said the general.

"This wing will be all yours. Captain—" She turned to Radnik. "Your rooms are behind. Shall I show you?"

"Thanks," said Radnik. Their glances met for just a fraction of a second before she turned and led the way toward the rear of the area, the swarthy, hard figure of the captain limping along beside her.

As they disappeared through the shimmering light-curtain of the wall, Mrs. Allson turned to the general. It was disturbing to him to see Sali, as it were, suddenly grown old and standing there in front of him.

"Is there anything you'd like, General?" Her voice was soft and deepened a little by age. She must, the general thought, be as much as a dozen years younger than himself, but she seemed older.

"A word with you, Mrs. Allson, perhaps," he said.

"Of course." She led the way to seats and waved him into one, seating herself. "Would you like anything to drink? You'll have dinner with us, of course, as soon as Sali gets your captain settled."

"Thanks," said the general. "I wonder if you could help me, Mrs. Allson, by telling me *your* point of view on the situation here."

She looked down at her skirt and smoothed it over her knees with one hand.

"I don't know what I could say that would help you, General," she said, quietly.

"Are people really as ready to give up as it seems?"

She looked up at him.

"Give up?" she echoed. "What, exactly, do people on the younger worlds expect of us, General?"

"I believe," the general said, slowly, "they expect you to live."

"But we are living," she replied.

"I mean," he said, "live in an active sense. Live in the sense of growth and replenishment."

"Oh, that," she said, vaguely. "I don't see how they can expect that. There's only a handful of children among us, you know—and most of the grown-ups are middle-aged or better."

"Then you think this attempt is destined to—not flourish?" asked the general.

"I really don't know about such things." She smoothed the skirt again. Then, suddenly, she looked back up at him. "You know, General," she said. "Sali's father was a fine man."

"I'm sure he was," answered the general.

"But neither he nor I were pioneers. We had never really been off Earth at all, except for quick trips to Arcturus. Frank had his business—and I had our home. It was what we had both grown up to, and what we both wanted. After he died, that part of my life ended, but the structure of it was still there until this—accident happened. I think you'll find that's the case with most of our five thousand population. With a few exceptions like my daughter, Coby, and Testoy Monahan, none of us are the sort of people to try to build a new world in the first place. For most of us, in this case, it would only be a futile attempt to keep the memory of our loss green."

"I see." The general nodded.

"I thought you would," she said.

"But," said the general, "did you ever stop to consider there might be another side to it?"

"What other side?"

"The side," said the general, choosing his words with care, "of instinct. The instinct to survive."

"I don't see where that applies," she answered. "If this little community of ours was all that was left of humanity—perhaps. But there's a number of younger worlds, and billions of people on them, altogether."

"Yes, but—" said the general, "man has been in constant conflict with his environment. It tried to kill him off, and he fought to survive. That's where the instinct comes in. It's a matter of principle. Man can't afford to admit defeat, the sort of defeat that destroys a world and all of his kind upon it—even if that's only one area of battle. I've been a military man all my life, Mrs. Allson. I know. Admit defeat in any one small part of yourself, and the seeds of cancer are planted. A cancer to eat up your will and finally destroy you."

She smiled.

"Are we that important to the race?" she asked.

"I think you are," replied the general, seriously. "What happened to Earth—and you—has become a test. Will man end by killing himself off, or by surviving his tendency to kill himself off? That's what the race wants to know—and why the peoples on twenty different worlds pitched in immediately to raise the tremendous amount of money needed to fund and furnish this world for those of you that were spared. The race has been challenged. The question has been raised. Can the will to survive be killed in a people? None of us dares face the possibility of an answer of *yes* to that question."

"That's very eloquent, General," she said. "But I don't believe you."

She sat, unmoved.

"Why not?" he asked.

"Because," she said. "I happen to read the newsfax, like everybody else. I happen to know about the Kalo uprising. And as a result, I know you to be the kind of man who determines to succeed at any cost, as long as it's not at his own. Well, you took care of the situation on Kalo. And now, because the press has put you on the spot, you'll take care of it here. You won't allow us the luxury of dying in peace, for your career's sake, will you, General?"

"It's not for my career's sake," he said.

"After Kalo?" she lifted her eyebrows.

"On Kalo," he said, feeling suddenly old and tired, "I was following orders."

She stood up.

"General," she said. "I don't believe you. About Kalo, *or* now."

And she left the room.

After a dinner at which only small, polite talk prevailed, the general borrowed Sali's platform and flew it over to the temporary barracks area that had been set up to house the military personnel concerned in setting up the city. He landed on the parking pad adjacent to the headquarters building and walked inside, returning the salute of the sentry on duty at the door. Radnik was not with him. He had given the captain the evening off on a sudden, curious impulse he did not care to examine at the moment. But now, as he walked through the door of the headquarters building, alone, he felt a definite and disturbing vacuum about that area to the left and a little behind him where his equerry was usually to be found in step with him.

"Colonel Soiv?" he said to the non-com at the desk just inside the door.

"Yes, sir." He was a corporal, a round-faced youngster. "In his quarters, sir. Right down the hall here, through the *Officers Only* door."

"Thanks," said the general, and walked on. The corridor echoed to his feet, and there was the door, as the boy had said. The general knocked and went in.

The outer room of the quarters was—as was customary on details of this sort—half office. It was also occupied. Colonel Soiv was seated in the reclining chair of a desk, in very unreclined argument with a thin, elderly civilian who sat facing him. The civilian did not appear disturbed by the colonel's tactics. He was a good-looking white-haired man with smooth, gray cheeks and a bony jaw.

"—and why can't you give me an estimate?" the colonel was saying angrily. "I'll tell you why you can't give me an estimate. It's because there's no estimate to give. You won't—Sir!" He fumbled to his feet in some embarrassment.

"Sit down, sit down, Colonel," said the general. "Sit down, both of you, please."

"Sir," said the colonel, still on his feet, "may I introduce Mr. Tam Yuler, Mayor of the Earth Survivors."

They shook hands. "I won't interrupt you," said the general.

"It's not interruption, General," said Soiv. "I've

been trying to get His Honor here to give me an estimate of the time it'll take to get his people to take over the running of this installat—city. He refused to give me one." The pink cheeks of the colonel were as insulted as a child's.

"My dear Colonel—my dear General," smiled the mayor. "How can I tell? I'm not expert at running a city like this. And I've no idea how people will take to the work."

"Yuler . . ." said the general, thoughtfully. "You were Mayor of New York, on the American Continent, weren't you?"

"I'm surprised you recognized me," said the mayor. "Oh, yes—I see. You're from Earth yourself." He smiled again. "Your accent gives you away."

"Do I still have an accent?" The general smiled himself.

"To the trained ear, yes. A hobby of mine. Well, you two gentlemen probably have something to discuss. I'll leave you." And with no further courtesy, the old man turned and walked out. The general turned back to Soiv, who spread his hands to the air, hopelessly.

"You see, General," he said.

"No," said the general, taking the mayor's vacated chair. "I don't see. Oh, *sit down*, Colonel!"

Soiv dropped back into the reclining chair.

"They're doing it deliberately," he said. "Deliberately. They're playing for time. They've got something up their sleeves, I know they have. They've *got* to care what happens to them, that's all there is to it!"

"Sure?" asked the general. Soiv stared at him in astonishment. "All right, Colonel," he went on. "The situation. Brief me on it."

"Well, sir." Soiv laid his short-fingered hands on the polished desk top. "You know we shipped them in here almost a year ago. I came along with an all-equipment construction battalion. We went to work right away. Construction's met all scheduling to date—*all*, General. If you'd care to check the records—"

"That won't be necessary. That's not my job here, Colonel."

Soiv's experienced military ear apparently caught the connotation. He hurried to repair the breach.

"Oh, of course not, General. I hope you don't think—I just wanted to point out that the military's done their end of the job in this thing. As I say, sir, we've filled the bill. These survivors just won't accept delivery, that's all."

"What bill?"

"You know what I mean, General. The city's completed. We're all done except for training key personnel among the civilians to take over the various necessary jobs and services. Out of the five thousand of them, all they need are about three hundred men or women to hold down the vital spots. Lord, General, an automatic sewage plant's a fine piece of equipment, but *somebody* has to keep tabs on it. The same way with the water system, the food processing plants—and somebody has to oversee the crop-growing. Then there's paving, lighting, some sort of civic body, legal staff, and so forth. Blast it, General, they're a community! Why can't they act like a community, instead of a lot of pensioners in an overage rest home?"

The colonel flapped his heavy hands in despair and sat frowning helplessly at the bright desktop.

"And you say they've given you no cooperation at all?"

"No sir, it's just—none of them volunteer. We can't line them up, army system, and pick them out—you and you and you, like that. But nobody offers himself."

"I see," said the general.

Soiv looked up at him.

"What can a man do, General?"

"I don't know," said the general, frowning. "I don't know at all."

When he got back to the Allsons', the living area was dark. But, going up the terrace alongside the landing pad, toward his rooms, the general saw Sali sitting in one of the long lounge chairs, smoking and gazing at the night sky.

"Good evening," he said.

She lowered her eyes from the region of the Pleiades and smiled at him.

"Good morning," she answered.

"Is it already?" said the general, feeling slightly confused. He sat down on the foot of the chair next to her. Her face in the shadow of the starlight was indistinct.

"You've been up conferring with our colonel," said Sali. "Cigarette?"

"No, thanks," he said. "Yes, I had to go over the military end of the situation."

"I'll bet that wasn't the only thing that got a going over." She sounded remarkably gay, and he peered at her through the darkness in surprise.

"Is there something I don't know about?" he asked.

"No," she said. "Yes," she corrected herself immediately. "I like your Captain Radnik."

"Do you?" replied the general. "He surprises me, sometimes." He was thinking of something else.

"You mean," she said, "by being the sort of man I could like?" He came back with a start from wherever it was he had been.

"Like?" he echoed, and blinked at her. "You are—pardon me," he said, "rather young, aren't you?"

She laughed.

"Thank you, General. I'm twenty-six. And how old is Charlie?"

"Why—late thirties, I believe," said the general. "I'm not sure as his officer if I ought to approve of this. We're guests in your home, here—"

"General," she said. "I love you." She got up lightly and kissed him on the cheek. Then, before he could move, she was gone, into the house. The general sat there under the stars and felt his cheek with startled fingers.

"I'll be damned!" he said.

CHAPTER III

The next day, the mayor called a meeting of the Earth Survivors, at the general's suggestion. The call was couched in strong language, and some eight hundred people did actually show up at the municipal amphitheatre. They were addressed by Colonel Soiv, who outlined the situation of the military and made a now-or-never plea for public-minded citizens to come forward and start learning how to take over the civic services. After he had finished, the eight hundred rose and drifted out, with the single exception of one man who came up to put his name down for work in the food-processing division. The following day, a different meeting was held—a collection of the so-called senior citizens, in the Allson home—which was addressed by the general himself.

"You fifteen men and women," he finished, "could pull these five thousand to their feet by their noses, if you wanted to. Why won't you do it?"

No one volunteered an answer. The general singled out a blocky gray-headed man.

"Judge?"

Seaman Bennet had been one of the World Supreme Court Judges on Earth. He shook his head.

"I don't believe we could; and I—for one—don't

want to," he replied, bluntly. "I think we've had enough of this urging. The plain fact of the matter is that this whole project is a farce dreamed up by the romantic popular mind of the younger worlds. And the only good reason you can give us, General, for trying to make a go of it, is to please that popular mind."

"And save the clusters on his shoulder-tabs," said an unidentified voice behind the general. He ignored it.

"No," he said. "New Earth, here, is a world worth having; and I cannot believe that some of you, at least, don't want it."

"And if we did," countered Bennet. "What's the use? I tell you if every one of us sat down and pushed like blazes, we'd still end up the same way. Earth is dead, General dead! You can't resurrect a corpse. It's been almost two years since the blow-up. How many of us have had children in that time? None. Not one out of more than five thousand people. On the other hand, we've had, since the beginning when we were gathered together, more than eight hundred deaths from suicides and ordinary natural causes. Do a little arithmetic, General, and see what it gives you. The so-called Earth Survivors have about six more years of survival left in them, before they dwindle to nothing. And you want these people to build a new world!"

"The death rate doesn't have to continue," said the general. "The younger couples can have children."

"What for?" demanded Seaman Bennet, leaning forward in his chair. "I ask you, General, *what for?*"

And that was that.

"Charlie," said the general to his equerry that night. "Do you suppose these people could be right after all? Maybe I'm the one that's wrong."

"Not by me," said Radnik. "We flew north to the mountains today, Sali and I. This is a world worth living in."

"Oh, yes—Sali," said the general. He frowned. "I hope you won't think I'm just being nosy, Charlie, but—"

"But you'd like to know what kind of hanky-panky I'm up to in that department, is that it?" said Radnik, grinning. "Shall I fix the general a drink and tell him all about it?"

"Cut it out," said the general. "And yes, I will take that drink. And have one yourself, Charlie."

Radnik limped over to a small bar in the wall, fixed the drinks, and brought them back.

"Luck," he said, sitting down opposite his superior officer and handing the tall glass over. They both drank to luck, in silence.

"All right, now how about it?" asked the general.

Radnik's face had gone serious.

"How hard would it be," he asked, "for you to wrangle me an immediate discharge?"

The general almost choked on his drink.

"Charlie!"

"I mean it, Sam," said Radnik. "Every frousting word of it. I like New Earth; and I like Sali Allson. If these other blasted fools want to fold up and die, let 'em. We don't need them. We've got an open planet, the best equipment money can buy and all the time in the universe. Our kids'll grow up free of conscript duty, taxes, fashions and other-world prejudices, and with whole continents of virgin mountain, forest and jungle. Who wants better than that?"

"I—I don't know what to say, Charlie," said the general. He was honestly shaken up. He set his drink down.

"If you don't like the idea of my abandoning you—"

"No, no," said the general, hastily, "that's not it—"

"—stay here yourself."

"I?" said the general.

"You," said Radnik. "You don't like staff work anyway, you know that as well as I do. When they took you out of the field, your hitch was finished for all practical purposes. What the hell do you want to juggle paper and play headquarters politics for, for the next twenty years? Quit, stay here, and put in some honest work, instead."

"Charlie," said the general, "you're drunk."

"General," said Radnik, "I'm as sober as a general."

"Nonsense!" said the general.

The beginning of the end arrived the next day, and the harbinger of it was Colonel Soiv. The general was just sitting down to breakfast when the colonel appeared with a sheet of newsfax from one of the top interstellar services.

The general took it and read it silently, while Soiv stood whitely by. It was there, much as the general had expected it from the beginning.

ATTEMPT TO MAKE MILITARY 'PROTECTORATE' OF NEW EARTH CHARGED

Arcturus Five World's Representative Allan Pike queried Staff Headquarters on that world today, concerning a rumor that General Samuel Tully had "pulled strings" for his present assignment to the New Earth Military Construction Unit. Pike announced to reporters that the same rumor, as it reached his office, predicted that the military occupation of New Earth would be strengthened and enforced and that there would be a resort to martial law on that planet.

* * *

It was not necessary to read any further. The general put the sheets of newsfax, still fresh-smelling from the duplicator, thoughtfully down on the table. On an afterthought, he glanced again at the story—yes, they had worked the Kalo business in, as he might have expected.

This power-hungry officer who had already demonstrated his indifference to human rights before during his career.

The colonel was talking.

"Why me? Why did they let me in for this? Why was I assigned—"

"Because, Soiv," said the general, and it gave him great satisfaction to be able to say it out loud at last, "you're a fool!"

"*Sir!*"

"Oh, shut up!" said the general. "Go on back to your headquarters and let me finish my breakfast. I'll be right over afterwards to take charge of things."

"But—"

"That's an order, Colonel!"

Blasted out of the room by the general's not inconsiderable voice, Soiv scurried off. Turning somewhat moodily back to his fruit and toast, the general pondered on the sad deviousness of official ways and the worth of a forty-six year career. Good enough. He had always been a fighting man. If fight was what they wanted . . . He picked up the communicator and buzzed for Radnik.

The dark man showed up, Sali with him.

"You've seen the newsfax?" asked the general.

Radnik scowled.

"Who showed them to you, sir?" he growled. "I thought—"

"You thought wrong," said the general. "I've always been able to take care of myself. Just answer me something about this discharge of yours. Still want it?"

"No, sir."

"Come off it," said the general. "I want a straight answer, Charlie."

Sali slid her arm through the captain's.

"Yes," said Radnik.

"And you, Sali," said the general. "How many of the Survivors, do you think, really want to leave this planet?"

"Why—I don't think any of them want to leave," she answered. "Really, they don't know what they want."

"All right," the general said. "Come on, Charlie, time to go to work." He stood up. "I'd appreciate it if you helped keep the Survivors as quiet about this as possible, Sali. Until—say—tomorrow night."

"General," replied Sali, "that's one thing I can promise you. These people don't want to be anything other than quiet."

"Fine. Come, Charlie."

They went out.

At the headquarters building, in Soiv's office, the three of them—the general, Radnik and Soiv— sat down to business.

"I don't know what to suggest," stammered the colonel. "General, I—"

"Don't bother," said the general. "Just tell me what I want to know. Colonel, you say the installation here is complete, physically speaking. Every piece of equipment's in and working?"

"Yes, but—"

"Never mind the buts. I think the work of this command is finished. How soon can you take off?"

The colonel stared at him in stunned silence.

"Did you hear me, Colonel? I asked how soon your personnel could enship and take off."

"Why—why—if we had civilians trained—" The

colonel winced away from the fire building in the general's eyes. "A week," he said hastily.

"A week!" snapped the general. "What kind of an outfit are you running, Soiv? You aren't taking any equipment here back with you, are you?"

"No sir. Orders were to leave everything for the Survivors—"

"The ships are ready to take off, I hope. New planet regulations call for a ship under these conditions to be ready for instant lift, except when undergoing repairs."

"Oh, the ships are ready. Only—"

"Only what?"

"Well, General, the men will have to—it takes about a week to move a command of this size, sir!" cried the colonel, in anguished protest.

"The devil it does," said the general, coldly. "I've moved flotillas on four hours' notice. Get your staff in here"

The colonel obeyed. The staff came, listened and went as if the devil the general had mentioned was on their tails. The colonel sagged weakly in his chair.

"That's that," said the general, signing some orders. "Now, one more thing. You've got your machine shop still operating. I want you to make and deliver five thousand axes."

Soiv sat up.

"A—five thousand whats, sir?"

"Axes. Axes!" The general drew the outline of a double-bladed woodsman's axe on a sheet of paper. The colonel stared at it as if he expected it to jump up off the surface and chop him.

"Yes, General," he said, at last, weakly.

"One for each of the Survivors, delivered to their homes, two more for Captain Radnik and myself, delivered here. By eighteen hundred hours tonight. You'll start loading personnel and what equipment belongs to the command, immediately. I'll expect everything ready for take-off by two thousand hours. Anything you can't enship is to be left behind for Survivor use. Now send me your medical officer."

"Medical officer?" But the general looked so explosive that the colonel hurried out without waiting for a response.

He was back in fifteen minutes with a major wearing the caduceus.

"Wait outside, Colonel," said the general. "Major, I want you to examine the captain, here. No, no—not a general examination, man. Just his heart. No, you don't need your stethoscope. What've you got an ear for? Listen to his chest."

Gingerly, like a man approaching a stick of dynamite, the broad-faced major bent his ear to Radnik's tunic jacket.

"Terrible shape, isn't it?" prompted the general. "Ready to quit at any minute, wouldn't you say?"

"Sir?" said the major.

"I said his heart's ready to give out—isn't it?"

The major stared at the general, and for once the general found his reputation standing him in good stead. The major's gaze wavered and fell away.

"Well, General, if you say so—"

"What?" roared the general.

"I mean—yes, General."

"A takeoff would kill him, wouldn't it?"

"Yes sir," said the major miserably.

"Very well. Under the special authority described in official regulations for situations such as this, I am hereby issuing Captain Radnik an emergency discharge for reasons of health. Prepare the proper papers for medical discharge, Major, and have everything here for my signature by fourteen hundred hours. That's all. Send the colonel in as you leave."

The major fled. The colonel stuck a worried face in through the door.

"Get me your power officer, Soiv—no, I take that back. Get me the first sergeant of the power company. Well, what are you waiting for?"

"Well—General—" The colonel clenched his hands. "About this order to abandon the installation."

"Yes?"

"Would the—would the general put it in writing, please?"

The general looked at him. The colonel's face went red, then white, then back to red again.

"Of course, Colonel," said the general, softly. "Have it written up and I'll sign it. Now—that sergeant!"

At about four-thirty that afternoon, Sali Allson managed to get into the colonel's office for a very brief moment, and talk to a very busy general. She found him still sitting at the colonel's desk, immersed in papers and the issuing of orders.

"Hello, Sali," he said, when she was let in after a short wait. You can go now; Lieutenant—sit down, Sali. This'll have to be quick. What's up?"

She looked troubled.

"General," she said. "I'm sorry. It seems I promised something I can't deliver."

"What's that?"

"You know, I promised that people would keep still until tomorrow night? Well, it seems I goofed. They aren't going to. I argued against it, but Mother's set on having some people over tonight. Mayor Yuler, Judge Bennet, Testoy, Coby. They're going to talk over this newsfax accusation of you and decide on what sort of a complaint to make to the World's Council about it."

"I see," said the general.

"I'm afraid—" She took a deep breath. "They're not on your side, General. They want you to be there and answer some questions. I was sent to ask you to come."

"Yes," replied the general. He gazed at her almost fondly. "You sure you didn't volunteer to carry the message—so as break it to an old man easily as possible?"

She gave him a wan smile and did not deny it.

"They're ready to throw you to the wolves," she said. "They aren't the bunch of people to agree on anything except a mutual enemy. Even Coby and Testoy. I'm sorry."

"That's all right," said the general, slowly. "I was thinking of dropping over this evening, anyway. Tell them I'll be there."

"All right." She got up. "Anything else I can do?"

He shook his head.

"Nothing," he said.

CHAPTER IV

The guests at the Allsons' had come for dinner. They had sat around the table through dinner, and completed the familiar process of talking themselves into what they most wanted to believe. Right now they had reached the convenient conclusion that all the problems of their situation here on New Earth probably had their roots in some long-term machinations of the general's. And that these machinations were probably the result of his wish to repair and forward his own military career.

Now that dinner was over, they sat on the terrace in the warm summer evening as the sunset faded, drinking after-dinner coffee and watching the slight breeze stir the tops of the pretty little trees about the garden pool, and continued their discussion.

"No," the judge was saying, to the mayor, "I can't go along with you on the notion that he thought it all up himself. The military mind is a little too limited in practice to work out something on this scale. I think he must have fallen into it."

"You've got a nerve, Sea," said Sali, evenly. "When the Worlds first offered us this new planet, you were one of the first to think it was a grand idea. It wasn't until we got here and everybody started expecting everybody else to take the responsibility that you changed over and went along with the idea we'd all been given a handout none of us wanted."

"Sali," said the judge, "you might allow for the fact that I'm human. At the beginning I didn't know what we all were getting into."

"Human!" she cried. "You're human, all right—all of you. Human and lazy! Human and mean!"

"That's beside the point." The judge's calm, rotund voice created a neutral background against which the violence of her emotion seemed juvenile and out of place. "The point is that General Tully saw his chance to profit by our situation—" He broke off suddenly. There had been a whisper of approaching airfoils above the landing pad, a white shape sinking through the encroaching gloom—and now the precise rap of military feet along the walk toward the terrace. "Here he comes now. He and that captain."

"That captain," said Sali icily, "is the man I'm going to marry!"

"Sali!" It was her mother's shocked and startled voice.

The general emerged into the garden and approached along the terrace. He was carrying a double-bitted axe in his hand, and swung it as he walked along.

"Good evening, good evening," he called cheerfully as he came up. "I see you waited for me."

Testoy Monahan laughed harshly.

"Did you think we wouldn't?" he demanded.

"I knew you would," replied the general, undisturbed. He leaned on the axe and looked about him. They found his regard disconcerting.

"What are you doing with that thing?" said the judge. "And while we're on it, why did you have one delivered to me?"

"Each of you should have gotten one," said the general. "To answer you—I thought you might find it useful. Still got it?"

"I tossed it in the utility room and forgot about it," said the judge. The general nodded.

"Listen—" said Testoy, coming forward from the wall against which he had been standing. "What's all this we've been hearing?"

As he spoke, the last rays of twilight faded. Mrs. Allson pressed a stud on the table beside her chair and soft lights glowed suddenly into being in the living area and around the terrace. The general stood revealed in them as a soft current of warmth eddied out from the living area to ward off the first chill of the evening breeze.

"And what have you heard?" asked the general.

"That you're going to move the soldiers out of here."

"Quite right," said the general. He squinted at the white glare off beyond the rim of the city, that was the landing field under lights. He turned back and began to examine the terrace border of trees, one by one.

"Just what do you think you're doing?" demanded the judge.

"I'll tell you," said the general, ceasing his survey for a moment to look back over his shoulder. "I'm checking a theory of mine about the human race." He turned back and picked out one of the small trees. "Ah, this ought to do."

*　　*　　*

He stepped back and hefted his axe. Mrs. Allson gave a little scream as the bright blade bit into the trunk of the tree.

"Are you mad, man?" shouted Testoy, taking a step forward. "Have you gone out of your mind, completely? Thinking of sending the ships off. Axes—chopping trees. You ought to be in a strait-jacket."

"I don't . . . think so . . ." said the general, grunting between swings. "One more . . . that does it . . ." The little tree came crashing to the flagstones of the terrace. The general put his foot on it and began to cut it into lengths.

"Call the colonel, someone," said the judge. "I believe the general's really—what Testoy says."

"No use," said the general between swings. "There's nobody in the headquarters building."

"Why not?" demanded Testoy. "You haven't moved them out yet."

"Yes, I have," answered the general.

There was a moment of complete silence from the group. Then, one of the figures present—it was the mayor—jumped up from his chair and bolted into the living area. The general continued to chop.

"Can I help you, sir?" asked Radnik, hefting his own axe.

"No thanks," panted the general. "The exercise is just the thing for me. Have to get back in condition."

After a moment, the mayor came running out again.

"He's right!" cried Yuler. "They've been loading for an hour. They're warming up the drives, now."

Testoy cursed.

"Marooned!" he cried. Before anyone else could move, he plunged one big fist in through a slit in his tunic and came out with a little handgun.

"You'll call them back!" he shouted at the general. "You'll call them back!"

Captain Radnik spun stiffly about on his short leg. He stood facing Testoy with about six feet between them, his own axe held crosswise in both hands before his waist. The gun in Testoy's hand shook.

"Get out of the way!" he said, in a sort of sob.

"I'd live long enough to reach you," said Radnik, coldly. "You wouldn't like that. Drop it!"

"No!" blurted Testoy; but his hand shook even more. The dry voice of Coby came from behind him.

"Give up, Testoy! Amateurs haven't any business going up against professionals, anyway. He means what he says. You don't."

Testoy's hand sagged and dropped.

"All the way," ordered Radnik.

The gun clattered on the flagstones.

The general had continued to chop imperturbably all the while this little byplay was going on. "You see," he said now, "it wouldn't do me any good to order them back, anyway. When an outfit is due to lift at two thousand hours, it lifts at two thousand hours." He paused to glance at his chronometer. "Any minute now. Besides, I've no authority to order them back any more. I've resigned my commission."

"You!" said the judge. And Sali gave a little cry.

"Me," said the general, now dividing the narrow top trunk of the tree into sections by single chops. "After all, you ought to remember I'm an Earth Survivor, myself. And it's time I retired. Captain Radnik—pardon me—Charlie and I are now civilians." He stopped working suddenly, glanced at his chronometer again and shaded his eyes with one hand, gazing off in the direction of the landing pad . . . "There they go now."

His ears had caught the familiar first rumble of the tubes a short second before the rest had. As he spoke, the white light around the pad washed out in brilliance, for a moment making the city roofs stand out as if in broad daylight. Then one great trail of fire shot up into the night. And another. And another—until all five were gone.

"And that's that," said the general, stooping to gather together an armful of the cut tree sections at his feet. He carried them into the center of the terrace and piled them there.

"You won't get away with this!" said the judge, a little hoarsely. "We'll message the World's Council. They'll have the ships back here in six weeks. Then we'll see what the courts do to you."

"No," said the general, going back for another armload. He grunted as he bent over to pick them up. "Stiff, by Harry! Too much desk work. No, I don't think so, Judge. Something else is due to happen soon."

He stopped and gazed expectantly to the north end of the city, but nothing happened. He went back to pick up the last of his butchered tree.

"I guess maybe the fuse—" A sudden, distant, dull explosion interrupted him. "Ah, there she goes. That was the communications center." He chuckled. "Don't look so upset, Mr. Monahan. It can be rebuilt in two or three years if we really settle down to work on it."

There were a few more isolated explosions at various points about the city. The lights dimmed and went out; a few seconds after that the small current of warm air circulating about them drooped and died—so that now, through the garden, they could feel the chillier touch of the evening breeze.

"Right on schedule," said the general's voice from the darkness. "If you'll hand me your lighter, Charlie." A little flame sprang into being from nowhere, fireflied over to the small heap of cut-up wood and crackled through the dry outer branches. There was a splash of something liquid and the flames flared up suddenly, lighting up the general, Radnik, and the rest of them with the same lurid glow.

"Those other shots you heard," said the general, smiling at them, "were the lighting, water and other services. The automatic machinery's been knocked out in each case. Your power pile's been damped and the automatic control there destroyed."

"You—you madman!" choked the mayor from a far corner of the terrace. "You've killed us all."

"Nonsense!" snapped the general, with the hint of exasperation in his voice for the first time. "Your warehouses are bursting with stored food and supplies that'll keep indefinitely. You've got a hundred years' supply of medicines, spare parts, everything in the universe. You've got the best of modern tools, the best of machinery, the best of everything. The only thing I've taken away from you is a soft place to sit and sulk. If you want to be warm from now on, you're going to have to build a fire. For hot food—cook. You're going to have to go to the reservoir after water, to the warehouses after food, and do your own housecleaning. And that situation is going to go on existing exactly as long as you all continue to sit still and put off rebuilding the equipment I've just now put out of action. And if you're expecting outside help, don't. The last message the communication center sent off before it blew up was the information, under the mayor's name, that it was shutting down for alterations. We're all on our own here until some ship happens to drop by—anywhere from two years to ten."

He finished, and there was a short silence. Surprisingly, it was Coby who broke it. The wiry artist stood up suddenly from his chair by the house wall.

"You win, General," he said. He paused. "I had a hunch you had from the way you walked in here.

Anyway, I've still got my north light. See you all in the morning. I've got a long walk home, and a fire to build before bedtime."

The sound of his footsteps moved off along the terrace into the night.

"You!" cried the mayor to the general. "You—you'll be lynched!"

"And will you help the lynchers or try to stop them?" said the general. "Charlie, here, and I might turn out to be the only ones with technical know-how enough to see the sabotaged equipment gets properly repaired."

Yuler glared at him, and then, finding the general's gaze did not falter, looked despairingly around the circle for support.

"Oh, for God's sake, Tam!" the judge burst out. "Make up your own mind for once!"

With one last, wild glance at them all, the mayor flung about on his heel and plunged off. They heard his steps beating away. The judge turned his eyes on the general.

"Tam's a fool," he said bitterly. "He always was, in spite of his background. I'm not—I can see it now, what you planned. And I should have known—I've met your kind before that don't care how the chips fall just so things go their way. Well, I wash my hands of it. You hear me? I wash my hands—" And, rising very quickly for such a heavy, old man, he was up and also gone.

There remained, besides the general and Radnik, only Mrs. Allson, Sali, and Testoy Monahan. Testoy had been staring at the general as if he expected him to sprout either horns or a halo.

"You're staying!" he said, at last. "You're going to make them work!"

"They'll work," said the general.

"Then I'm a dog!" cried Testoy, slapping himself violently on the forehead. "And you're a great man!

I'll just go after that slippery mayor and do a little of the setting these people straight my own self."

He left, and the sound of his going died away on the night air. For a moment after the last sound had ceased, the four who remained stayed caught and immobile, as if they had suddenly reached together some echoing point of time too great for any single heart and mind to disturb. And then the general broke the silence.

"All right, Sali—Mrs. Allson," he said briskly. "Both of you go now and wrap whatever personal things you feel you absolutely have to have in hand towels, and take them to your front door. Charlie has field packs there for you. Dress warmly and put on the best footgear you've got for rough hiking."

They both stared at him, still in shock.

"Footgear—" said Sali's mother, dazedly.

"You're taking to the hills. You've got three—maybe five minutes to get ready. Mrs. Allson—*please!*" The snap of authority was back in the general's voice. Mrs. Allson turned uncertainly and went back into the house. Sali did not move.

"Taking to the hills?" she said.

The general considered her in the firelight.

"You'll have a better chance of surviving back there. Charlie's had field training with the expeditionary forces."

"Of surviving?" She stared at him. "You just finished telling them—"

"That the elements of survival were here and they just had to make use of them. Of course," said the general. He reached behind him for a chair and sat down in it. "That woodchopping—" He warmed his hands at the fire. "Nothing was said about the human element. This community must disintegrate before it can cohere again." He glanced at her. "You know, Sali, I spoke to your mother my first day here. She said that most of the people here were not the people to build a new world from scratch. She was right, of course."

"What do you mean?" she whispered.

"A necessary element was lacking here, one that's present in an ordinary pioneering community," said the general. "The *need* to succeed. They've got it now. For all practical purposes their protective civilization has been destroyed. They will fall back into essential savagery; of necessity, the weaker will go to the wall, but the fittest will survive and build."

She shrank from him.

"But—you know this!" she said. "Why did you do it? Why—did they give you orders—"

"No," said the general wearily. "No. You misunderstand the limits of military authority, Sali. When the service has a job to do, they send out a man in whom they have confidence, and simply order him to get results. I made up my own mind. As for the necessity of it—" He picked up a branch and poked at the fire. "There was a question in the minds of some of our best qualified authorities in the field of human survival. It was questioned whether the human seed our race has spread to various other worlds was truly viable. Our race, you know, might be like a spreading vine that needs its original root system to survive. For all we knew some of the necessary traits for racial survival might be the exclusive property of those who had a horror of being transplanted from their native Earth."

"But a question—" Sali moved her head as if it rolled on a pillow, in pain. "—only a question. And you did this. No decent man could sleep nights—"

"I have my duty," said the general. "Certainly, only a question—but who would want to take the chance it was right? The instinct of racial survival is a strong, deep thing; and civilization is only painted on us—"

"You *monster!*" Though she only breathed them, the words cut at him out of her white face.

The general winced.

"So they called me on Kalo," he murmured. "It was the very word—and still, someone had to do it—" He stopped suddenly, and slowly raised his head in the silence of the night, listening. "Charlie!" he said sharply. "There's no more time. You can't wait for her gear. You'll have to take them both as they are."

He stopped, and now they all heard it, a far-off confusion of voices, such as from a ball park on a summer's evening, distant, but coming nearer.

Radnik nodded. His eyes met the general's. They did not move to shake hands.

"We'll name the first after you, Sam," he said.

"Thanks," said the general.

Radnik's hand closed on Sali's arm, and she cried out at his touch.

"Come on!" snapped Radnik.

"But you—" She hung back, staring at the general. "You aren't coming! What are you going to do now, then? What are you planning for them now?"

"Don't be a fool!" said Radnik roughly, jerking at her. "Listen to them! Do you think they're going to pin roses on him?"

The general returned her gaze more gently.

"I'm their last excuse," he said. "For not saving themselves. When they destroy that last excuse—"

He paused, and smiled at her a little apologetically.

"And as you say," he said, "I don't sleep well, nights. Good luck, my dear. Go on, take her now, Charlie."

And Radnik took her away.

Savage beasts have been known to share the same floating plank in a flood.

BUTTON, BUTTON

The music blared. The Phobos night club chorus line advanced, female bodies shapely under an artificial one-half gravity, brilliantly dancing. They attracted male gazes among the tourists all around the room; but they did not attract the Assistant Engineer.

"Goddam button-pusher!" glowered the AE. He was staring across at the bar, where stood a ship's First Officer of his own youthful age—but tall, polished and handsome in dress whites and with the fine manners of a graduate from a private academy. The AE was short, sandy-haired, mastiff-tempered, and lapsed into the slum argot of Greater Chicago, Earth, under the influence of stress or alcohol. And he had been drinking double champagne cocktails for the last two hours—ever since finishing up the very dirty job of checking over the converter, on orders from the captain delivered by that same First Officer, as he left ship on his own port leave, some eight hours earlier.

"Listen," said the Chief Engineer, "don't sneer at button-pushers."

"No?" said the Assistant, swinging around with half-drunk belligerence before he remembered who it was he was talking to.

"No," said the Chief.

"Anybody can push a button."

"You think so?" said the Chief. He pointed across the room. "Look at those two over there."

The Assistant looked. At a small table for two, he saw a gross, hog-faced man well into middle age, and a woman verging on it, but yet startlingly beautiful with the sharp, thin beauty of a high-fashion model in a woman's magazine ad. The man was eating something elaborate with gusto; the woman, sipping an emerald drink in a fragile cocktail glass. They looked as badly matched as swine and pearls.

"I see them," growled the Assistant. "They're no button-pushers, either one of them."

"That's the point," said the Chief. "Let me tell you about those two."

The hog-faced man [said the Chief] is named Craigo DelMyer. He is also from Chicago. He came up the hard way as an odd-job business representative, got in with the labor and guild organizations, and ended up as top man for the Interplanetary Freight Handlers' Union. Which as everybody knows, is no small pickings.

However, it took him nearly twenty years to get there. He had been a pretty rough customer to start off with, and he ended up like a bear on top of the mountain—in fine position, but hardly the sort of character anyone could love. The only trouble was that, like the bear, he had no place else to go from where he was, but down.

He tried to think about this. When he did, he was liable to smoke too many cigars, or drink too many martinis; and then his indigestion would start in on him again.

However, for years he was not threatened. Things went normally until about six years ago, when there was that sudden surge of government investigations. One of the organizations that came under the glare of the investigating committees' spotlights was the Interplanetary Freight Handlers Union. And Craigo sweated.

The queries flew thick and fast. Craigo woke up nights, parrying questions in his sleep. The Committee was on his tail. The press was on his tail. His old enemies among management were out to nail him while opportunity offered. And then, somewhere along the line, they all three got together. What came out of their collaboration was a question put to Craigo in a press conference.

"—and do you hold a union card yourself, Mr. DelMyer?" asked a reporter.

Craigo laughed like the jolly man he was on these occasions.

"A union card? You're asking me—" Laughter made him quiver all over like a well-dressed blanc mange. "Had one nineteen years, guy, that's all!"

"Would you say that present union members work as hard for their pay as they did in your day, Mr. DelMyer? The work was more physical then, I understand?"

"Not a bit! Same thing. Different ships, same duties!"

"Enough the same, would you say, so that you, yourself could take charge of a ship on a regular run right now, if you had to validate your card?"

Craigo saw the trap then; but he saw it the same way a packing-house-bound steer sees the chute to the killing room.

"Well now—" he chortled. "Well, now, I'm not just as young as I was once, guy. Twenty years—"

"But assuming your health was—"

When cornered, Craigo, for all his other sins, was not one to turn belly-up and beg for mercy.

"Assuming my health's still good!" he interrupted, bringing his thick fist down with a crash on a handy table, "I'll buck a freight to anywhere in the Solar System, guy. And you can tell'm I said so!"

But he lost no time in terminating the interview. And the minute he was alone in his hotel suite, he put in a furious call to the head of the Union's legal department.

"Get me a doc says I can't lift a freight two inches!" he yelled into the phone. And then sat back to gnaw a cigar. The legal head obliged; but by the time the doctor arrived, Craigo had heard the evening news on his wall screen, and recognized the inevitable. He sent the doctor back to his office.

The Committee, officially informed of the interview, had announced that Mr. DelMyer's statement was very interesting. It might, said a committee spokesman, tend to show whether he was an honest working member merely representing his fellows—or a slick opportunist, living high off the fat of the men who really did the work. If Mr. DelMyer meant what he said. . . .

A hundred years before, Craigo would have had his doctor's prohibition and a rigged vote of confidence to shut up the squawkers. But nowadays the voting was government-supervised.

Craigo spat out his chewed cigar butt, faced up to the situation as he had faced up to many since he had first opened his eyes under Chicago's looming skyline—and left for Earth Outer Station Number Five, while the commentators were still wondering whether he would go through with it.

At the station, they picked him the easiest immediately available run—a medical supplies shipment to Venus Orbital Dockage; and a sharp young union member took him out to look over the ship he would be handling. A freight ship, as anyone in the business knows, is nothing much more than a tin can full of goods, with a thrust unit forty meters off at the end of a steel rod. In the tin can part are a control panel, living space for a single crewman, and the freight. Craigo, once he was in the ship, stared rather closely at the control panel. Things *had* changed a bit, in the last twenty years.

"Don't let it bother you," the sharp young union member reassured him. "The minute they give you a green light, punch for start. Six days out, punch for turnover. Eight days after that, punch for park. The computer'll do it all but park—Venus Orbital Dockage'll take care of that."

"WhaddaIdoincaseofanemergency?" demanded Craigo, around his cigar.

"Forget it? There aren't any emergencies, nowadays. Just push the start button when they give you the green—"

"What," repeated Craigo, taking the cigar out of his mouth and speaking more distinctly, "do I do in case of an emergency?"

"But there aren't—" began the young man; and stopped on suddenly finding Craigo's boar-like features uncomfortably close to his own. He gulped, and started to explain. Half an hour later, Craigo interrupted him with an upraised hand.

"All right, arright!" said Craigo. "Let's make it simple, hey? Let's get down to the important parts. This here button takes it off the computer and puts it on manual. Right?"

"Right—"

"And this here lever lets me unlock the regular manual controls. I know how t'use *them!*"

"Yes, sir."

"The buttons for the gyros, here. The picture

model shows my inclination to line of course. Ship-to-station phone controls, here. Ship-to-ship, here. Computer logs and allows for change of course. It controls here. Punch this if I want back on course—"

"Well, yes, but—"

"Don't give me no more buts. I got your buts and excepts and only-ifs up to here. What I wanted to know was what do I do in case of an emergency. All right. I know."

When it was time to leave, he left. He did not curse his fate as he went; but its touch was heavy as the incipient indigestion on his stomach. At that, he should have been more chary of letting his resentment ride him.

For Fate had barely started with him.

At the moment Craigo was taking his seat before the controls of his ship, a certain well-known but temperamental opera star was giving her steward final directions for a buffet lunch to be served aboard her private ship (*yacht* was a word rather sneered at in spacing circle) as soon as they were underway from Venus Orbital to Earth Station.

". . . and salmon mayonnaise," she was saying. "I can't stand the stuff myself, but the Senator wants it. And so we'll give it to him." She fixed the steward with a green and glittering, if beautiful, eye. "Won't we?"

"Well, ma'm—I haven't checked the stores; but I think—"

"You think? Don't you know? I pay you to know, I pay you very well to know, I believe!"

"Yes, ma'm."

"Salmon mayonnaise, then."

"Yes, ma'm."

"And right next to the salmon mayonnaise, on its right . . .

Meanwhile, Craigo was watching the traffic light on his panel. It blinked on, suddenly green. He punched the start button, got up, lit himself a fresh cigar and began to mix himself a martini. . . .

One day went by. Craigo's ship, computer-run, burned its way through the hollowness of space on a conventional course.

Two days went by. Craigo began playing solitaire. Because he cheated, he invariably won. When he won, he bought himself a drink.

Five days out. Craigo gave up cheating.

Six days out. Craigo punched the turnover button and had another drink.

Eight days out. Craigo, who was sleeping off a middling-to-heavy hangover, was suddenly blasted out of sleep and bunk alike by the clamoring of an alarm bell that nearly deafened him. He rose and blundered his way to the panel and finally shut off the alarm by keying in the ship-to-ship phone to which it belonged.

Blessed silence suddenly filled the freight ship. But hard on the heels of it, a female human voice blasted out of an overhead speaker.

"Answer me! Answer me—I know you're there. I can see by the light on the dingus you're in range. Oh, come in, come in—whatever they say—Mayday! S.O.S.! *Help!*"

The final word burst from the speaker with all the range, power, distinction and point of a fine lyric soprano.

Meanwhile, Craigo, half-hungover, half-asleep, bleary-eyed, cotton-fingered and cursing, had been simultaneously trying to find the talk button on the ship-to-ship phone and the volume control that would allow him to tone down this blasting banshee of a woman. As luck would have it, he succeeded in doing both at once; so that the voice from the speaker suddenly faded away to a whisper, and then abruptly cut off altogether, as he, himself, started transmitting.

"Shut up!" bellowed Craigo. "Who're you?

Where're you? What the—" Craigo lapsed into gutter profanity— "goes on here, you?" He released the transmit button.

He sank back in the control chair; and sat there, sweating and waiting. After a minute, he remembered; and turned up the volume on the speaker.

"—at once!" belled out the female voice. "Everybody on board here had food poisoning; and one by one we put them in freeze-sleep until we could reach Earth Station One and a doctor! Only me! That filthy salmon mayonnaise! I knew it wasn't fit for people to eat. But I'm alone! Do you hear me, out there. Everybody's in freeze sleep but me! Oh, help!" The tone of the voice changed suddenly and became haughty. "Do you hear what I'm saying? Come at once! I am Taina Scarloff, of the North European Opera Company. Do you hear that? Who are you?"

Craigo fumbled about, found a package of unlighted cigars and pinched one alight. He shoved it into his mouth and pushed the talk button on the phone.

"Who?" he roared.

"*Taina Scarloff!*" trumpeted the speaker in furious silver tones.

"Never heard of you!" shouted Craigo, to whom opera was something, you put the word soap in front of it, old ladies listened to it all day. "Listen, this is Craigo DelMyer."

"What?"

"Craigo DelMyer, Mr. Interplanetary Freight Hand—Listen you drab!" roared Craigo, what she had said suddenly registering on him, "whadayou mean, *what?*"

"I don't care if you are a freight handler! I didn't mean what! There'll be a good tip in it for you if you'll just come and get me and—"

The volume of sound from the speaker suddenly began to decline rapidly and be lost. Craigo grabbed for the control and twirled it upwards—then suddenly realized he must be passing out of range of the other ship. He swore, punched the controls over to manual and clumsily and inexpertly began to fumble with the manuals.

Fifteen minutes later, sweat standing out like oil on his face, he had the bright idea of turning the whole problem over to the computer. He did so, cut out the manuals, and went back to finish his nap.

Five hours later, when the alarm bell rang once more, he had finished his sleep, had a meal and was well into his second shaker of martinis since waking up. This time, since he was making the call, he took his time about sitting down at the panel and pressing the talk button.

"Now shaddup!" he said, without preamble.

Having said it, he released the button. The speaker burst to life overhead.

"Oh, it's you again! I thought I'd lost you. Where are you now? Where—"

The speaker broke off suddenly. There was a moment of tense breathing and then the voice continued in a tone of hard-held restraint.

"I'm listening."

"All right," said Craigo. He reached for his martini and took a swallow from it. "Now listen. I am Mr. Craigo C. DelMyer, Legal Representative of the Interplanetary Freight Handlers Union. You, I take it, are some moldy singer." Craigo released the button to hear if there was any reaction to the last part of this statement. Only the tense breathing sounded. Satisfied, he continued, "Where do you think you're going?"

To Earth Station One!" snarled the speaker.

"No you aren't," said Craigo, happily. "You're headed in the other direction. Unless you're in a solar orbit, that is."

"I never pretended I could drive this monstrosity!" flared the speaker. "Just who do you think you—"

"Cool off," growled Craigo. "I'm going to save you."

"You are!" Joyously, from the speaker.

"Could I leave you here to perish?" said Craigo, in his public voice—the one he used for press interviews. There was more truth to that question than he cared to admit to this frill. The automatic log had taken note of his contact with the other ship. If he came back without it now, questions would be asked as soon as he hit Venus and the log was examined. Legal questions. On the other hand, turning up as a hero wouldn't do him any harm in the investigation back on Earth.

"So listen," went on Craigo. "I'll find you and bring my own ship alongside. Then I'll get a cable on you and tow you in."

"Yes, yes. Just get busy and *do* it!"

"Slow down," snarled Craigo. "First you got to tell me where you are."

"But I don't know where I am!"

"You're at the panel!" yelled Craigo. "You're standing in front of it, aren't you? Aren't you?"

"I'm not deaf! Where else would I be standing?"

"So look for the green buttons—all the controls colored green!" shouted Craigo. "Stupid frill!" he muttered.

"All right. I found them."

"Right below them's a coder and tape spill. Now, here's what you do—" And Craigo proceeded profanely to coach her on how to demand her ship's present position from its automatic log. It was not an easy, nor a polite process, but eventually he got a reading.

"All right," he growled, finally. "Now, sit down and cool off. I'll give your course and position to my computer, and it'll bring us close enough so that I can make contact by the manuals."

He turned to go to work with his own computer—after first thoughtfully cutting off his phone, so that he would not be disturbed any more than necessary by this Scarloff frill. When he had the figures set up he took another little nap.

He was awakened somewhat later by the alarm bell; and sat up to shut it off. Then he took a look at the computer which told him that his destination had been reached. Craigo grunted; and flicked on the outside viewers. He began to scan about for Taina's ship.

It was nowhere in sight.

Craigo went over the area three times on full magnification before he could believe it. When he did he swore loud and long. He turned viciously on his controls panel to hunt for the radar controls.

He couldn't find them.

Craigo admitted this, finally; but he was close to foaming at the mouth by the time he did. He gave up and sat seething before the forest of unknown buttons and dials on the panel. The radar controls were just not there. Or maybe they had been combined with some other control function. Or maybe modern ships didn't have radar. Or maybe—

Craigo jammed down the ship-to-ship button with a heavy thumb. There was a moment's pause; and then the speaker burst into hysterical life, overhead.

"Oh, there you are! Where've you been? How dare you cut phone contact with me? I thought something had happened. What do you mean—"

"Shaddup," said Craigo automatically, almost thoughtfully. He let her run on for a few minutes while he mulled things over. After a few moments she became apprehensive, and paused to listen. "Hey," he said then. "Were these the figures you gave me?" He reeled them off back to her.

"Say it again. Slower," she said.

He repeated them, more slowly. There was a pause from the far end.

"That's right," said Taina, suddenly. "What about them?"

"I'll tell you what about them," growled Craigo, clamping down on a fresh cigar. "Those are the figures I gave my computer, so I'm where you're supposed to be. And where are you?"

"Me?"

"You heard me."

"But I'm right here."

"The hell you are!" roared Craigo, losing his temper completely. "I'm here, and you're not. I can't see you anywhere. You're lost!"

Taina's voice went up on a shriek, like an ascending rocket.

"Oh! I knew this would happen! You brute! You fool! You idiot! I might have known no stupid freight handler could—"

Craigo bit his cigar in two, jammed down his send button and began to shout back at her, half in ordinary English, half in Chicago argot—

"Don't ky me none of your fat lip, scorby! I got better things to do than dingle no cash-seed wen . . ."

After about two minutes of this, they both began to run out of breath. Also it began to occur to each of them that probably their choicest insults were being wasted on empty vacuum, since both were sending and neither receiving. Accordingly, they almost simultaneously switched to receive—and of course heard nothing.

"Hey," said Craigo transmitting cautiously after a moment of this, "You still there?"

There was a second of silence. Then—

"Of course," said the speaker, coldly.

Neither one made an effort to renew the slanging sessions. They had burnt up their emotions for the moment; and were thinking sensibly, coolly, and a little uncomfortably.

Craigo was reflecting that after this, after getting this close to another vessel in distress, no lawyer in the Solar System could get him off a verdict of at least manslaughter if he tried to abandon Taina now. Taina was thinking with a touch of something like panic that he might do just that, and she had certainly better throttle back her temper until she was safe. But then, give her ten minutes with this lout, and—

Meanwhile, Craigo had got around to considering in what other ways contact between the ships could be made. His was the more practical mind.

His thoughts at the moment ran more or less to the effect that, since human beings were fallible but computers were not (at least, modern computers were not supposed to be), the two ships must actually be within a reasonable distance of each other. A reasonable distance, that was, as distances in space go. Say, a few hundred miles—certainly less than a thousand.

It all revealed the interesting fact that he knew a lot less about handling a freight ship than he had ever dreamed he did. In fact, when you got right down to it, it amounted to what the sharp young union member had told him about start, turnover, and stop—and how to work the manual controls. The last was the only thing about this ship that bore any resemblance to the ones he had worked on.

"Mr. DelMyer?" said the speaker, perhaps a little too sweetly.

"What?" grunted Craigo.

"Oh, that's all right. I just wondered if you were still there."

"I'm thinking," said Craigo.

The speaker wisely said nothing. Craigo half-closed his eyes and thought—how to get next to a ship you can't even see?

It was not as if this was the first time in his life Craigo had been forced to think. Craigo's life had been one series of problems after another, clamoring to be solved. But these problems had generally been human problems—in the sense that they concerned themselves with the way so-and-so would jump, if Craigo did this, or that. However, he was used to using his wits. He even had a technique; an ancient practice which at one time had gone by the name of brainstorming, but which Craigo, like a great many people before and since that time had simply discovered for himself.

Consequently, he began to list off solutions practical, impractical, and downright nonsensical; in the hope that by keeping the ideas flowing he would turn up one that was workable.

He thought of signal guns. Roman Candles, lassos, magnets, smoke signals . . . and, after about five minutes of this sort of mental pyrotechnics, came up with a notion.

He thumbed the phone.

"Hey!" he said.

"What?" responded the speaker, promptly.

"You sing. Right?"

"I," said the speaker, icily, "have a voice. Yes."

"All right," said Craigo. "You sing. Into the phone. I'll start hauling this ship of mine around on manuals. If your voice starts to fade, I'll turn another way. After a while, you'll start growing louder. Then I'll be heading toward you. Get it?"

"I see," said Taina. "Very well." And, warming up with a few scales, she burst into *"Ardon gl'incensi—"* the mad scene from Lucia Di Lammermoor. She sang it all the way through, and finished feeling better than she had in some days. Automatically she switched the phone over to receive as she finished, to hear the applause.

"No! No!" Craigo was bellowing. "How can I check the cashseed volume on the floddy speaker with you screeching all over the goddam place, like that? Forget the singing! Cut it out! Talk—just talk! And keep your voice steady!"

For a second the speaker above him was silent. The insult was simply too enormous to swallow in a second. Screeching—!

"And what, may I inquire, would you wish me to say?" she snarled at last in a tone which, while pitched to a conversational level, was so reeking with venom that it was an artistic achievement all by itself.

"Anything you scorby well feel like," replied Craigo coarsely.

To Craigo, women fell into two classes. Those you didn't need to slap down every time you looked at them; and those you did. He had already placed Taina in the second class, not realizing she fitted neither. He was far from understanding this woman. For example, he was blissfully ignorant of the fact that the worst of his gutter insults had simply gone over her head. Taina had never learned Chicago slang—for roughly the same reason she had never got around to learning Eskimo, or Mandarin Chinese.

So, without bothering about it, she began talking; choosing, out of sheer shrewishness, however, to discuss current women's fashions. But here she missed her mark as badly as Craigo had missed it with her. In Craigo's opinion women did not talk, they made noise. He did not expect her to make sense; and he would have been more than a little surprised if she had. Noise, he had requested—a good, constant steady level of noise to check his volume by—and noise he was getting. So, for the present, anyway, he was not concerned with what words she made it with.

Later, it was to be different. After being talked

at long enough anyone will listen. But for the present it did not bother him.

Meanwhile, she continued talking and he listening and moving around in space for a couple of hours. At the end of that time he had made some small movement in her direction, he thought, but it was going floddy slowly. Just then, however, he heard her break off in mid-sentence.

"My voice is going," she told him. "I can't go on. I've got to rest my throat."

"Rest!" yelped Craigo. "Rest?" She did not answer. "Are you crazy? You want to get rescued, or don't you? Talk!"

But here he was up against more than he had bargained for. It was opposition on the instinctive level. To protect her voice was a reflex with Taina. She could no more entertain the possibility of life without the silver trumpet of her vocal cords than he could accept losing the title of Mr. Interplanetary Freight Handlers. After a good half hour of haggling, it was finally decided that Craigo would tell her how to use the manuals (they were simple enough for a child to manipulate, anyway) and he would talk for a while, while she listened and tried to steer in his direction.

"—all right," growled Craigo at last. "You got the controls?"

"I've got them," replied Taina. "Start talking."

"Right—uh—" Craigo fumbled for a moment, then he chortled. "There was this guy walking down the street, see, and he sees this three-legged dog . . ."

And on and on he talked. But a man, even a man like Craigo who has spent most of his life in bars and hotel rooms, knows only so many jokes. He began to realize he was running dry when he was forced to delve back into his childhood and come up with clean ones. He switched over to speech-making. There were a number of these he could reel off almost in his sleep. He gave Taina the *Welcome, Visiting Brothers* speech, the *How Can We Keep The Welfare Fund Going Without Support?* speech, the *What Has Management Actually Done For Us? I'll Tell You What Management Has Actually Done For Us* speech . . . and a host of others.

But eventually his voice, too, began to tire. He stopped and Taina took over again. She ran down a list of music critics, giving her acid-dipped opinion of each one. Then she did much the same for a number of conductors . . .

Craigo took over once more and gave her a rundown on all the women he had ever known . . .

Taina took over . . .

—What I want you to do [said the Chief Engineer to the Assistant] is get the picture of this. The two of them, hating each others guts by this time, bobbling around in the middle of nowhere and talking, talking, talking—about ships, about shoes and sealingwax, Moussorgsky, smoke-filled rooms, dressing rooms, backstage vendettas, strong-arm methods, artistic suicides that might have been murders, about acid thrown in the face, about acid poured into a throat-spray atomiser—about personal history, slander, enemies, triumphs, disaster; in short, about everything and anything that comes into the head of a man or woman who have been talking for hours and for the sake of their lives must still go on talk-talk-talking forever.

Because this twin filibuster of theirs went on and on. They did not find each other in the first four or five hours. They did not find each other by the tenth hour, the fifteenth, or the twenty-first. Three times Craigo had to threaten to leave Taina to strangle or starve, depending on whether her air or food gave out first. Once, he had to pretend actually to leave, before she would put the hope of rescue ahead of the thought of irreparable damage to her voice.

Finally, twenty-nine hours and some minutes after Craigo had begun talking them together, blood-shot of eye, light-headed from exhaustion and croaking murderously at each other, they came at last to the moment in which Craigo, looking in his forward viewscreen, saw the dark cylinder of Taina's ship occulting the bright view of stars dead ahead.

It was all over.

The Chief Engineer stopped talking and poured himself some whisky; and drank it straight. He had been talking steadily himself, and it had made him thirsty.

"Well?" barked the Assistant, impatiently, his last champagne cocktail untouched and forgotten in its glass before him. "Well? Then what happened?"

"Well, then," said the Chief, slowly wiping his lips with the back of a hairy hand, "they got married."

"*Married?*"

"Well, not right away, of course," said the Chief, pouring himself a drop more whiskey. "They had to wait until they reached Venus Orbital Dockage before they found someone with the authority to marry them. But when they did, there was no time wasted. And there you are. That's why I say, don't sneer at button-pushers."

"Button-pushers—" echoed the Assistant, bewilderedly.

"Certainly. The autopilot controls for ship-to-ship contact were right in front of Craigo all those hours, just waiting to be pressed after the computer pilotage brought him to a safe distance from Taina's ship, not far outside viewing range. That's why I say—never sneer at a button-pusher. It's not pushing a button that counts—it's knowing the proper button and the right time to push it that makes them worth their wages."

"But kag that scorby flod!" shouted the Assistant, "What I want to know is—why did they get *married?*"

"Why, they couldn't afford not to marry," said the Chief. "A wife can't testify against her husband in court, and vice versa—you know the System Laws. They'd both had just too much time to talk during those twenty-nine hours in space. They'd both said too much, told each other things they wouldn't admit to their closest friends—if either had a friend—things the very limit of which to a newspaper man would see them spending the rest of their lives in jail. They didn't dare *not* get married. Even now, after all these six years, they don't let each other get very far out of sight. And all," said the Chief, driving the point home with a thick finger jabbed at the Assistant's chest, "because Craigo didn't know what button to push."

The Assistant stared back at him, his jaw shoved forward in an expression seemingly caught between insult and disbelief. Then his face seemed to split apart all at once like a shattered window. He began to laugh. And then he began to roar.

Salvation and destruction may depend on one's point of view.

RESCUE

It was at noon of the third day that the four hunters of Amuk came upon the fallen star. It had not buried itself as deeply in the earth as most of its kind, but it was very shiny and hard; after trying unsuccessfully for a while to break off a piece, the hunters gave up and left it alone.

There was, however, a trail leading away from it, as of a beast that went on two legs, like the men, like the hunters themselves; out of curiosity, as much as out of their need for meat, they followed it. It led them into the jungle for some little ways, wandering here and there as if the beast was wounded, but there was no sign of blood to be seen; indeed, when the hunters finally caught up with the thing it turned out to be perfectly whole.

They came upon it at last in a clearing, where instead of running away from them it ran toward them. And so they waited for it—for indeed they were four, and all hunters—and it came up within a spear's length and faced them and they talked with it.

It was, indeed, very like a man; it called itself a man, and claimed to have been seeking the men over great distances. But no one would have taken it for a man. For one thing it was too tall for a man, and too light, and had no beard. Also it wore the clothing of no tribe. However, it spoke a variant of the Old Language, which the tribe itself had jealously preserved; and so the hunters decided to take it back to the king for instructions on what to do with it.

The king of the Men of Amuk at that time was Pibo; he was very old and had a reputation for being wise. He did not come at once to a decision, but ordered the hunters to step back and told the thing that talked like a man, and walked like a man, to seat itself and talk with him.

The beast opened the neck-part of its strange clothing and sat upon the ground; Pibo seated himself upon the black rock of judgment and questioned it, drawing his robes around him as he talked. "Where do you come from?" he asked, in the old language.

"From Earth," said the beast, "Scout Lieutenant Holroyd Aldo at your service."

These words, of course, made no sense, but Pibo had not come by his reputation for wisdom by admitting ignorance. He nodded and went on.

"What are you doing in the neighborhood of the Tribe of Amuk?" he asked.

The beast settled himself more comfortably on the ground. "I was looking for you," he answered.

These words were understandable, but pretty obviously a lie. However, Pibo's wrinkled brown features gave no sign of what he thought of such a transparent falsehood; he merely nodded to the beast to go on.

"It's going to come as a bit of a shock to you, probably," said the beast, "but we've been hunting you, along with the other lost worlds, for the last eighty years. You're just lucky I found you; I'd already made my sweep of this system and was just about to give up when my drive by-pass conked and I had to flop in for an emergency-landing. The reason I missed you on my first sweep must have been because your cities are all gone. I didn't see a sign of any buildings. What are you people living in?"

"We live in trees, of course," said Pibo. He swayed a little on the black judgment-rock, considering which of many questions to ask. He finally seized on the one understandable statement out of the beast's last speech.

"You have been looking for the Tribe of Amuk eighty years," he said. "You mentioned others; who are they?"

"The people of Earth and of the twenty systems," replied the beast. "The people of forty-eight worlds; but they're all from Earth of course, just like you are."

"But *you* have been looking for eighty years," said Pibo, cunningly.

The beast laughed. "Not I, myself," it said. "I've only been searching personally for five of your years. After all, I'm only thirty-five years old."

Pibo stifled a smile of triumph. He began to feel more sure of himself, and sat on the black stone in more relaxed fashion. He began to feel almost indulgent toward the beast for letting itself be tricked into such a clumsy lie. No man lived to be thirty-five. Pibo himself was an ancient twenty-seven, three times the average age of the hunters; and no tree or bush or animal lived half the age of a man. He looked at the beast fondly. Now that he had proved his superiority by catching it in a lie, he could afford to let it string tales at will. He encouraged it with a lazy nod. "Tell me more," he commanded.

"Anything you want to know," said the beast, cheerfully, "but I ought to be asking a few questions myself. How many are there of you people?"

"Five hundred thousand," lied Pibo.

"That many?" said the beast, with a look of astonishment. "It'll be some job to reorient your bunch. Well, if you've got that many, you ought to be able to spare me about twenty men to dig my ship out. I've got to get her upright before I can extend my antenna and call my mother ship."

Pibo nodded; but said nothing. The beast looked relieved. "I suppose you wonder how this all came about?" he asked. "How much do you people remember of the past?"

"We know all our history," said Pibo. "Nothing that ever happened to Men has been forgotten by the Tribe of Amuk."

"That so?" inquired the beast. "Tell me, just how does your history run?"

"From the beginning to the present," replied Pibo. "It is all remembered. From the time the earth split open and gave forth the first man, to the end of the world when the sun will trip his feet on the mountains as he passes and fall into the jungle, setting the world on fire."

"My God!" said the beast. Then it checked itself and said no more. Pibo looked at it curiously, wondering if perhaps he had not made a mistake to say what he just had. Then he remembered the stupid lie of the beast about the years it had lived, and felt reassured. Still, it was a very strange beast, and it behooved him to find out about it. Also, Pibo was very old and the old are inquisitive.

"Are you surprised?" Pibo asked the beast.

The beast looked at Pibo cautiously. "I see I've made a mistake," it said. "You people are in for extensive reorientation. It was the fact you spoke such good lingo that fooled me."

"Eight and eighty-eight are the tongues of men," said Pibo, automatically, "but there is only one Old Language. How could there be more?" He looked at the beast. "How did you learn to speak it, beast?"

The beast jumped a little at the last word. He looked around and saw where the hunters had drawn close and leaned upon their spears, listening. He put his hand to the middle of his body as if searching for something; but the hand found nothing and he pulled it away again. There was a little sweat that came out of his forehead and the hunters scented Fear.

"Hold on, there," he said. "I'm a man just like the rest of you. I learned what you call the Old Language the same way you did—by growing up with other human beings."

"What are human beings?" asked Pibo. The hunters moved closer.

"People like yourself," cried the beast. "Men— and women and children."

"There are the Men, and there are beasts," replied Pibo; "these others I have never heard of." He made an imperceptible little gesture to the hunters, that they should draw back, for their nearness was alarming the beast. Then he went on. "Tell me about them."

"Well, I'm not supposed to," said the beast, "I'm just a scouting pilot; you ought to be told these things by the reorientation-crew." He looked Pibo in the face and continued a little helplessly. "Well, I'll try."

Pibo nodded.

"You see—" began the beast stumblingly. "We are all Earthmen once—"

"That indeed would be so," said Pibo. "For did not the first man come out of the earth?"

"But—well, anyway," went on the beast. "We grew in numbers and—er—developed until we could fly in the air; then we got better so that we could fly between the stars."

"Truly," said Pibo, "truly that is some feat, for the stars are very close together, as any man by himself may see by looking."

"No," said the beast; "no, that is one thing you must change your mind about. You see, those stars that look so small when you look at them from here, are really great big places where other men live."

"Now this is impossible," said Pibo. "How can something so small be so big?"

The beast thought for a minute and the hunters smelled Fear again. "Look," he said. "If you stand and watch a man go away from you, doesn't he get smaller the farther away he goes?"

"That I have seen," said Pibo.

"Then these big places look so small because they have gone so far away from your—the world that they have grown very small, and everything on them."

"Now, this is indeed something new," admitted Pibo. "And to me it sounds like the truth; for since the earth is the center of all bigness, since it is from what everything came, things do get smaller as they get away from it. For are not the leaves near the top of the trees smaller than those below, and do not all birds grow smaller as they rise in the sky? But—" he added struck by a certain thought, "how is it that you are so large, if you come from so tiny a place?"

The perspiration shone greasily on the beast's forehead. "Why," he said, "when I got closer to the earth, I got bigger, of course."

Pibo thought this over in the time it took for an insect to crawl halfway across the clearing. Finally he spoke again. "You must understand," he said, lowering his voice to a confidential tone that the hunters could not overhear, "that I can't just accept something like that just on your say-so. I am the King of the Men of the Tribe of Amuk. If you were not from so far away, you would have heard of me. It is my job to sit here on this black stone and pronounce solemn judgments. But I'm also an individual, aside from my official position—an individual with an individual's interest in what may be of personal benefit. Now, I'd like to hear more of all these interesting things you talk about; but before we go any further, do you happen to have any small item of proof with you that would indicate that more talk would be to both our advantages?"

The man—as he called himself—sitting on the ground, nodded. He reached through a slit in his strange clothing. "I have here—" he began.

"Just a minute," said Pibo. He motioned for the hunters to draw further away, which they did without protest. They were all healthy young men without too much in the way of brains—interested in the more concrete verities of food, women and hunting, and quite willing to let the King settle matters. "Go ahead," said Pibo.

The other drew out a small rounded object, about the length shape of a thumb-sized piece of peeled stick. It shone like calm water in the sunlight. "This is a very useful thing," said the man. "And if you'll supply me with twenty men to put my ship back on its feet, I'll give it to you and show you how to use it."

"It strikes me," said Pibo, rubbing his old chin, "that something that small could hardly be worth twenty men; I might give you one or two."

"Twenty," said the man. "There's lots of men in the world, but there's only one of these."

"Oh, well," said Pibo, "why quibble? You and I are above such things. What does it do?"

"This," said the man. He turned one end of the stick that seemed to rotate separately from the rest of it and a faint beam sprang from it to strike the ground a few feet from Pibo's feet. Almost immediately, the ground began to smolder and smoke. Little flames sprang up from the humus of dead leaves lying close. The man turned the end of the stick back, the light winked out, and he stamped on the ground to kill the flames.

"What is it?" demanded Pibo eagerly, feeling greed curl within him like a hungry snake.

"We call it a small hand-torch for cutting metal parts, but it has many uses," explained the man.

"It would be very useful for setting fire to the forest to drive game." said Pibo. "Even I could go hunting with it in my hand."

"Do I get my twenty men?" asked the other.

"You do," said Pibo. He stretched out his hand toward the object. "Give it to me."

The man withdrew his hand. "When my ship is set back upright," he said.

Pibo concealed his disappointment. He made a deprecating gesture with one dark and skinny old hand. "However you wish it," he said; "these things are mere details. How is this thing constructed?"

"It is made with other things called tools in a place called a factory," said the man. "There are no words in the Old Language for how it is done."

Pibo almost sulked. The man was either very stupid, or very smart to withhold information so neatly. "What were you doing when my hunters found you?" he asked.

The man considered his answer before replying. "I will try to explain," he said. "My ship comes from a bigger ship which we call the mother ship. When I was forced to make an emergency-landing here in the jungle, and saw that my ship was so placed that I could not extend my antenna to call my mother ship to come and rescue me, there was only one thing I could do. That was to locate some high place like the top of a mountain, and there set off a mechanism that would go high in the air and then fly apart, into countless little bits. The winds would carry these little bits all over the world in the air. These little bits are what we call radio-active; and there is a mechanism on the mother-ship that can smell them from a great distance. When I do not return, the mother-ship will come looking for me. They will listen for my radio-signal; and if that does not come, they will look for the little bits—using their smelling-apparatus. If they smell them, they will stop and search the world closely until they find me."

Pibo nodded, absorbing this all with his black, button-bright eyes.

"These others on the mother-ship," he said, "they are men, too—they are not beasts?"

The man chuckled. "They're men; I give you my word on it," he answered.

"Good," Pibo said, "we could use another tribe around here; the Men of the Tribe of Amuk often go footsore and hungry."

The man looked surprised.

"With five hundred thousand of you," he began. "I should think—"

Pibo instantly saw the error of his earlier lie. "Do not all men go hungry at times?" he countered. "When a man is far from home and hunting is bad, is he not often hungry?"

The man laughed. "That's something that's going to be changed for you and your people, oldtimer," he said. "Out where I come from nobody ever has to go hungry."

"Is that the truth?" said Pibo.

"Of course," said the man. "We have something

which we call civilization, which means people-and-machines-working-together. There are great artificial places to live where the weather cannot get at you."

"Even the thickest trees," interjected Pibo, "will not shelter a man from a heavy rainstorm."

"The great caves we have built do that," replied the man, "for I suppose you'd call them caves. The great places which make food produce for all."

"Who hunts?" asked Pibo, dubiously. "Who goes tired and thirsty while ranging the jungle?"

"There is no jungle," cried the man. "There is no need to hunt."

Pibo laughed. "This is foolish," he said. "The jungle is all about us. Look for yourself."

"But the jungle will be there no more when my mother-ship comes, and others like it," said the man. "They will clear out the trees and the undergrowth. They will heal your sick people. They will give you machines to build great structures, and other machines to fly you through the air like a bird. You will live longer and be happier. You will be safe from all dangers and fears. There will be shade for the day and light for the night."

"Bah," said Pibo. "This is impossible."

"Impossible?" said the man—and there was the light of triumph on his face. "How about that cutting-torch I showed you and promised you for the men you will lend me? Do you have anything like that? If that is real and does what you saw it do, then everything else I say must be real and true, also."

His voice rang out over the clearing; and Pibo did not answer. Instead he sat like an old idol in black stone, perched on his seat of judgment and thinking deeply. He sat in this fashion, pondering what the man had said; the slow minutes crawled past, and crawled past, one after the other, like worms that travel in a long line, the nose of each to the tail of the one before it. He thought of what the man had said, and he thought of the stick that set fires; he thought of the future the man had painted and he thought wryly that he was probably the only man in the tribe with wit enough to consider the implications of the situation.

At last, when the sun had moved a good forefinger's distance across the sky, he gave over his thinking; turning to the hunters, gave them an order in their own language to kill the man. And the four of them leaped upon him and pulled him down on the ground, to cut his throat. The man screamed.

"Why are you doing this?" he shrieked at Pibo. "It was the truth I told you; the truth!"

"I don't disbelieve you," replied Pibo, not moving from his judgment seat. "What you had to say was fantastic; but there is enough evidence in the form of the Old Language, and certain almost-obsolete tribal customs, to convince me that what you picture is probably the truth. After all, I have always been a wise man and age has mellowed my thinking-processes. I realize that nothing is impossible.

"However—" continued Pibo, rather unnecessarily—for the jagged stone knives of the hunters had done their work and the man from the stars was busily engaged in gasping out the last of his life into a widening pool of his own blood on the ground—"there is the moral question to consider.

"I cannot honestly see but what a transition to such a paradise as you picture would be destructive to the ancient and honorable virtues of our independent way of life. The social-structure of the Tribe of Amuk might well collapse. Possibly the hunters might not even need me to think for them any more. And the Gods forbid," finished Pibo, folding his robes around himself judicially, and looking at the now-dead man from the stars, "that I should do myself out of my job in the summer of my old age."

Thornton Wilder said, "There is a land of the living and a land of the dead and the bridge is love, the only survival, the only meaning." But what if that bridge be rotted out?

FRIEND FOR LIFE

It had been sixteen years, and here Jimmy was dead. Holter Lauren sat with the body in his arms in the bare living room of the small, two-room house of the Daclan sea-farm. Outside, the cold waves of the globe-wide Daclan ocean beat like heavy, grey ghosts on the rocky slopes below the house. Jimmy's fishing boat, laden with its nets, rocked at the dock's end.

Jimmy would be over thirty now, Holter thought. But under the stubble of blond beard, the dead face was still youthful . . . relaxed and innocent, gentle. Jimmy had not bled much—where the slim curve of the nethook entered his body below the left shoulder blade, the heavy coat of coarse sisal fiber was marked by only a small stain of red.

It had happened with such impossible swiftness. *Jimmy*, Holter had been going to say, *remember when they shipped us back from the Belt stars? Remember when we were orphans together, after an epidemic that killed off the grown people on Belt Four? How's it been with you since, Jimmy? What friends and neighbors you got, Jimmy boy? How's Dacla as a place to call home?* But he never had a chance to say any of it. Holter was rich now, a ship-hopper, a perambulating tourist who wandered where his whims took him. They had brought him to Dacla now, after sixteen years—hours too late.

He had come directly here from the ship. He had waited in this cold little room until Jimmy's fishing boat came into the dock. He'd heard Jimmy's uncertain footsteps up the rocky walk to the house, and seen the front door open.

"Hi, Jimmy," Holter had said, "long time no see, kid."

And Jimmy had looked at him and coughed a little blood. Then he fell forward into Holter's arms and died, with nine centimeters of steel and the plastic handle of a net-hook sticking out of his back.

Holter Lauren had never known anything could touch a man like this. Rich man, poor man, beggarman, thief, Holter had been all of those. But always on the bright, slick surface of life. Now he crouched like a dog above another, dead dog, with a dog's dumb, savage misery in his heart. Sixteen years he had followed the dark angel of his own dark spirit until it no longer had anything more to give him. So he had come back to what might have been his bright angel, one day too late.

There was a small sound beyond the front door. Sudden new purpose flamed up in Holter. He reached to the net-hook in Jimmy's back and with easy strength drew it gently out. Dark and slim and hard, he moved noiselessly to the wall alongside the door and flattened himself out. The stained net-hook twitched in his hand.

There was a shuffle on the doorstep, a hesitant sound. Then, slowly, the door began to open. There was a movement—

Holter leaped. A flurry of action, and he slammed a slight form against the inside wall; and held it there, the needle point of the net-hook centimeters from a throat. A rabbit face with thin strands of black straggling beard gabbled in terror at him.

"Who're you?" whispered Holter.

"Dummy . . . don't hurt Dummy . . . no, no, please don't hurt Dummy . . ."

Slowly, but keeping the net-hook close, Holter released his grip. The obvious half-wit sagged against the wall. His eyes went to the body of Jimmy, and he began to cry.

"Oh no . . . oh no . . . oh no . . . oh—"

Holter dropped the hook to lift both hands and fit them around the narrow neck. The idiot reiteration died and for a minute something like intelligence gleamed in the black, vacant eyes.

"Don't know you—" whispered Dummy through the strangling hands.

Holter forced himself to let go and step back.

"I'm Jimmy's friend," he said. "Do you know what happened? Tell me!"

"No. Dummy don't know. Jimmy say stay home. Dummy couldn't go today in boat. Jimmy come home with hook in back. Oh no . . . oh no—"

"Shut up!" said Holter. The singsong voice cut off as if a switch had been snapped. Holter lifted the body of Jimmy with smooth strength.

"Where you take my Jimmy?" whimpered the half-wit, scrambling after him.

"To the police," said Holter.

The Daclan police lieutenant, an older man who wore his sisal-cloth uniform carelessly, but neatly, sat on the corner of his desk.

"What are you going to do first?" asked Holter.

"Don't worry," said the lieutenant. His grey eyes under faded brows considered Holter. "We'll check into it."

"Check into it?" Behind Holter, standing half-crouched in a corner, the half-wit, Dummy, stirred. "Damn it!" burst out Holter. "This is murder!"

The lieutenant drew a long breath.

"Look, Mr. Lauren," he said. "You're a tourist. No offense—but you don't know Daclan. We're a young world, geologically as well as colonially. Our land is rock and we make our living from the sea. We're over-worked and under-populated." He stood up from the desk. "I'll do what I can."

Holter stood up also. With the fury in him, he felt taller even than he was.

"What did you have against Jimmy?" he asked softly.

"Have against him?" echoed the inspector. "There wasn't anyone I liked better than Jimmy. Everybody liked him—loved him. You come here after all this time and ask me what I had against him. How good a friend were you, these last sixteen years?"

Holter turned on his heel and walked out, down concrete corridors and into the cloud-broken sunlight of the street. He stopped, undecided; and in that moment he heard the hesitant scurry of feet behind him. He turned and saw the half-wit.

"Come here," Holter said.

The little man sidled closer.

"All right," said Holter, impatiently, "I won't hurt you. Now listen. Who was Jimmy's closest friend?"

Dummy didn't understand, put his thumb in his mouth to bite it.

"How about girl friends? A girl—did Jimmy have a girl?"

Dummy's thin face lit up. "Mincy!" he cried; and clapped his hands. "Mincy!"

Dummy led him by narrow, pedestrian streets between the blocky concrete buildings of the business section down to the harbor, past countless wharves and many ships until they came at last to a cordage warehouse. In the interior, the dim outlines of men at work moved to and fro; on the dock itself, a young girl in rough work pants and shirt sat on a coil of rope cable, gazing toward the sea. As soon as he caught sight of her, Dummy gave a little whimper, ran ahead and knelt down beside her. He hid his face in her lap and she put one hand on his head and stroked it absently. She did not look away from the sea.

Holter hesitated, then approached slowly. The hand which stroked Dummy's tangled black hair was brown and hard, with short, blunted nails; her hair was yellow and alive and her face beautiful with fine, strong bones. She had not been crying but her face was stony.

"I see you've heard," said Holter.... "I'm an old friend of his."

"They were all his friends," she said. After a moment she added, "Would you leave me alone, please. I'd like to be alone."

"I want to do something about it!" Holter broke out, angrily. "That lieutenant I talked to—he's worse than nothing. I want to find the man who did it."

"You can't do anything," she said, expressionlessly. "You're a tourist."

"What's that got to do with it?" he demanded. "He was the only—the best friend I ever had. I'm going to get the man that did it. You can give me a lead."

"Please," she said. "Go away."

"What's wrong with you?" he shouted at her.

"You're as bad as the lieutenant. Weren't you his girl?"

"His girl?" she said. "I was his wife."

"His wife—" Holter stared at her and the mounds of sisal cable on the dock. "What are you doing here? The sea-farm—"

"That was his work. This was mine," her voice had the eternal greyness of the sea in it. "I have to get back to work soon. Will you go now?" She spoke with infinite weariness.

Holter stood like a wild animal, baffled by its chains, for a second. Then he turned away, his fists clenched.

Dummy clung to the woman's knees. She patted him gently.

"Go with him, Dummy," she said. Reluctantly, the little man got to his feet.

For the first few moments, Holter strode along automatically, without plan. Then he saw a knot of men ahead of him, congregated on a dock above one of the little fishingboats. When he reached the group, Holter saw that a stretcher was just being lifted by block and tackle from the low deck of the boat.

"Easy," said one of the men on the dock, catching at one end of the stretcher. "Easy, don't jolt him now."

They unhooked the stretcher and four men took the handles of it. Holter could see that it held a boy of about sixteen. He seemed to be unconscious; his eyes were closed and his face white. But his head turned from side to side as he was carried past and suddenly a low moan seemed to bubble from his lips. The whole right side of his body was stained with blood.

"For God's sake!" said Holter. "Why don't they give him a shot of morphine?"

"What morphine?" said the man beside him and

turned. He recognized Holter as a tourist and his lips spread in a humorless grin. "Sure, morphine," he said. "And some wire cable that wouldn't have parted and let the sheave block drop on him in the first place." He spat on the dock.

Holter held his anger capped within him by force of will.

"Say," he said. "Do you know Jimmy Molloy?"

The other looked up at him with new curiosity. "Sure. Sure, I know Jimmy. What about him?"

"He's dead," said Holter.

The wind-toughened face stretched with surprise. "Jimmy? No!" He stared at Holter.

"He came home with a net-hook in his back."

"Net-hook—" the other's eyes narrowed. "Today? That huncher Bollen, huh?"

"I don't know," said Holter, as calmly as he could. "Was it?"

They eyed each other for a waiting moment; and, slowly, a curtain seemed to draw across the eyes of the other man.

"I wouldn't know," he said, and turned away. Holter reached out and caught his arm and swung him back.

The man looked down at Holter's hand on his arm.

"That's no good," he said.

There was a shifting of feet on the planks around them; and Holter looked up to see himself surrounded by a ring of weather-scarred faces. They said nothing, only waited; and after a second he let go. He turned away and went across the dock to the landward stairs and climbed them to the street. He looked back. Dummy was following.

Holter felt weary with the weariness of the great, frustrated rage. Down the street was a bar. He went toward it, turned in, and seated himself on a stool at the narrow, empty counter. The bartender came gliding down behind the bar to him—gliding sideways.

Holter glanced over the bar, saw that the bartender was legless, and sitting on a sliding platform that ran on two rails.

"What for you?" asked the bartender.

"Anything," Holter said. "Booze—anything." He looked at Dummy. "And whatever he wants."

"Coffee!" crowed Dummy, excitedly. "Hot coffee!"

Holter sipped his drink and felt it bite and burn on his tongue.

"Pretty busy on the docks this time of year," he said.

The bartender flushed.

"Go to hell!" he said.

Holter stared at him. "What's the matter with *you?*" he said.

The bartender grunted. "Forget it," he said. "You're a tourist. You don't know any better. If I had two good legs I'd be out there—nobody loafs on this world unless they have to."

"All right." Holter swallowed his own gall. "I'm sorry. Maybe you'll tell me why."

The bartender reached for a barcloth.

"Know anything about economics?" he said. "This here's no industrial world. There's no surpluses. We live on a subsistence level, and that's all. We got to work that hard to stay alive, day by day."

"I still don't get it," said Holter, watching him. "Why do things the hard way? Why weave cloth out of vegetable fibers? Why rope cable? Why don't you set up a plastics plant and a steel industry?"

"Who's to do it?" the bartender swept the cloth in sharp circles. "Food's the main thing. Food comes from the sea. To put people on plastics and steel we'd have to take them off the boats. Take them off the fishing boats and there's not enough food coming in. Then we starve. You can bring in only a few emergency things by ship."

There was a moment's silence. Dummy sucked at his cup.

"All right," said Holter. "I said I was sorry."

The bartender made a half-ashamed gesture.

"Forget it. I sit here all alone all day and I get to feeling—ah, forget it."

"Sure," said Holter. He leaned a little forward over the bar. "Do you know a man named Bollen?" he asked.

The bartender's head came up.

"Bollen? You mean Tige Bollen? Yeah, I know him."

"Where would I find him?"

"Up on the sisal farms, this time of year," answered the bartender. "They're harvesting, now. He works on Farm One Eighty-nine."

"Know him very well?"

"I know him," he reached out with the barcloth. "He's a tough huncher, that motherson."

"That's what I hear," said Holter. "I heard he's liable to use a net-hook."

"He'll use a net-hook. He'll use anything," replied the bartender, dispassionately, as if considering the instincts of some remote animal. "He's got plenty of guts; but if he can't take you with fists and feet, he'll take you with anything that's handy."

"He took Jimmy Malloy," said Holter, harshly.

"Jimmy?"

"He's dead," said Holter. "With a net-hook in his back."

The barcloth was stopped now.

"I suppose," said Holter, "you don't give a damn, either."

"Want another drink?" asked the bartender.

"What's wrong with you?" grated Holter. "All of you? You scared of something? Everybody claims they liked Jimmy, but nobody'll move a finger after this bastard that killed him."

"You better pay me for what you got," said the bartender. "That'll be twenty-two fifty."

"For that rot-gut you sold me?" Holster said. "Fleece the tourist, eh?"

"The rot-gut's fifty cents," said the bartender. "The twenty-two's for the coffee. I thought you knew what the price was here when Dummy ordered it."

Holter threw down a twenty-five-credit note and walked away.

Out on the street, he turned to Dummy, who shrank from him.

"It's all right," said Holter, sharply. "I'm not mad at you. Listen, do you know this Tige Bollen?"

Dummy nodded, huddling against the wall.

"Good," said Holter. "You come along. I want you to point him out to me."

They went back to the transportation center next to the spaceport.

"Sorry," the one man on duty told Holter. "All the rentals are out."

"How about those?" said Holter; and pointed to a row of the light craft parked under a weather overhang.

The thin face of the other smiled placatingly, but without regret. "Those there are private craft."

"I see," said Holter. He thought for a second. "Look—" he said, digging into a pocket and coming out with an envelope. "I have to get moving right away. Here, look at this."

He opened the envelope and took out a sheet of paper which he unfolded and passed to the transportation agent. The man glanced at it.

"But this is just a passp—"

Holter hit him before he finished the sentence

and caught the limp body in time to ease it to the ground.

"Come on!" he cried at Dummy, and ran for the nearest of the flyers.

"Which way?" demanded Holter when they were aloft. "Where's Farm One Eighty-nine?"

Dummy fearfully raised his head and pointed north. Holter swung the nose of the flyer in that direction, a tight smile on his face.

It took them about half an hour to reach the farms. Air markers had been set out plainly. Farm 189 was a sprawling patch of rosettes of thick, fleshy leaves spaced in staggered orderly rows. Along one side of the farm ran a deep river of clear water, flowing down to the sea. Near the buildings of the farm was a dock, and beside this Holter set the flyer down.

The farmyard was filled at the moment with great stacks of the broad leaves. Beyond, the greenish black of the artificial soil of the fields began; and from within the scraping house came the steady whirr and thump of machines pulling the pulp and waste material of the leaves from the fibers. No one was in sight. Motioning Dummy to silence, Holter stole up behind one of the leaf piles and peered through the open door into the dim interior of the scraping house. Here and there were shadowy bulking machines; and among them came and went the dim outline of a short, broad, busy figure.

Holter turned to Dummy. "That Bollen?" he whispered.

Dummy nodded, his eyes big.

"Stay here," Holter ordered Dummy. And he strolled openly forward.

Prepared as he was, the abrupt change from brightness to gloom was still so startling that Holter had to stop and blink for a moment. For a second he was blind; and then the first thing the expanding pupils of his eyes revealed was a short, broad face, not a yard from his own, that seemed to hang there, regarding him with light green eyes.

"What d'you want?" said the face.

"I'm off the space ship," said Holter. "I wanted to see how they made rope from plants." He added, "My name's Lauren. Holter Lauren."

Bollen's face did not change. The lips were full without being loose, the nose slightly pug with wide nostrils. A face that might look cheerful, or sullen, or indifferent as it did now—but hardly any way else. The face of a healthy human animal. The body was slightly round-shouldered and thick-waisted, broad-chested, short-armed. All this Holter saw in one automatic instant of appraisal.

"Look around if you want," said Bollen, in a voice that was hoarse and rough, as if dust had gotten into the vocal cords. "I got work to do."

He was turning away, when Holter spoke.

"Wait," he said. It seemed to Holter that there was something lacking, as if a high religious sacrifice had turned out to be a simple butcher's job.

"Do you know Jimmy Molloy?" he said.

Bollen's face did not change.

"Sure I know him," he answered.

"I used to know him—we were kids together—" Holter was talking without paying any attention to the sense of his words. "We were orphans together, from Belt Four. Everybody liked Jimmy. He was that kind of guy. I talked to his wife today. She was sitting on the dock there, looking at the sea—"

"Say—" said Bollen suddenly, harshly. "What're you talking about?"

Holter looked at the shorter man calculatingly. Bollen was a full head in height less than himself, but their weights must be close to equal. The sisal farmer was tough; and the bartender had said he could be a dirty fighter.

Well, thought Holter, so could he. He had not bummed around on a dozen different worlds without learning a few things. He saw that Bollen was watching him with the careful balance of a man expecting action. Maybe though, he might be led to think that Holter could be taken by surprise.

"Why—nothing—" he answered, with the little quaver of a man whose nerve might have failed him. "Ah—come to think of it, it's later than I thought, I—I guess I'll be going."

He turned away, started to walk off. And in spite of the fact that he was braced for it, still he almost did not hear the soft, rapid thump of boots running up behind him. There was only that small warning—and then the sudden shock, the short man's arms clamped around his body and the whole weight of the charging body against him. But Holter was ready, crouching, reaching back over his shoulder to seize and flip the short man pinwheeling through the air to the ground ahead.

Bollen landed hard; and instantly Holter was diving on top of him, digging his knee into the other's middle. His knee bounced off surprisingly hard stomach muscles. He rolled hastily clear.

Holter kicked out at the kneeling man's chin; but Bollen grunted and swayed his body sideways. He caught Holter's boot as it shot past, seized and twisted it, throwing him. Holter kicked the hands loose with his other foot and rolled over onto his back, getting his knees up just in time to ward off the short man's diving body. They scrambled apart and to their feet; and faced each other.

There was a wariness in them both now. Each had been surprised by the quality of the opposition. They had rolled out of the scraping house into the brilliant sunlight and they stood between the wall of the house and a long high pile of leaves. Slowly, step by step, Bollen began to back away along the wall.

Cautiously, looking for an opening, Holter followed. Slowly, like rhythmic ceremonial dancers in a pageant of ancient passions, they moved together back along the loose plank wall until Bollen reached its end. Holter crouched to spring, tensed for an attempt by the other man to break and run; but instead, Bollen's arm flashed out of sight behind the corner of the building, to reappear all in one sweep of motion, swinging the bright flat blade of a machete high through the air.

Only the fact that he was already tensed to leap saved Holter. Instinctively he drove forward, inside the swing of the weapon, catching Bollen's wrist in his left hand and bringing his right hand and arm around the other's body to reinforce his left as he strove to bend Bollen's machete wrist back.

Bollen was inconceivably strong. Even with the power of both Holter's arms against his single one, the farmer's wrist resisted stubbornly before it began slowly to yield. The long blade drooped like a brilliant flower for one long second before Bollen's fingers loosened and it fell.

Triumph boiling inside him, Holter twisted about to drive his right leg between Bollen's to trip him up and throw him down. And then, in the second before Holter could accomplish this, he felt a terrific explosion of pain as the sisal farmer drove his knee upward into Holter's groin. The sky above Holter seemed to blacken with his agony. He felt his grip loosen; he fell, rolling into a ball on the ground.

A shattering kick on his shoulder sent him tumbling. Instinctively, he continued to roll, over and over, in an attempt to get away; but the boots of Bollen found him, in great hammer blows that jarred his undefended body and shook his brain into dizziness. He had one wild melange of impressions—the choking dirt in his nostrils, the flashing picture of Bollen towering above him; and the racking kicks that drove through all his attempts to escape . . . And then, suddenly, they ceased.

Gasping, Holter managed to focus his swimming eyes. He saw Bollen walk away from him over to the fallen machete, pick it up, and turn back toward him. Holter strained to move, but his muscles responded with agonizing slowness.

From the corner of the pile of leaves there was a flicker of sudden motion, and a shrill wordless cry from Dummy. A pitifully ineffective rock bounced off Bollen's shoulder—but it was enough to stop him. He swung angrily, raised the machete threateningly at Dummy's retreating back.

Holter drove his battered body as he had never before in his life. He forced it to his feet and into a lunge for Bollen. Chest slammed against back, and Bollen was banged against the wall, dropping the machete, stunned by the impact. Holter jerked him around and clubbed his fist again and again against Bollen's jaw.

Bollen sagged and they both fell, Bollen still struggling. Kneeling Holter twined the fingers of both hands in the dark, thick hair of the sisal farmer; and, raising the shorter man's head, drove it against the wall of the building. He lifted and slammed it down again, and Bollen stopped moving.

Panting, Holter forced himself to stop. Murder was in *him*, now—but he wanted to take Bollen alive. He breathed deeply for several seconds; then he stripped off the sisal farmer's belt and tied Bollen's wrists behind him. A shadow fell across him. Dummy had stolen back and stood hunched above them.

"Bad—bad . . ." said the half-wit, scolding at the unconscious Bollen like some small, nervous animal.

Holter laughed grimly.

* * *

Bollen came to on the flyer ride back to Dac City.

Holter flew directly to the city hall and landed on the grass before it. He hauled Bollen from the flyer and thrust him ahead of him, up the steps and in through the doorway of the city hall. Dummy trotted along behind.

They went down the long concrete corridors until they came to the office where Holter had talked to the lieutenant of police that morning. Holter opened the door and pushed Bollen inside.

The lieutenant was at his desk. There also, seated in a chair facing him, was the girl Mincy. Two uniformed policemen stood against a wall.

Holter gave Bollen a shove that sent him half-sprawling across the desk.

"Here's your murderer," he said. "The man that killed Jimmy. I brought him in for you. And don't tell me you can't convict him; because if I have to, I'll bring in the best talent in the galaxy to dig up evidence he did it."

"I know he did it," said the lieutenant. He walked around the desk, helped Bollen upright, and with a knife cut the belt binding his wrists.

"You knew!" said Holter. "You admit it!"

"I never denied it," said the lieutenant, wearily. "Jimmy thought Tige had been short-grading him on the fiber he consigned to Mincy's warehouse. Jimmy went out to talk to him about it. It must have come to a fight between them. . . . Am I right, Tige?"

"That huncher!" growled Bollen, rubbing his wrists.

"Shut up, Tige," said the lieutenant. "Jimmy was worth three of you. As for you—" he turned to Holter— "your landing privileges are canceled here. I'm sending you back to the spaceliner you came on, under guard."

"But what are you going to do about him?" Holter almost screamed the words. "He's guilty! You got to make him pay!"

"Got—" the lieutenant put both fists on the desk top and for a moment leaned on it like a very old, very tired man— "give me patience. Make Tige pay for it? Sure. And who takes over Farm One Eighty-nine? You fool, you tourist fool," he said to Holter, "what do you know about it?"

Holter stared at him.

"No," said the lieutenant, savagely, "you don't understand. You can't see that here there's no cash value on being a nice guy, on being kind, or gentle, or a good husband. All that counts here is how much work your two hands can do. Sure, we all loved Jimmy. He was a good man—but he's dead now. There're men and women and children on the farms and on the docks and in the quarries, and right here in the city, who'll be missing the catch that Jimmy would have brought in today. Who do you think fed them—who do you think feeds me, God help me? I've got a double hernia, and this is the best I can do."

"I—" began Holter.

"Shut up," said the lieutenant, softly. "Listen to me. We're on our own here. We're too far out and too isolated to be rescued if anything goes wrong. We're too many to feed if our food supply fails. We can't afford an abstract justice to pamper our moral values or our emotions. Tige killed Jimmy, and nobody likes him for it—but what's to be done? We've lost one worker. Would you take another one from us? God in heaven, there isn't a person in this room, except yourself, that doesn't work fourteen hours a day or better and consider himself lucky to have three meals and a bed to sleep in for it. What can we do to punish Tige that wouldn't punish ourselves at the same time? Rehabilitate him? We haven't got the time. Imprison him? We haven't got the jailer. Sentence him to a lifetime at hard labor? What do you think he's got now?''

Holter sagged. He made a little defeated gesture with one hand.

"I give up," he said, and he turned away. "Let me out of here. I'm going back to the ship."

He took one lagging step forward and made as if to push between the two uniformed policemen. Then, abruptly, he had spun like a cat, shoving one man away from him and clawing at the gun in the other's holster. He had the weapon half-dragged clear before hard arms clamped about him, wrestled him down. He hung pinioned between the two men. The lieutenant walked slowly around the desk to face him.

"You would, would you?" said the lieutenant with a strange quietness. "You'd be your own judge and executioner. You'd risk being deported in irons, knowing that's the worst I could do to you. I suppose you think you've got guts."

He turned about and walked back to the desk. From a drawer he pulled out a sheet of printed paper and scratched briefly on it with a pen. He came back with it to Holter.

"Let him go, boys," he said. "Here." He drew his own sidearm and extended it, butt foremost, together with the paper. "Citizenship application. Sign it—and you can have *my* gun."

The hands on Holter's arms fell away. A sudden silence filled the office.

"Here, take them," said the lieutenant. "One for one's not a bad trade; and we badly need someone to replace Jimmy. Sign—and you can have his boat and his house. You can probably have Mincy, too. She's going to have to marry again, and she feels about Tige the way you do. She's young and healthy and that's a good sea-farm. You could do worse on this planet."

Holter did not answer. They were all looking at

him; Mincy, the lieutenant, Dummy and Bollen. Bollen did not avoid his gaze—he stared back at Holter without emotion, without fear.

"Or is that too much to ask?" demanded the lieutenant, softly. "Is that too high a price for you to pay for your revenge—to freeze at the nets and sweat in the sisal fields? Because that's the price, Lauren. Take over the work that Jimmy did and you can have everything he had, and more—you can have justice as well."

Holter still did not move, or speak. He stood before them now with all the brittle casing of his dark soul broken and stripped away. High on the wall of the office a clock ticked once, marking a minute gone—a long, long minute dwindling off into eternity, an eternity as grey as the sea, cold as an empty house, agonizing as an injured child, bitter as a legless man. After a while, the lieutenant lowered gun and paper.

"Take him away," he ordered the two policemen. "Take him back to his spaceliner."

The hands of the police closed on Holter's arms. Bollen's face still showed no emotion. Dummy gazed with wondering animal eyes, and the expression of the lieutenant was now indifferent. It was the eyes of the girl Mincy, as the policemen led him out the door, that made a mark deep on Holter's naked soul.

The look on *her* face he would never forget. . . .

As long as the memory of man runneth, love of homeland has spurred heroes to "uttermost endurance in the service of indomitable will."

CARRY ME HOME

Partially, it was the youth of Jason Jonasse that made it difficult for him to understand his fellow man. But mainly, it was his background.

His family was of the military. From their native city on Kilbur Two, during the past hundred years or so, had come a steady stream of Jonasses. Mostly, they died, in one way or another, while serving humanity on the Frontier of man's expanding spatial area. Those who did not, won through to advancement and posts of high honor. All, however, without exception, made the first step of transfer from the backwaters of military duty, earning their right to carry their officer's buttons to Class A Service in the Frontier Zone.

It was this transfer that Jason had just received and which was propped now on the toilet shelf beside the shaving mirror in his quarters, where he could feast his eyes on it during the process of trimming the straight black lines of his little mustache, with the aid of that self-same mirror. The mustache was an index of his character, so essentially Kilburnian, so uncompromisingly military, so uniquely Jonasse. It was the final seal upon his difference, the crown upon his height and the lean good looks of his breed, and the uniform of which tunic cape and boots were custom-tailored.

There was no one thing about him which did not set him off from the other officers of this small military garrison on Aster. For this small lost planet out in the Beltane Quadrant was class C duty; and the other officers were Class C officers, as Jason had been, serving his apprenticeship in a sort of police duty, until the blessed arrival of the transfer, welcome as a pardon to a life sentence prisoner. Jason beamed at it, working the clippers carefully over the ends of the mustache, for his baggage was packed and ready for the next courier ship that came and the transfer was his passport to the future.

A buzzer rang through his room, and Jason jerked at the unexpected suddenness of the sound. For a split-second the clippers slipped, chopping a little, ragged v out of the top line of the mustache, a v unfortunately beyond the ability of any clipping to disguise and anything but time to mend. For a moment, Jason stared at its reflection in the mirror. Then he cursed, threw down the clippers and thumbed the switch of the intercom.

"Officer Five Jonasse here," he said.

"Headquarters, Chief Troopman Basker, Sir," said the Speaker. "The Commandant would like you to report to his office right away, Officer."

"It'll be right there, Chief."

"Right, sir."

Scowling, Jason buttoned his tunic and clipped his cape about his shoulders. There was no good reason why the Commandant should want to see him, unless there had been some change in his orders directing the transfer. And if that . . .

Jason clamped down on the speculative section of his mind and left his quarters, hurrying across the drill-ground to the Headquarters Building.

Hot sunlight hit him a solid blow as he stepped out of the shade of his quarters. The Timudag, as the plains country of Aster's one large continent was known, broiled during the summer months under a cloudless sky. Jason strode across it and stepped gratefully into the air conditioned coolness of the Headquarter's Building.

The Commandant was waiting for him in the outer office. Like Jason, a Kilburnian, but without the Jonasse family tradition of Service, he had won little recognition during his short term of Frontier Class A Service; and, having no prospects to speak of on retirement from that, had fallen back on Class C duty, where the retirement age was much higher. A thin, cold man, he did not particularly like Jason though a scrupulous sense of fairness forced him to admit that the younger Kilburnian was far and away the most valuable of his men.

"You messaged for me, sir?" said Jason.

The Commandant took Jason's elbow and drew him aside, out of earshot of the troopmen at work at clerical tasks about the outer office. "Something has come up, Jason."

Jason felt cold apprehension and hot resentment. But he held it locked within him.

"The courier ship has just arrived," the Commandant said. "It brought your replacement—and another man."

The Commandant looked out the window and back to Jason again.

"The other man's an officer retired from Class A Service," he went on. "And he carries a request from the General Commander of our Quadrant to give him every assistance in returning home."

Jason looked at the Commandant in puzzlement. This was nonsensical. If the man was from Aster, he was already home. If he was not from Aster, why had he come to Aster, to this outlying station to obtain assistance?

"I don't understand," he said honestly.

"His home," explained the Commandant briefly, "is in the Timumang."

At that, Jason began to understand.

North of the Timudag, on Aster's one large land mass, lay the Timumang, the Mountains of the People. Boulder-strewn upthrust of the continental geosyncline to the north, it housed the degenerate descendants of an early abortive attempt at colonization, four hundred years before the coming of civilization proper to Aster. Wild and suspicious, these forgotten people had backslid to a clan-tribal form of organization. They warred on each other, lived off their inhospitable country in the course of nomadic wanderings, and shunned their latter-day cousins of the lowlands as if they had been plague-ridden.

The Timumang ignored the Timudag. Jason had not, in his term of service guarding the Interstellar Message Station and the few raw little towns of the Timudag, been anywhere near the Mountains of the People. Nor, as far as he knew, had any of the other men at the station. But of course he had heard stories.

There were other worlds where the tragic accident of too-early colonization had taken place, and the settlers had backslid to savagery or near-savagery. They were the cobwebbed corners that the Central Headquarters on Earth, like a busy housewife, was always planning to do something about and never getting to. From them, every so often, would come the rare case of a degenerate who ran away or escaped from his own people to join the ranks of civilization. Sometimes such men rose to respectable positions. But the tendency of ordinary people was to feel some repugnance toward them—reminders as they were of the fact that the human race was not completely without exception shooting up the dizzy stairs toward the millenium.

"A degenerate!" Jason muttered.

"An ex-officer," corrected the Commandant coldly.

Jason felt his temper rising, but held it back. He returned to the crux of the matter.

"I interrupted you, sir," he said. "Pardon me."

"Well," said the Commandant. "He'll need an escort and an officer to command the escort."

"You don't mean me, sir?" said Jason, aghast. "My orders—"

"I've no choice," said the Commandant, irritably. "And the delay in your transfer needn't be fatal. I've got no one else I can trust with such a job. He won't take more than twenty men."

Jason stared, incredulous.

"You can't go into the Timumang with just twenty men," he said, at last.

The Commandant snorted.

"Come and talk to him, yourself," he said, turning and leading the way toward his private office. "And remember, the Commander General requests our assistance. There's no dodging this."

Bitterly, Jason followed him, the sour anger of the betrayed curdling in his stomach. Mere hours from shipping out, they had to send him off on a what sounded like a suicide mission. Not that Jason had any objections to dying, if the time and place were right—but to be possibly clubbed to death in what amounted to a backyard brawl!

The Commandant ushered him in and a man sitting in one of the easy chairs of the office rose to greet them. He was a curious figure, as tall as the two Kilburnians, but so broad of shoulder and long of arm that he seemed much shorter. In the dark skin of his face, set above flat, heavy cheekbones and beneath pronounced brows, his brown eyes looked out at them with the soft liquidity of an animal. There was something yielding and sad about him. No guts, thought Jason, harshly, out of the fury of his resentment. No backbone.

The Commandant was introducing the two men. Jason shook hands briefly.

"Mr. Potter, this is Officer Five Jason Jonasse," said the Commandant. "Jason, this is Mr. Kerl Potter, formerly an Officer Three."

"Honored to meet you," said the degenerate. His voice was husky and so deep that he almost seemed to croon the words.

"Pleasure is mine," replied Jason briefly and mechanically. "The Commandant tells me you think twenty men is a sufficient escort into the Timumang."

"Yes," replied Potter, nodding.

"Why, that isn't nearly enough strength," said Jason. "The average clan usually musters at least a hundred fighting men."

"I know," Kerl Potter smiled, a warm, but deprecating smile. "I grew up in the Timumang—or had the Commandant told you?"

He didn't have to, thought Jason, looking at the man with disgust and disfavor. Aloud he said, "Any single tribe would be more than a match for us."

"Please——" Kerl held up his hand. "Let me explain."

Jason nodded, curtly.

"I wish to get back to my own clan—the Potter Clan," said the dark man. "For that we must go in on foot and search, because the clans move constantly, and from the air—which would be the quickest way of going—there is no way to tell which

tribe is which. They go to earth when they see a
flyer."

"I'll admit that—" began Jason.

"So we must go in on foot," continued Potter,
his deep voice like distant summer thunder in the
office. "We must hunt for campsites until we find
Potter sign at one. And then we must trail the clan
until we catch up with it." He paused, looking
at Jason and the Commandant to see if they
understood.

"Now," he said, "that means we must go through
much Timumang territory. If we are too large a
group, the word will go ahead of us and all the
clans will hide and we will never catch up with
the Potters. If we are too few, the first tribe we
meet with will destroy us. Therefore the solution
is to have enough men to discourage attack, but
not enough to frighten the clans into moving out
of our way. When we have found the Potter Clan,
you can drop me off and call for air transport to
pick you and the men up and bring you back."

Kerl wound up the argument and smiled at Jason as if to soften the young man's opposition with
good humor. Jason looked helplessly at the Commandant, who shrugged and looked out the window,
washing his hands of the matter.

"Look, Mr. Potter," said Jason, turning back to
the man and making an effort to be reasonable.
"These men of ours are all Class C. They know
something of police duty in the towns here, and
maintaining order generally. What they know about
expeditioning is nothing—"

"You can take your pick of the station, Jason,"
said the Commandant.

It was the culminating blow, the stab in the
back. Turning to look at his superior officer, Jason
realized finally that he was not to be allowed to
avoid this expedition, nor to alter the conditions of
it. For some reason, some intricacy of interbranch

politicking, it had become necessary for the General Commander to oblige Kerl Potter and for the Commandant to oblige the General Commander. It struck him as symbolic. As the degenerates were a clog and hamper upon the progress of humanity, here was Kerl Potter, their representative, to be a clog and hamper upon the progress of Jason, representative of the out-seeking spirit of Man. His spirit bent under the blow, but pride held his body upright.

"Well, thank you, Commandant," said Kerl, turning to the commanding officer. "I'll look forward to leaving tomorrow then." He turned back to Jason. "Until then, sir."

"Until then," said Jason, and watched him leave. When the door had shut behind the broad back, he turned once more to the Commandant.

"This is unfortunate," said the Commandant, reading his eyes. "But into each life some rain must fall, eh?"

Damn him! thought Jason.

"Yes sir," he replied woodenly.

Jason picked the twenty men for the expedition with the same lack of sympathy the Commandant had shown in the choice of Jason, himself. He was curt with the Quartermaster, harsh with Ordnance, and unfeeling toward Transportation. At the end of the day the expedition had been outfitted with brilliant organization and Jason returned to his quarters to write a letter to his family on Kilbur Two, explaining that his expected entrance into the realm of glory would be somewhat delayed.

". . . the duty (he wrote his father, after the usual family well-wishes) is hardly one that I would have wished for at this time. Aside from the fact that I am naturally eager to enter on my Class A assignment at the Frontier, I do not expect to find it pleasant to be cooped up, possibly for weeks, with such a man. Your instincts, I know, would cause you to advise me to treat him with respect for his former rank as an Officer Three. Ordinarily, such respect would be automatic on my part. However, this is no ordinary case. In the first place, he has obviously left the Service long before the earliest age of retirement, which argues a lack of courage, or at least of character. And in the second place, to meet the man is to realize there is nothing at all to respect about him. And finally (if any more were needed) the fact that he is turning his back on the competition of civilized life and running back to hide in the stagnant safety of the primitive. If there is one thing that revolts me, it is a lack of courage . . ."

And more in that vein. By the time Jason had filled a couple of micro-reels, he was more resigned, if not reconciled to his task. He got to bed and managed to get to sleep.

He awoke to the day's duty. The men were mustered on the drill field under the leadership of Chief Troopman Acy, a non-commissioned officer who had grown up in the foothills of the Timudag to the north, and whose knowledge of local conditions, slight as it was, might prove to be useful. Looking the detachment over, Jason had to admit that if any men from the station could do this job properly, these were the ones. All were fit professionals with more than one hitch to their credit and a few had even had some combat experience. Jason nodded and ordered Chief Troopman Acy to move them over to Transportation.

Kerl Potter was waiting for them when they arrived, his dark figure a still monument of patience in the clear morning sunlight. A transport was waiting for them, already loaded with two man cars and supplies. They embarked.

The transport flew them to a spot where the foothills gave way to the mountains. Here they landed and transferred all personnel and equipment to the two man cars. When all was ready, Jason signed off the transport and gave the order to mount, taking the lead car himself, with Kerl in the bucket seat beside him. The transparent tops of the cars were shut and the caravan led off up a steep and unmarked valley toward a pass into the mountains.

"Now," said Jason, turning to his passenger as they topped the pass. "Where to?"

Kerl turned brown eyes to him and away and pointed out and ahead to where a long canyon that lay like a knife slash through the mountains, its further end lost in distance.

"North," he said. "Straight north until we pick up sign."

Jason nodded and turned the car off in the direction of the canyon. Like obedient mechanical sheep, the cars behind swung through the turn, each in their proper order, and followed him.

It was about an hour's run to the beginning of the canyon. From there, the route they were following sloped down and the steep walls rose high and forbiddingly above them. Gazing at this barrenness and the apparent lack of life, with the exception of the stunted bushes clinging in the cracks of the boulders, Jason felt his stomach turn over at the thought of deliberately spending a lifetime, *by choice*, in such an environment. It would be worse than being dead. It would be hell without a purpose. How did these people live?

"Mainly off game," said Kerl beside him; and, turning with a jerk, Jason realized he had spoken his last thoughts aloud. "There's quite a bit of it. Wild mountain sheep and goats descended from stock the early settlers themselves brought in. Native species, too, of course, but they aren't edible. Only their furs are useful."

"I see," said Jason, stiffly.

"It's not a bad life when you're used to it," Kerl went on. "You'd be surprised, Jason—you don't mind me calling you Jason, do you? Seems foolish to be formal when we're cooped up like this—but if you like the mountains and like to hunt, it can come close to being ideal."

Jason had meant to keep his mouth shut; but this last statement was too much.

"Exactly," he said, bitterly, "and let the rest of the race take care of you."

Kerl looked at him in surprise.

"The Peoples of the Mountain don't ask help from others," he protested, mildly.

"How about the Frontier?" demanded Jason. "How about the Class A troops that protect the inner worlds like this from attack by some inimical life form?"

"What inimical life form?" countered Kerl. "We've never run across one intelligent enough to be a threat."

"That's no sign there isn't one," said Jason.

"Nonsense," said Kerl, but without heat. "The Class A troops have only one real function and that's to clean up planets we want to take over. You know that."

"I—" Jason realized he was getting into the sort of argument he had promised himself to avoid. He bit his tongue and closed his mouth. Two seconds more and he would be telling this man what he thought of degenerates in general.

"The mountaineers are a sturdy self-sufficient people," Kerl went on. "They even have a few virtues that are largely lacking in the outside world."

"Virtues!" said Jason.

His hard-held temper was about to snap when an interruption occurred that saved him from himself. From nowhere there was suddenly the sound of thin, crescendoing screams. Something slapped with sickening violence against the transparent cover of the car, leaving a small grey smudge; and half a second later came the sound of a distant report.

"What was that?" Jason snapped.

Kerl pointed away and up to the high rim of the canyon where a tiny plume of white smoke rose lazily in the still air.

"They're shooting at us," he said. "They use chemical firearms, you know, with solid missile projectiles. We've moved into the area of one of the clans."

Jason's hand shot toward the intercom button that would activate the speakers in all the cars behind him. Kerl caught his fingers before they could activate the mike.

"Let it go," he said. "That was just a warning to make sure we keep traveling. If they meant to attack they wouldn't give themselves away by shooting from a distance." He pointed at the smudge on the overhead transparency. "No harm to it. The plastic is missile proof."

Jason looked at him icily for a minute then continued to reach for the intercom. His fingers touched the button.

"All cars," he said, into the mike. "Keep your tops up. There'll be sporadic shooting at us from now on."

Kerl smiled a little sadly, and looked away, into the distance of the canyon, winding out of sight ahead.

For a week they searched, always headed north. They traveled by day, barracking at night, sentries posted, and sleepers locked in their individual cars. By night, the stars glittered, cold and frosty and distant, far above the jagged tops of the mountains; and every rattle and slither of falling stone made the sentries jerk nervously and grab their power rifles in sweat-dampened hands.

By day it was better only because of sunlight and company. The eleven cars jolted and rocked their way down one valley and up the next, moving in single file. From time to time they would run across the cold ashes and litter of an abandoned clan campsite and halt for a few minutes while Kerl prowled about it, sifting the ashes with his finger, sniffing like a huge black bear at any discarded equipment. Then they would rebark and be moving again.

Every so often from the cliff tops above them would spurt a little puff of grey smoke and seconds later would come the report of a chemical energy missile firearm and the whack and scream of a solid slug as it bounced off the transparent cover of one of the cars. The shooting ground on the nerves, a constant reminder of the unseen, inimical, mountain dwellers waiting just out of sight and reach for something to happen to the detachment.

It was hard on the nerves of the men of the detachment. And it was hard on Jason, chafing at the bit to be free of this degrading duty, faced with the responsibility of holding untested troops to their work, and forced to live cheek by jowl with a man whom training and his own inclinations forced him to despise.

It was a situation with explosive potentials. And the first touch of violence brought these out into the open.

On their seventh day out and some nine hundred miles north and slightly west of the point at which they had entered the Timumang, they were proceeding down a long narrow valley. To the left, a small stream marked their road for them, clear water singing down the narrow, level throat of the valley. Beyond it, a series of slopes faded up and back to the skyline. To the right, the cliffs rose more steeply, sharp, pitching angles rubbled with boulder and sharp-cornered loose rock. Jason had been guiding the caravan of cars as usual, his hands on the controls, his mind a dozen light years off on the Frontier and the job he had yet to do there.

Abruptly he felt a hand on his arm.

Yanked abruptly back to the present and the Timumang, he turned with no great pleasure to see Kerl staring at him with a frown line deep-graven between the brown eyes.

"What is it?" said Jason.

"I've got a hunch," answered Kerl. His deep voice filled the interior of the little car with hollow sound. "I think we ought to turn back."

"Turn back?" echoed Jason.

"This valley," said Kerl. "I don't like it. I don't like the feel of it. We could go back and take another one."

Jason throttled down the speed of the car but kept it moving forward.

"Now let's get this straight," he said, impatiently. "You don't think we ought to go any farther down this valley. Why?"

"We may be attacked," answered Kerl. "We haven't been shot at for some hours now. That's a bad sign."

"Couldn't we be traveling through an area where there are no people?"

"Could be," admitted Kerl. "But I've got this hunch—"

Jason considered, keeping his face blank. On the one hand, the man beside him was supposed to know these mountains. On the other hand, the little knowledge he had so far gained of the mountaineers had given him a kind of contempt for them.

"Tell me," said Jason abruptly, "have you any

definite reason for warning us out of this valley?
Any—'' he stressed the word slightly—''*real* evidence?''

''No,'' said Kerl.

''We'll go on,'' Jason said flatly.

The detachment proceeded without trouble. As
they approached the far end of the valley, it became too narrow for two of the cars abreast.
Abruptly, Kerl shot out an arm and skidded the
car to a halt. Behind them the rest of the detachment slammed brakes to keep from piling up.

''What now?'' demanded Jason, exasperated.

''I was right. Look—'' Kerl pointed directly ahead
to a low mound of stones that half-blocked the
route. ''A food cache. The tribe around here has
been on a hunting sweep.''

''What's that got to do with us?'' demanded Jason.
''We don't want their food.''

''But they don't know that,'' said Kerl.

Jason looked at him; and the thought crossed his
mind that the other man was pushing his point
home out of sheer stubbornness. It bolstered his
belief that there was a cowardly streak in Kerl.

''We'll go forward,'' he said. ''If trouble comes,
it'll be time enough to turn back.''

''I don't—'' said Kerl; and suddenly his face
twisted in alarm. He thrust out with both hands,
slamming home the throttle and activating the
intercar communicator.

''Forward! Full speed!'' he yelled. And, Jason,
slammed back in his seat by the acceleration, had
just time to grab for the steering bar as the little
car leaped forward.

As he shot past the cache, the reason for Kerl's
actions became horribly apparent. High up the
steep slope to the right the top of the cliff seemed
to be bowing forward like the head of an old man
and crumbling slowly and majestically into a thousand pieces. Distance lent it a gentle air as if the

whole process was taking place in slow motion, but Jason realized suddenly with a sickening sense of shock that thousands of tons of rock were in that landslide, tumbling down upon him and upon the detachment that was his responsibility. With no time for cursing fate or bawling orders, he hung grimly to the controls of the car and prayed that the men behind him had followed.

For an agonizingly long time it seemed that they would make it. And finally, when the dust and the rattle of smaller stones closed about them, it proved impossible to tell. At that moment a huge rock came springing out of nowhere at Jason's car, and he felt a terrific blow that flung him into darkness.

Late that night, after two dead troopers had been buried in the shattered frame of one of the cars, Kerl went hunting Jason.

He found the young officer standing off by himself, wrestling with his devils in the darkness. It is not easy at any time, but particularly the first, to have to face the fact that an arbitrary decision of yours has cost two men their lives. And this becomes worse when there is ground for self-blame in the reasons behind that decision. Rightly or wrongly, Jason believed, and would go on believing for the rest of his days, that his dislike of Kerl had killed two men. He was not particularly glad, therefore, when Kerl loomed up out of the darkness beside him.

"Well?" he said.

"The men are pretty well bedded down," replied Kerl. "I thought you'd like to know. They've got the last car fixed, so we can go on with nine of them, tomorrow."

They stood in silence for a little while.

"I know how you're feeling," volunteered Kerl, finally.

"Do you?" said Jason, savagely.

"I did the same thing myself once," said Kerl. "Shortly after I was taken into Class A Service. I was on Kelmesh and I thought I'd save time by fording a river. It was shallow enough and the water was clear enough, but there was more current than I thought and I hadn't the foresight to rope the men together. I lost five troopers."

Jason said nothing.

"You'd better come back inside the ring of cars," said Kerl.

Jason looked up at the cliff. And then, just at that moment, the moon crept into sight, bathing the whole long valley suddenly in silvery luster. And in that same split second, born almost it seemed of the light itself, came a long, keening, wavering cry, that quivered out alone over the valley for a minute and then was taken up by many voices in something half-song, half-wail.

Jason halted as if struck.

"What's that?" he said, staring at Kerl.

The dark man's face in the bright moonlight was etched and hollowed by mysterious shadows. He looked off at the hills.

"There was some shooting while you were unconscious," he answered. "One of the men evidently hit and killed the clan's head. That's the lament for a chieftain."

They turned in silence and went back to the cars. The voices followed, crying on their ears.

The men in the cars were somber and quiet as they broke camp the next morning. Once they were moving, their little car trundling up out of the valley to head into the next one, Kerl spoke to Jason.

"Things may start occurring to the men," he said.

"Things?" repeated Jason, sharply. "What things?"

"That if I was out of the way, they could start back to the lowlands."

Jason stared at him.

"What?" he said, half-unable or unwilling to believe he had heard right.

"Don't look so shocked," said Kerl. "It's a natural reaction."

"These troops are completely trustworthy!" Jason felt his face warming with anger.

Kerl shrugged and looked away, out front at the barren cliffs.

"It's something to think of," he said. "It's important to me to reach my destination."

Jason felt words coming to his lips. He tried to check them, but the pressure inside him was too great.

"More important than men's lives?"

Kerl turned to face him again. His features were unreadable.

"To me," he said, "yes."

For what seemed a very long moment they seemed to sit poised, staring at each other. Then Kerl said, very softly:

"You don't understand."

"No," said Jason.

"Tell me," said Kerl. "What do you intend to do with your life?"

"I am a career officer," answered Jason stiffly.

"Serving humanity on the Frontier, eventually, no doubt?"

"Of course." Effort kept Jason's voice level. "I was ready to leave for the Frontier when you arrived."

"And I held up your transfer," said Kerl, thoughtfully.

Jason could think of no rejoinder to this that would not be explosive; and so said nothing.

"Each to his own," Kerl went on, after a pause.

"I was a Frontier officer myself, as I said. On Kelmesh."

It was the one weak spot in the armor of Jason's resentment. This man was a former officer. To Jason the words implied the very opposite of all that the word degenerate implied. He felt his fury ebb with a rush leaving him floundering in uncertainty.

"I don't understand you," he said helplessly. "I don't understand you at all."

The new valley dipped abruptly before them and Jason found that all the attention of his eyes was required to guide the car.

"Let me tell you about myself," he heard Kerl say.

"I was a chief's son," said Kerl. "I am still, for that matter, for there is nothing that can take that away from you. If my father has died while I was gone I am chieftain; my people will offer their hands to me as if I had never been away. But I am also a deserter."

"Deserter," murmured Jason, finding the military ring of the word odd in context with the mountain people.

"Deserter," repeated Kerl, strangely, as if for him the word had some hidden, personal meaning. "I ran away. I wanted to go down to the lowlands. I wanted to go to civilization and become famous. Not that being famous in itself was important. It was what it stood for. I wanted to leave my mark on the race."

"So you ran away?"

"We were camped one day near the southern foothills. My father had refused permission for about the thousandth time. That night I went. Three days later I was wearing a uniform back at your station there. That was twenty years ago. I was fourteen years old."

Jason shot him a glance of shocked surprise.

"You were in the service for twenty years?" he asked.

Kerl shook his head.

"I put in three years and saved my money. Then I took off toward the frontier as a civilian pioneer. I bounced from new planet to new planet, doing everything—mines, timber, weather, construction. It was a rough life, but I liked it. It was like home."

He means the Timumang, thought Jason, looking bewilderedly at the bleak mountains.

"Then one day I woke up. I was twenty-eight and I hadn't even started to do the things I wanted to do. I hadn't left my mark on the progress of civilization, but it had left its mark on me. Suddenly all the wishing dreams I'd had as a boy came back. I just had to build something permanent and lasting that would be my own."

He paused.

"I went to Kelmesh," he said. He turned his head to look at Jason. "You've heard of Kelmesh?"

Jason nodded.

"A good world," said Kerl, his voice thoughtful as if he was half-talking to himself. "A fine world. Sweet water and clean air and all the natural resources. Nothing but little harmless life-forms as far as we could see. Everything was beautiful. I looked at Kelmesh and I told myself that here was where I would make my mark and finish my days. Someday Kelmesh would have schools where history was taught. And near the beginning of that history would be the name of Kerl Potter." He sighed, a thin husk of a sound.

"I went to work," he said. "People were pouring into Kelmesh in those first couple of years after the planet was cleared and opened up. I bought land. I bought into the new towns and started things—an ore processing plant here, a tool factory there. I backed prospecting expeditions, and news services and everything else that I had the time or finances for." He looked down at his big hands in his lap with something like satisfaction. "I got a lot done."

"I suppose you made money," said Jason, thoughtlessly.

"Oh, I made it, all right," said Kerl. "But I ploughed it back in, every cent of it, as fast as I got my hands on it. It was history I was really after. And I made it, too, until the hordes came."

"Locusts, weren't they?" asked Jason, his eyes on the ground as he guided the little car through a small scattered forest of huge boulders.

"No," said Kerl, "they just resembled them in their life habits. Like the seven year (is it seven years?) locust. Millions of eggs were buried as much as ten feet underground. Every forty years they worked their way to the surface as worms and came out as little, hopping creatures as big as a small frog. Then they grew. They swelled up to the size of a grown sheep and spread out by the millions all over Kelmesh and devoured everything."

His voice stopped on a flat note.

"Everything," he repeated.

Jason had the good sense to keep his mouth shut. After a little bit, Kerl went on again.

"The colonists ran," he said. "God, I didn't blame them. Homes, lands, the grass, the trees, everything up to and including the clothing they wore was meat for the hordes. But I hated them for it. I stood on the spaceport landing stage with a silicoid jumper over what was left of my clothing and a thermite gun in my hand and cursed the last ship out of sight."

"You didn't leave?" asked Jason, incredulously. "I thought everybody left."

"Not I," said Kerl. "And not some others. It took us about two weeks to find each other for we were scattered all over the planet. But at the end of that time there were sixty of us gathered together in what was left of Kelmesh's governing city hall. Sixty-odd lousy, dirty, hungry men, with just one thought in common: that the hordes might chew the planet to the bone this time around, but the next generation wasn't going to live to boast about it."

The fierce note on which Kerl ended rang through the little car. He stopped, as if abashed by it, and then went on in a mild voice.

"They live for five years, you know," he said, "and lay their eggs at six week intervals all during that time. They don't all lay at once, either. A bunch go off somewhere by themselves and bury themselves alive. The body of the parent is food for the grubs when they hatch."

Jason shivered.

"Well, our first plan was to take to the air and track down a group that was about to lay and incinerate it. The first few months we tried it. Then we woke up to the fact that the job was too big and started just tracking them down and marking the laying areas. When the hordes began to split up and the individuals began to spread all over the place, we finally yelled for help. By that time we were down to about eighteen men."

Jason glanced sideways at him in surprise. Kerl caught the look.

"Lack of food," he explained. "Long hours in the air. Men would go asleep at the controls and crash. On foot you couldn't count on lasting very long. A human being's organic, and anything organic suited their appetites.

"We messaged our story out to the nearest Message Relay Station. Three months later a spruce Frontier Cruiser dropped down on our spaceport. I was there to meet it with two other men. A neatly tailored little commandant came down the landing ramp and looked me over.

" 'Where is everybody?' " he asked.

" 'Dead,' I said."

"He looked at me as if I was pulling some kind of joke on him."

" 'Well, come on inside,' he said. 'We'll fix you up with some food and clothes.'

" 'The hell with food and clothes,' I said. 'Give us thermite recharges for the guns.'

"He peered at me.

" 'You're out of your head, planter,' he said. And I took a swing at him and woke up in the ship's hospital two days later.

"Well, they wanted to send us back to civilization, but none of the three of us would go. So we compromised all around by having us sign on as Frontier Special Troops. Then the war began.

"It wasn't what Sector Headquarters ten light years away had thought it would be. It wasn't even what I thought it would be. It was worse. The whole thing tied in with the evolution process of these critters. They had no natural enemies, so they weeded each other out on a survival of the fittest basis. Within a few months after they came out of the ground—inside half a year at the latest— they'd cleaned up everything else worth eating. That meant the only source of food was—each other.

"Sounds good, doesn't it?" Kerl smiled briefly at Jason. "Sounds as if they were helping us along in our extermination program? But it turned out that this process had bred some intelligence into them and with that intelligence, the ability to learn—fast.

"They had no use for brains when the whole planet was one big dinner table. But when the numbers began to thin out—when they were down to the last few millions of them—intelligence began to show up.

"First, they took to cooperating. Each little group

began to show signs of internal organization. Then the groups began to work together, and we woke up to the fact that the critters were fighting back; what had started out as a fumigating project had turned into a war."

Kerl broke off suddenly to stare intently out the transparent front of the car. The seconds lengthened into minutes, and finally Jason spoke.

"What is it?" he demanded.

"Potter sign, I think," said Kerl. "A campsite about five hundred yards ahead. Drive on up to the foot of that big rock and halt the detachment."

The sign was Potter sign. Kerl toured the area of the camp, like a hunting animal, running the cold ashes from the cooking fires through his fingers, and raking through the discarded litter around them. His investigation kept him occupied until noon, so the midday meal was eaten where they stood. They pushed on after lunch, covering another fifty miles before night brought them to a stop.

The going was slower now, for Kerl was forced to watch the ground and the rocky walls closely to make sure that they were staying on the Potter trail and not drifting off on the track of some other clan that might have crossed or paralleled the same route. Consequently, there was no further chance for conversation between him and Jason and it was not until that evening that Jason had an opportunity to draw him aside.

They sat down in their car and closed the top— that being the only meager means to privacy the situation afforded.

"How much farther before we catch up with them?" asked Jason.

"Not far," replied Kerl. His voice seemed to have grown old and weary since the morning. "Say thirty miles. We should catch up with them tomorrow afternoon."

"Good," said Jason.

They sat in silence for a little while, each occupied by his own thoughts. Finally Jason broke the pause.

"You were telling me about Kelmesh earlier today—"

"Oh—yes," said Kerl, abruptly, like someone whose thoughts are suddenly recalled from a great distance. "I was. Well—right now I'm a little tired. If you don't mind—"

"Of course," replied Jason promptly. He threw back the lid of the car and stepped out. "Good night."

"Good night," said Kerl, from the interior shadows of the car.

Jason did not feel like sleeping. He had always been a straightforward man, as honest with himself as nature permitted. He believed thoroughly in the solid universe that he knew. It contained space and the human race, whose manifest destiny it was to occupy space. Occasionally, among the teeming hordes of mankind emerged those who perceived this destiny. These went out and dedicated themselves to it. The rest lived and bred in happy ignorance. To them, no blame, but no glory.

But among the dedicated— By no possible stretch of the imagination could Jason imagine a man who saw the light, followed it, then turned his back on it, and went again to dwell in darkness. What flaw in the ideal of man's manifest destiny could prompt such an action? The thought was very disturbing to Jason. After all, this was the ideal he was probably going to get himself killed for—unless good luck and skill preserved him.

Jason could no longer write Kerl off as a man basically lacking in courage and the virtues that the frontier demands. Jason had read and heard enough about Kelmesh to recognize that the other man was speaking the truth. Had Kerl's nerve finally broken under those conditions? Jason could not believe it. There was nothing broken about the big, dark man.

What then? Pacing the narrow circle of the camp, Jason looked up at the stars and did not know the answer.

But he would find out tomorrow, before Kerl parted company with them for good—he made himself that promise.

Morning came bright and sudden. A little of the sparse rain that fell upon these mountains had fallen during the night, and the rocks around them were dark and had a damp smell that began to fade quickly as a thirsty sun licked up the moisture through the dry air. Camp was struck, and the circle of cars took up the trail again in customary file.

For four hours, the going was the same as it had been the day before, the detachment crawling along slowly, with Kerl in the lead car tensely scrutinizing the ground for sign. They crossed out of the valley and into another that ran parallel for some twenty miles. This at a point where the mountains split three ways, Kerl called a halt.

He got down from the lead car and began to examine the little open area where the four valleys came together. For some time he combed the area minutely, eyes bent on the rock at his feet; long arms dangling loosely from hunched shoulders, so that he looked almost more ape than human from a distance. Finally, he returned to the car where Jason waited.

"There," he said, pointing to the rightmost of the three new valleys as he climbed into the car.

"And about thirty miles off. I know where they're headed, now."

Jason looked at him; then closed the open top of the car and gave the order to move out over the intercom. They rolled ahead between the rocky walls that had been steadily about them since the beginning.

In his bucket seat in the car, Kerl leaned back and sighed, rubbing one big, square-fingered hand across his eyes.

"A strain, that tracking, I suppose," said Jason.

Kerl turned to look at him. He managed a tired grin.

"I'm out of practice," he replied. "Too much being done for me by gadgets has spoiled the senses."

His eyes had wandered off to look at the mountains. Now he brought them back again to Jason.

"You've done a good job for me," he said. "I'm grateful."

"My duty—" said Jason, with a little deprecating shrug. He half-turned to look at the other man.

"Can I ask you a question?" he said.

"Go ahead," Kerl told him.

The strict Kilburnian ethics of Jason's upbringing fought a momentary, short and silent battle with his curiosity and lost.

"Why are you going back?" he asked.

Jason could see the sharp barb of his question strike home. Kerl did not answer. And, as the seconds slipped past and were lost in silence, he began to think that he had, indeed, stepped beyond the bounds of all propriety and right. And, then, just as he was about to apologize, words did come from the other man.

"You asked me to tell you about the rest of what happened to me on Kelmesh," said Kerl.

"I—yes," replied Jason. "Yes, I did."

"I'll tell you now," said Kerl. "You've heard what it was like, no doubt."

"I had a cousin who came in on the tail end of it," said Jason. "I read some letters from him."

"A lot of men died," Kerl spoke softly, "more men than I could ever have imagined dying in one place at one time. That's why I earned rank so quickly. They discharged me as an Officer Two, but I was acting Commandant for the last six months."

"You know," Jason said, "I have trouble understanding how creatures like that, even with a little intelligence, could stand up to our war equipment so long, and cause such trouble."

Kerl chuckled a little bitterly, "Sector Headquarters had trouble understanding it, too. But then, they weren't on the planet."

Jason blinked at such open criticism of the Frontier's military leadership. Kerl went on:

"It was easy enough to understand when it was under your nose. There were two reasons. One was that we were not fighting a war, we were conducting an extermination project, in which all of those critters had to be killed off. The second was that we couldn't defend, we had to attack. Impose those conditions on men fighting in what amounted to a wasteland, and what did you have?

"You had small patrol action and nothing but small patrol action. There was so much ground to be covered and so many of the things to be killed. You called in your junior officers and lined them up in front of a map and drew out their routes for them. Then out they went to make their patrols on foot—on foot, mind you, because the critters buried themselves in the ground during the daytime and even in a two man car you'd drive right over them.

"They'd take off—" Kerl's eyes had grown bleak and distant, seeing again the bitter plains of his memories. "—extended in a skirmish line, looking for spots where the earth was loose. And when they found one, they'd dig it out and incinerate it, unless it woke up first and got away before the thermite charges could cripple it enough to make escape impossible.

"When night came the men would bivouak and dig in, with their guns charged and portable searchlighs illuminating the ground all around them. And they'd try to sleep—but the night would be one long battle.

"Nothing kept the critters away. The searchlights even attracted them—but what could you do? The men needed light to shoot by, and some warning when they came. For they came at top speed. They must have been crazy mad with hunger, during this period when there was nothing for them to live on but each other and us. One would spot the light and come up quietly, then suddenly charge in as fast as it could. And they could move fast. The idea seemed to be to pick up a man and carry him off into the darkness.

"Sometimes, two or three would work together and we'd have them charging at once. The horrible thing was, there was a sort of instinct in them that made them try to continue eating even when they were dying. If they grabbed a man and couldn't make it out of the circle, they still tried to make a meal of him, even while being burned by the gun charges.

"Their notion of fighting was just to start eating their enemy. In fact, fighting and feeding was the same thing. In the beginning the losses from night attacks were fantastically high. But after a while we began to keep them down to a minimum. The men kept their lives, but they lost their nerve—"

This was so close to what Jason had been thinking about Kerl himself the night before, that the young officer started involuntarily. Kerl, however, went on without noticing.

"—and cracked. And the commonest form of cracking was to blow up some night when the patrol was dug in, to jump out of the hole you had dug and go running off into the darkness to hunt down the critters that were prowling out there. That waiting—" Kerl shuddered, "—it was bad. Sooner or later, the men would lose their self-possession and go to meet them halfway." He turned to look at Jason. "They estimate around a hundred thousand men were lost that way."

"A hundred thousand!" Even Jason's military-conditioned mind was shocked by the number. "But not all of them. Not—" his tone was almost accusing, —"not you."

"No, not me," said Kerl. He sighed. "I was the exception—the freak. It bothered me, but I lasted through five long years of it. I even kept other men from cracking up as long as they were with me. Nothing particular I did—just knowing I was around seemed to brace them."

Jason stared at him.

"But that was marvelous—wasn't it?" he said. "I mean, they could study you and find out what was needed to keep other men from cracking up. You could turn yourself into Service Research and . . ." his voice faltered, died before a supposition so monstrous that it overwhelmed him. Finally he put it into words. "You aren't—that isn't what you're running away from?"

Kerl laughed.

"Nothing so melodramatic," he said. "Research didn't even wait for the business to finish on Kelmesh before pulling me back to Earth. They tested me and worked me over and scratched their heads and finally came up with an answer. In plain words, what was happening was that the civilized man of today was many times as susceptible to the emotional strains of war as his remote ancestor. It was a matter of environment—what the psychologists called having a 'wider mental horizon'."

"But what are they going to do about it?" asked Jason.

"There isn't too much they can do," said Kerl soberly. "There are two obvious solutions. One is to return to the environment of eighteenth-nineteenth century Earth, which is impossible. The other is to freeze the present environment long enough for the human race to mature up to it. Which is unpalatable and which people won't stand for."

"Of course not!" cried Jason. "Why, that'd be ridiculous! It—it'd be fantastic. To hold up our proper and necessary expansion for a little problem like that. The human race solves problems—it doesn't knuckle under to them."

A shadow passed across Kerl's face for an instant, saddening it.

"You're right," he said. "The race does."

"There must be some practical steps they can take," continued Jason. "Some conditioning process, or such."

Kerl shrugged.

"Some factors seem to help a little," he said. "You may have wondered why you've been held in Class C duty so long when it's usual to promote to Class A Frontier posts fairly quickly."

"They have been slow with me," frowned Jason.

"And with a lot of others in your class," said Kerl. "That's one of the little things that seems to help some—a longer tour of garrison work."

"Look here!" said Jason. "*I'm* not liable to crack up. My mental health is excellent."

"A fresh water fish," replied Kerl, "can be in fine shape. But put him in salt water and he sickens and dies."

"But this is all backward!" exploded Jason. "You're supposed to have come through on Kelmesh. To you that environment should have been much more of a shock than to a man like me—I take new and different worlds for granted. I grew up with an open mind. Why, if what you say is true, then these mountain people of yours—"

He broke off abruptly, a realization taking startling form in his mind. In the little silence that followed, Kerl's voice answered him.

"It *is* the opposite from what you might expect," he said. "Early in the beginnings of psychology, men began to notice that some primitive peoples were amazingly well adjusted. Not all primitive peoples, of course. The majority ran the scale from bad to worse. But a few stood out."

"But you can't scrap civilization!" cried Jason, desperately.

"I don't know," answered Kerl. "Can't you? I can't. You can't. No government or controlling power can—or wants to. Maybe we won't have to. But when Research dug into the matter they came up with some funny answers. For instance—the individual has a survival instinct. They've known that for a long time. Now they think the race has one, too."

"Of course," said Jason. "Survival of the fittest—"

"No," said Kerl. "Think of the race as a single individual with instincts. And one of the instincts is not to put all his eggs in one basket."

Jason merely looked puzzled. Again, that shadow crossed Kerl's face, shading his eyes with an obscure pain.

"Never at any time," Kerl said, "have all the people been all alike. Some were more one way than another. Geographical accident, they used to think—and of course it was, largely. But there's a real instinctive tendency for groups to be different, even as there is for the individual to be different— and for the same reason, survival. It wouldn't be good for them all to be alike. Then, some new thing that could wipe out one, could wipe out all."

"Do you mean to tell me," said Jason, spacing the words slowly, and, he thought, calmly, "that the trillions or quadrillions or whatever it is we have of people on all the civilized worlds, are an evolutionary dead end; that you and these mountaineers squatting on their rocks represent the future of the race?"

"No," Kerl shook his head, "not *the* future. A possible future. A remotely possible future. One of nature's extra strings to its bow. Imagine civilization breaking down. Would that make any difference to my people here? Not a bit. They're completely self-supporting. They don't need and don't want the rest of you. They might pull humanity back up out of the mud again."

Kerl's words died in the car. For what seemed a long while, Jason sat thinking. Finally, he turned to Kerl.

"But *you* think your people will make the future," he said. It was an accusation. "That's why you've come back."

Kerl's dark face was suddenly ravaged with sorrow.

"No," he said. "No. I came back for an entirely different reason."

Jason waited.

"Research turned me inside out," said Kerl, painfully. "When they were through with me, I knew myself—too well. I knew myself inside and out. And I realized—" his voice faltered, then picked up with a new strength "—that I was different. From the time when that difference came home to me, living in civilization became living among strangers. There was a barrier there I could not cross because it was inside me and now I knew it was there." He stopped.

"I had no choice," he said suddenly. "I had to go home."

He let out his breath and looked down at his hands, big and dark, folded in his lap.

"I—am sorry," said Jason, stiffly. "I beg your pardon."

"That's all right," said Kerl. "It's almost over now." He raised his eyes from his lap and looked out ahead. "You can stop anyplace along here. We don't want to drive up to the camp. We'll stop a bit short and let them find us."

"All right," said Jason. He switched on the intercom and gave the necessary orders.

The cars circled in the light of the afternoon sun, halted, men got out, and camp was made.

About an hour before twilight, the Potter clan put in its appearance. One moment, the valley was empty beyond the camp and then—it seemed, almost without transition—a small host of rough-clad figures had sprung into view, on the valley floor and down the rocky slopes some two hundred yards from the circle of cars. They stood silent, waiting. Two groups with centuries of apparent difference between them. Silent, they stood and watched. Jason went to get Kerl and found him sitting in their car, chin on hand, his eyes absent and thoughtful.

"Well, they're here," said Jason.

Kerl nodded.

"I know," he answered.

"They've come right out in the open," continued Jason. "Almost as if they knew you were with us."

"I imagine they do," said Kerl. "Other tribes will have seen me with you and passed the word along." He got heavily to his feet and stepped out of the car. Beyond the cars were the troopers. Followed by Jason, Kerl walked to an open space where a number of the men of the tribe stood waiting. Kerl turned and looked at the troopers.

"Goodby," he said. "Thanks."

The men murmured self-consciously. Kerl turned again and started off, stepping surely down the rugged path. Jason followed, without quite knowing why.

Where the rough going ceased and the valley began to broaden out, Kerl stopped again and turned to Jason as the younger man came up level with him. They were far enough from the troopers now so that low voices would not carry their words back.

"Goodby," said Kerl.

"Goodby," Jason replied. Kerl put out his hand and Jason took it. They shook briefly, but Kerl held on to Jason's hand for a minute before releasing it.

"Don't—" he began earnestly, but the words seemed to stick in his throat.

"Yes?" said Jason.

Kerl's face was twisted as if with a mighty inner effort.

"Don't be afraid of the future," he said, tightly. "Keep going. Keep looking. There's nothing so wonderful as that."

Jason stared at him.

"*You* say that?" he could not keep the incredulity out of his voice. He nodded toward the waiting mountaineers. "But you're going back!"

"Yes," whispered Kerl. "I told you. I have no choice."

Jason swallowed.

"Come back with us," he said. "I didn't know. But if it's our future you want, not theirs, come back. You can if you want to."

"I can't."

"Why not?" cried Jason. "It's all a matter of what you want. I thought you wanted this."

"This?" echoed Kerl, looking bleakly about him at the mountains. "This?" His face worked.

"God, *no!*" he cried. "The only thing I ever wanted was Kelmesh!"

He turned, tearing himself away from Jason and facing towards the clansmen. Pebbles rattled and rolled under his uncaring feet as he lurched away.

Walking like a blind man, he went down the valley.

> *"And how can men die better*
> *than facing fearful odds,*
> *for the ashes of his fathers*
> *and the temples of his Gods?"*
> —Lord Macaulay

JEAN DUPRES

Anything that man can imagine is theoretically possible. We have made the first giant-step of space flight to the moon. The planets will be next and then—the stars? We have the feeling that, unreasonable as it appears to be in the light of present knowledge, this voyage will someday be possible. What will we find there? What kind of life forms? These are classic science fiction questions that have been answered in exhausting detail down through the years. Yet very rarely is the more important question asked: What will happen when our culture brushes up against an alien culture? "Jean Duprès" is a well-considered, moving answer to that question. For there will be poeple who will form a bridge between ours and theirs.

*   *   *

The way I met Jean Duprès for the first time, I was
on independent patrol with a squad of six men,
spread out, working through the green tangle of
the Utword jungle. I came up to the edge of a
place where the jungle was cut off sharp, and looked
through the last screen of scroll-edged, eight-foot
ferns at a little room of pounded earth, the vesti-
bule of a larger, planted field I could see beyond.
Near the opening in the larger field sat a riding
macerator with no one in its saddle; and right
before me—not five feet beyond the ferns—a boy
not more than four years old stood leaning on a
rifle that was such a good imitation of the real
thing that I could hardly believe that it was a fake.

Then I saw it was not a fake.

I went through the last screen of ferns with a
rush and took the gun away from the boy even as
he tried to swing it to his shoulder. He stood staring at me, blinking and bewildered, trying to make
up his mind whether to cry or not; and I looked
the rifle over. It was a DeBaraumer, capable of
hurling out anything and everything, from a wire-
control rocket slug to any handy pebble small
enough to rattle though its bore.

"Where did you get this?" I asked him. He had
decided not to cry and he looked up at me with a
white face and round, desperate eyes.

"My daddy," he said.

"Where's your daddy at?"

Without taking his eyes off my face, he half-
turned and pointed away through the opening into
the larger field.

"All right," I said. "We'll go see him about this."
I unclipped the handmike from my belt and told
my six men to close up and follow me in. Then I set
my telemeter beacon and turned to go with the
boy to find his daddy—and I stopped dead.

For there were two of the Klahara young men

standing just inside the edge of the small clearing about twenty feet off. They must have been there before I stepped through the last ferns myself, because my scanner would have picked them up if they had been moving. They were seniors, full seven feet tall, with their skins so green that they would have been invisible against the jungle background if it hadn't been for their jewels and wepons and tall feather headdresses.

When you were this close it was obvious that they were humanoid but not human. There were knifelike bony ridges on the outer edge of their fore and upper arms, and bony plates on their elbows. Their hands looked attenuated and thin because of the extra joint in their fingers. Although they were hairless their greenish-black crests were rising and quivering a bit. Whether from alarm or just excitement I couldn't tell. They were nothing to bother me, just two of them and out in the open that way—but it gave me a shock, realizing they'd been standing there listening and watching while I took the gun from the boy and then talked to him.

They made no move now, as I nudged the boy and started with him out of the clearing past them. Their eyes followed us; but it was not him, or me either, they were watching. It was the DeBaraumer. And that, of course, was why I'd jumped like I had to get the weapon away from the boy.

We came out on to a plowed field and saw a planter's home and buildings about six hundred yards off, looking small and humped and black under the bright white dazzle of the pinhole in the sky that was Achernar, old Alpha Eridani. The contact lenses on my eyes had darkened up immediately, and I looked at the boy, for he was too young to wear contacts safely—but he had already pulled a pair of goggles down off his sun-cap to cover his eyes.

"I'm Corporal Tofe Levenson, of the Rangers," I

said to him as we clumped over the furrows. "What's your name?"

"Jean Duprès," he said, pronouncing it something like "Zjon Du-pray."

We came finally up to the house, and the door opened while we were still a dozen paces off. A tall, brown-haired woman with a smooth face looked out, shading her eyes against the sunlight in spite of the darkening of her contacts.

"Jean . . ." she said, pronouncing it the way the boy had. I heard a man's voice inside the house saying something I could not understand, and then we were at the doorway. She stood aside to let us through and shut the door after us. I stepped into what seemed to be a kitchen. There was a planter at a table spooning some sort of soup into his mouth out of a bowl. He was a round-headed, black-haired, heavy-shouldered type, but I saw how the boy resembled him.

"Corporal—?" he said, staring at me with the spoon halfway to the dish. He dropped it into the dish. "They're gathered! They're raiding—"

"Sit down." I said, for he was half on his feet. "There's no more than four Klahari young men for ten kilometers in any direction from here." He sat down and looked unfriendly.

"Then what're you doing here? Scaring a man—"

"This." I showed him the DeBaraumer. "Your boy had it."

"Jean?" His unfriendly look deepened. "He was standing guard."

"And you in here?"

"Look," he thought for a minute. "Corporal, you got no business in this. This is my family, my place."

"And your gun," I said. "How many guns like this have you got?"

"Two." He was out-and-out scowling now.

"Well, if I hadn't come along, you'd have only

had one. There were two Klahari seniors out by your boy—with their eyes on it."

"That's what he's got to learn—to shoot them when they get close."

"Sure," I said. "Mr. Duprès, how many sons have you got?"

He stared at me. All this time, it suddenly struck me, the woman had been standing back, saying nothing, her hands twisted up together in the apron she was wearing.

"One!" she said now; and the way she said it went right through me.

"Yeah," I said, still looking at Duprès. "Well, now listen. I'm not just a soldier, I'm a peace officer, as you know. There's laws here on Utword, even if you don't see the judges and courts very often. So, I'm putting you on notice. There'll be no more letting children handle lethal weapons like this DeBaraumer; and I'll expect you to avoid exposing your son to danger from the Klahari without you around to protect him." I stared hard at him. "If I hear of any more like that I'll haul you up in Regional Court, and that'll mean a week and a half away from your fields; even if the judge lets you off—which he won't."

I understood him all right. He was up out of the chair, apologizing in a second; and after that he couldn't be nice enough. When my squad came in he insisted we all stay to dinner and put himself out to be pleasant, not only to us, but to his wife and boy. And that was that, except for one little thing that happened, near the end of dinner.

We'd been comparing notes on the Klahari, of course, on how they're different from men; and the boy had been silent all through it. But then, in a moment's hush in the talk, we heard him asking his mother, almost timidly . . . "Mama, will I be a man when I grow up?—or a Klahari?"

"Jean—" she began, but her husband—his name

was Pelang, I remembered and hers was Elmire, both of them Canadian French from around Lac St. John in Quebec, Canada, back home—interrupted her. He sat back in his chair, beaming and rubbing the hard fat of his belly—swell under his white glass shirt, and took the conversation away from her.

"And what would you like to be then, Jean?" he asked. "A man or a Klahari?" and he winked genially at the rest of us.

The boy concentrated. I could see him thinking, or picturing rather, the people he knew—his mother, his father, himself, struggling with this macerated earth reclaimed from the jungle—and the Klahari he had seen, especially the senior ones, slipping free through the jungle, flashing with jewels and feathers, tall, dark and powerful.

"A Klahari," Jean Duprès said finally.

"Klahari!" His father shouted the word, jerking upright in his chair; and the boy shrank. But just then Pelang Duprès must have remembered his guests, and caught himself up with a black scowl at Jean. Then the man tried to pass if off with a laugh.

"Klahari!" he said. "Well, what can you expect? He's a child. Eh? We don't mind children!" But then he turned savagely on the boy, nonetheless. "You'd want to be one of those who'd kill us—who'd take the bread out of your mother's mouth—and your father's?"

His wife came forward and put her arms around the boy and drew him off away from the table.

"Come with me now, Jean," she said; and I did not see the boy again before we left.

As we did leave, as we were outside the house checking equipment before moving off, Pelang was on the house steps watching us, and he stepped up to me for a moment.

"It's for him—for Jean, you understand, Corporal," he said, and his eyes under the darkened contact glasses were asking a favor of me. "This place—" he waved an arm at cleared fields. "I won't live long enough for it to pay me for my hard work. But he'll be rich, someday. You understand?"

"Yeah. Just stay inside the law," I said. I called the men together and we moved out in skirmish order into the jungle on the far side of the house. Later, it came to me that maybe I had been a little hard on Pelang.

I didn't pass by that area again that season. When I did come by at the beginning of next season I had a squad of green recruits with me. I left them well out of sight and went and looked in from behind the fringe of the jungle, without letting myself be seen. Pelang was seeding for his second crop of the season, and Jean, grown an inch or so, was standing guard with the DeBaraumer again. I went on without interfering. If Pelang would not give up his ways on the threat of being taken in, there was no point in taking him in. He would simply pay his fine, hate me, and the whole family would suffer, because of the time he was absent from the planting and the place. You can do only so much with people, or for them.

Besides, I had my hands full with my own job. In spite of what I had told Pelang, my real job was being a soldier, and my work was not riding herd on the planters, but riding herd on the Klahari. And that work was getting heavier as the seasons approached the seventeen-year full-cycle period.

My squad had broken out mealpaks and were so involved in eating that I walked up on them without their being aware of it.

"And you want to be Rangers," I said. "You'll never live past this cycle."

They jumped and looked guilty. Innocents. And I had to make fighting men out of them.

"What cycle?" one of them asked. All of them

were too young to have remembered the last time it came around.

"That and more. You are going to have to understand the Klahari. Or die. And not just hate them. There is nothing evil in what they do. Back on Earth, even we had the Jivaros, the head-hunting Indians of the Amazon River. And the Jivaro boys were lectured daily while they were growing up. They were told that it was not merely all right to kill their enemies, it was upstanding, it was honorable, it was the greatest act they could aspire to as men. This code came out of the very jungle in which they were born and raised—and as it was part of them, so the way of the Klahari young men is out of their world and part of them, likewise.

"They were born outside of this jungle, well beyond the desert. They were raised in cities that have a civilization just above the steam-engine level, boys and girls together until they were about nine years old. Then the girls stayed where they were and started learning the chores of housekeeping the cities. But the nine-year-old Klahari boys were pushed out to fend for themselves in the desert.

"Out there, it was help one another or perish. The boys formed loose bands or tribes and spent about three years keeping themselves alive and helping each other stay alive. Their life was one of almost perfect brotherhood. In the desert, their problem was survival and they shared every drop of water and bite of food they could find. They were one for all and all for one, and at this age they were, literally, emotionally incapable of violence or selfishness.

"At about twelve or thirteen, they began to grow out of this incapability, and look toward the jungle. There it was, right alongside their sandy wastes with nothing to stop them entering it—nothing except the older Klahari from age thirteen to seventeen. At this stage the young Klahari males shoot up suddenly from five to about six and a half feet tall, then grow more gradually for the remaining four years in the jungle. And, from the moment they enter the jungle, every other Klahari boy is potentially a mortal enemy. In the jungle, food and drink are available for the reaching out of a hand; and there is nothing to worry about—except taking as many other lives as possible while hanging on to your own."

"*Klahari* lives," a worried Ranger protested. "Why should they trouble us?"

"Why shouldn't they? It's eat or be eaten. They even join into groups of up to a dozen, once they get older and more jungle-experienced. In this way they can take single strays and smaller groups. This works well enough—except they have to watch their backs at all times among their own group-members. There are no rules. This jungle is no-man's-land. Which was why the Klahari did not object to humans settling here, originally. We were simply one more test for their maturing young men, trying to survive until manhood, so they can get back into the cities."

They digested this and they didn't like it. Jen, the brightest in the squad, saw the connection at once.

"Then that makes us humans fair game as well?"

"Right. Which is why this squad is out here in the jungle. Our job is simply that of a cop in a rough neighborhood—to roust and break up Klahari bands of more than a half-dozen together at once. The young Klahari know that their clubs, cross-bows and lances are no match for rifles, and there has to be at least a half dozen of them together before they are liable to try assaulting a house or attacking a planter in his fields. So the arrangement with planters, soldier squads and Klahari is all neat and tidy most of the time—in fact all of the time except for one year out of every seventeen that makes up a generation for them. Because, once a generation, things pile up.

"It's the five-year Klahari that cause it. Post-seniors some people call them, as we call the younger Klahari freshmen, sophomores, juniors and seniors, according to the number of years they have been off the desert and in the jungle. Post-seniors are Klahari who are old enough to go back to the cities and be allowed in—but are hesitating about it. They are Klahari who are wondering if they might not prefer it being top dog in the jungle to starting out on the bottom again, back in the cities. They are Klahari toying with the idea of settling down for life in the jungles and their impulse to kill any other Klahari is damped by maturity and experience. They, unlike those of the first four years of jungle experience, are capable of trusting each other to gather in large bands with a combined purpose—to seize and hold permanently areas of the jungle as private kingdoms."

They were listening closely now—and no one was smiling.

"In the old days, before we humans came, this process once a seventeen-year generation would end inevitably in pitched wars between large bands largely composed of post-seniors. These wars disposed of the genetic variants among the Klahari, and got rid of those who might have interrupted the age-old, cities-desert-jungle-cities-again pattern of raising the Klahari males and eliminating the unfit of each generation. Before we came, everything was tidy. But with us humans now in the jungle, the post-seniors in their bands every seventeen years turn most naturally against us."

My talk had some good effect because the ones who stayed on made good Rangers. They knew what they were doing—and why.

One season followed another and I had my hands

full by the time I saw young Jean Duprès again.
My squad of six men had grown by that time to a
platoon of twenty, because we were now closing the
second and final season of the sixteenth year of the
cycle and we were having to break up Klahari
gangs of as many as fifty in a group. Not only that,
but we had the cheerful thought always with us
that, with the post-seniors running things, most of
the groups we broke up were re-forming again, the
minute we'd passed on.

It was time to begin trying to hustle the planters
and their families back into our Regional Installations. Time to begin listening to their complaints
that their buildings would be burned and leveled,
and half their cleared land reclaimed by the jungle
when they returned—which was perfectly true.
Time to begin explaining to them why it was not
practical to bring in an army from Earth every
seventeen years to protect their land. And time to
try to explain to them once again that we were
squatters on a Klahari world, and it was against
Earth policy to exterminate the natives and take
over the planet entire, even if we could—which we
could not. There were millions of the mature
Klahari in the cities, and our technical edge wasn't
worth that much.

So by the time I came to the Duprès property,
my patience was beginning to wear thin from turning the other cheek to the same bad arguments,
dozens of times repeated. And that was bad. Because I knew Pelang Duprès would be one of the
stubborn ones. I came up slowly and took a station
just inside the ferns at the edge of one of his fields
to look the place over—but what I saw was not
Pelang, but Jean.

He was coming toward me, a good cautious thirty
yards in from the edge of the field this time, with
his scanner hooked down over his eyes and that
old, all-purpose blunderbuss of a DeBaraumer in

his arms. Three years had stretched him out and leaned him up. Oddly, he looked more like his mother now—and something else. I squatted behind the ferns, trying to puzzle it out. And then it came to me. He was walking like a Klahari—in the cautious, precise way they have, swinging from ball of foot to ball of other foot with the body always bolt upright from the hips.

I stood up for a better look at him; and he was down on his belly on the earth in an instant, the DeBaraumer swinging to bear on the ferns in front of me, as my movement gave me away to his scanner. I dropped like a shot myself and whistled—for that is what the Klahari can't do, whistle. The muscles in their tongue and lips won't perform properly for it.

He stood up immediately; and I stood up and came out onto the field to meet him.

"You're a sergeant," he said, looking at my sleeve as I came up.

"That's right," I said. "Sergeant Tofe Levenson of the Rangers. I was a corporal when you saw me last. You don't remember?"

He frowned, puzzling it over in his mind, then shook his head. Meanwhile I was studying him. There was something strange about him. He was still a boy, but there was something different in addition—it was like seeing a seven-year-old child overlaid with the adult he's going to be. As if the future man was casting his shadow back on his earlier self. The shadow was there in the way he carried the rifle, and in his stance and eyes.

"I'm here to see your daddy," I said.

"He's not here."

"Not here!" I stared at him, but his face showed only a mild curiosity at my reaction. "Where is he?"

"He and my ma—mother"—he corrected himself—"went in to Strongpoint Hundred Fourteen for supplies. They'll be back tomorrow."

"You mean you're here alone?"

"Yes," he said, again with that faint puzzlement that I should find this odd, and turned back toward the buildings. "Come to the house. I'll make you some coffee, Sergeant."

I went to the house with him. To jog his memory, on the way I told him about my earlier visit. He thought he remembered me, but he could not be sure. When I spoke to him about the Klahari, I found he was quite aware of the danger they posed to him, but was as strangely undisturbed by it as if he had been a Klahari himself. I told him that I was here to warn his father to pack up his family and retire to the Strongpoint he was currently at for supplies—or, better yet, pull back to one of our base installations. I said that the post-senior Klahari were grouping and they might begin raiding the planters' places in as little as three weeks' time. Jean corrected me, gravely.

"Oh, no, Sergeant," he said. "Not for the rest of this season."

"Who told you that?" I said—snorted, perhaps. I was expecting to hear it had been his father's word on the subject.

"The Klahari," he said. "When I talk to them."

I stared at him.

"You *talk* to them?" I said. He ducked his head, suddenly a little embarrassed, even a little guilty-looking.

"They come to the edge of the fields," he said. "They want to talk to me."

"Want to talk to you? To *you*? Why?"

"They . . ." He became even more guilty-looking. He would not meet my eyes, "want to know . . . things."

"What things?"

"If . . ." he was miserable, "I'm a . . . man."

All at once it broke on me. Of course, there could only be a few children like this boy, who had never seen Earth, who had been born here, and who were old enough by now to be out in the fields. And none of the other children would be carrying rifles—real ones. The natural assumption of the Klahari would of course be that they were young versions of human beings—except that in Jean's case, to a Klahari there was one thing wrong with that. It was simply unthinkable—no, it was more than that; it was inconceivable—to a Klahari that anyone of Jean's small size and obvious immaturity could carry a weapon. Let alone use it. At Jean's age, as I told you, the Klahari thought only of brotherhood.

"What do you tell them?"

"That I'm . . . almost a man." Jean's eyes managed to meet mine at last and they were wretchedly apologetic for comparing himself with me, or with any other adult male of the human race. I saw his father's one-track, unconsciously brutal mind behind that.

"Well," I said harshly. "You almost are—anyone who can handle a scanner and a rifle like that."

But he didn't believe me. I could see from his eyes that he even distrusted me for telling such a bald-faced lie. He saw himself through Pelang's eyes—DeBaraumer, scanner, and ability to talk with the Klahari notwithstanding.

It was time for me to go—there was no time to waste getting on to the next planter with my warnings. I did stay a few minutes longer to try and find out how he had learned to talk Klahari. But Jean had no idea. Somewhere along the line of growing up he had learned it—in the unconscious way of children that makes it almost impossible for them to translate word by word from one language to another. Jean thought in English, or he thought in Klahari. Where there were no equal terms, he was helpless. When I asked him why the Klahari said that their large bands would not form or attack until the end of the season, he was absolutely not able to tell me.

So I went on my way, preaching my gospel of warning, and skirmishing with the larger bands of Klahari I met, chivvying and breaking up the smaller ones. Finally I finished the swing through my district and got back to Regional Installation to find myself commissioned lieutenant and given command of a half company. I'd been about seventy percent successful in getting planters to pull back with their families into protected areas—the success being mainly with those who had been here more than seventeen years. But of those who hesitated, more were coming in every day to safety, as local raids stepped up.

However, Jean turned out to be right. It was the end of the season before matters finally came to a head with the natives—and then it happened all at once.

I was taking a shower at Regional Installation, after a tour, when the general alarm went. Two hours later I was deep in the jungle almost to the edge of the desert, with all my command and with only a fighting chance of ever seeing a shower again.

Because all we could do was retreat, fighting as we went. There had been a reason the Klahari explosion had held off until the end of the season—and that was that there never had been such an explosion to date. An interracial sociological situation such as we had on Utword was like a half-filled toy balloon. You squeezed it flat in one place and it bulged someplace else. The pressure our planters put on the maturing Klahari made the five-year ones, the post-seniors, organize as they had never needed or wanted to do before.

The number of our planters had been growing in

the seventeen years since the last Klahari generation. Now it was no longer possible to ignore the opposition, obvious in the cleared fields and houses and Strongpoints, to any post-senior Klahari's dream of a jungle kingdom.

So the Klahari had got together and made plans without bunching up. Then, all in one night, they formed. An army—well, if not an army, a horde—twenty to thirty thousand strong, moving in to overrun all signs of human occupancy in the jungle.

We, the human soldiers, retreated before them, like a thin skirmish line opposed to a disorganized, poorer armed, but unstoppable multitude. Man by man, sweating through the depths of that jungle, it was hardly different from a hundred previous skirmishes we'd had with individual bunches—except that the ones we killed seemed to spring to life to fight with us again, as ever-fresh warriors took their place. There would be a rush, a fight, and a falling back. Then half an hour, or an hour perhaps, in which to breath—and then another rush of dark forms, crossbow bolts and lances against us again. And so it went on. We were killing ten—twenty—to one, but we were losing men too.

Finally, our line grew too thin. We were back among the outermost planters' places now, and we could no longer show a continuous front. We broke up into individual commands, falling back toward individual Strongpoints. Then the real trouble began—because the rush against us now would come not just from the front, but from front and both sides. We began to lose men faster.

We made up our ranks a little from the few planters we picked up as we retreated—those who had been fool enough not to leave earlier. Yes, and we got there too late to pick up other such fools, too. Not only men, but women as well, hacked into

unrecognizability in the torn smoke-blackened ruins
of their buildings.

. . . And so we came finally, I, the three soldiers
and one planter who made up what was left of my
command, to the place of Pelang Duprès.

I knew we were getting close to it, and I'd evolved
a technique for such situations. We stopped and
made a stand just short of the fields, still in the
jungle. Then, when we beat back the Klahari close
to it, we broke from the jungle and ran fast under
the blazing white brilliance of distant Achernar,
back toward the buildings across the open fields,
black from the recent plowing.

The Klahari were behind us, and before us. There
was a fight going on at the buildings, even as we
ran up. We ran right into the midst of it; the whirl
of towering, dark, naked, ornamented bodies, the
yells and the screeches, the flying lances and crossbow bolts. Elmire Duprès had been dragged from
the house and was dead when we reached her.

We killed some Klahari and the others ran—they
were always willing to run, just as they were always sure to come back. Pelang seemed nowhere
about the place. I shoved in through the broken
doorway, and found the room filled with dead
Klahari. Beyond them, Jean Duprès, alone, crouched
in a corner behind a barricade of furniture, torn
open at one end, the DeBaraumer sticking through
the barricade, showing a pair of homemade bayo-
nets welded to its barrel to keep Klahari hands
from grabbing it and snatching it away. When he
saw me, Jean jerked the rifle back and came fast
around the end of the barricade.

"My mama—" he said. I caught him as he tried
to go by and he fought me—suddenly and without
a sound, with a purposefulness that multiplied his
boy's strength.

"Jean, no!" I said. "You don't want to go out
there!"

He stopped fighting me all at once.

It was so sudden, I thought for a moment it must be a trick to get me to relax so that he could break away again. And then, looking down, I saw that his face was perfectly calm, empty and resigned.

"She's dead," he said. The way he said them, the words were like an epitaph.

I let him go, warily. He walked soberly past me and out of the door. But when he got outside, one of my men had already covered her body with a drape a Klahari had been carrying off; and the body was hidden. He went over and looked down at the drape, but did not lift it. I walked up to stand beside him, trying to think of something to say. But, still with that strange calmness, he was ahead of me.

"I have to bury her," he said, still evenly empty of voice. "Later we'll send her home to Earth."

The cost of sending a body back to Earth would have taken the whole Duprès farm as payment. But that was something I could explain to Jean later.

"I'm afraid we can't wait to bury her, Jean," I said. "The Klahari are right behind us."

"No," he said, quietly. "We'll have time. I'll go tell them."

He put the DeBaraumer down and started walking toward the nearest edge of the jungle. I was so shaken by the way he was taking it all that I let him go—and then I heard him talking in a high voice to the jungle; words and sounds that seemed impossible even from a child's throat. In a few minutes he came back.

"They'll wait," he said, as he approached me again. "They don't want to be rude."

So we buried Elmire Duprès, without her husband—who had gone that morning to a neighbor's field—with never a tear from her son, and if I had not seen those piled Klahari dead in the living room before his barricade, I would have thought that Jean himself had had no connection with what had happened here. At first, I thought he was in shock. But it was not that. He was perfectly sensible and normal. It was just that his grief and the loss of his mother were somehow of a different order of things than what had happened here. Again it was like the Klahari, who are more concerned with why they die than when, or how.

We marked the grave and went on, fighting and falling back—and Jean Duprès fought right along with us. He was as good as one of my men any day—better, because he could move more quietly and he spotted the attacking Klahari before any of us. He had lugged the DeBaraumer along—I thought because of his long association with it. But it was only a weapon to him. He saw the advantage of our jungle rifles in lightness and firepower over it, almost at once—and the first of our men to be killed, he left the DeBaraumer lying and took the issue gun instead.

We were three men and a boy when we finally made it to the gates of Strongpoint Hundred Fourteen, and inside. There were no women there. The Strongpoint was now purely and simply a fort, high, blank walls and a single strong gate, staffed by the factor and the handful of local planters who had refused to leave before it was too late. They were here now, and here they would stay. So would we. There was no hope of our remnant of a band surviving another fifty kilometers of jungle retreat.

I left Jean and the men in the yard inside the gates and made a run for the factor's office to put in a call to Regional Installation. One air transport could land here in half an hour and pick us all up, planters and my gang alike. It was then that I got the news.

I was put right through to the colonel of the Rangers before I could even ask why. He was a balding, pleasant man whom I'd never spoken three words to in my life before; and he put it plainly and simply, and as kindly as possible.

". . . This whole business of the jungle Klahari forming one single band has the city Klahari disturbed for the first time," he told me, looking squarely at me out of the phone. "You see, they always assumed that the people we had here were *our* young men, our equivalent of the Klahari boys, getting a final test before being let back into our own civilization elsewhere. It was even something of a compliment the way they saw it—our coming all this way to test our own people on their testing ground here. Obviously we didn't have any test area to match it anywhere else. And, of course, we let them think so."

"Well, what's wrong with that, now—sir?" I asked. "We're certainly being tested."

"That's just it," he said. "We've got to let you be tested this time. The city Klahari, the older ones, have finally started to get worried about the changes taking place here. They've let us know that they don't intervene on the side of their boys— and they expect us not to intervene on the side of ours."

I frowned at him. I didn't understand in that first minute what he meant.

"You mean you can't pick us up from here?"

"I can't even send you supplies, Lieutenant," he said. "Now that it's too late, they're working overtime back home to figure out ways to explain our true situation here to the Klahari and make some agreement on the basis of it with them. But meanwhile—our investment in men and equipment on this world is out of reach—too much to waste by war with the adult Klahari now." He paused and watched me for a second. "You're on your own, Lieutenant."

I digested that.

"Yes, Colonel," I said, finally. "All right. We'll hold out here. We're twenty or so men, and there's ammunition and food. But there's a boy, the son of a local planter . . ."

"Sorry, Lieutenant. He'll have to stay too."

"Yes, sir . . ."

We went into practical details about holding the Strongpoint. There was a sergeant with the remnants of a half company, maybe another twenty men, not far west of me, holding an unfinished Strongpoint. But no communications. If I could get a man through to tell that command to join us here, our situation would not be so bad. One man might get through the Klahari . . .

I finished and went outside. Three new planters were just being admitted through the gate, ragged and tired—and one was Pelang Duprès. Even as I started toward him, he spotted Jean and rushed to the boy, asking him questions.

". . . but your mama! Your mama!" I heard him demanding impatiently as I came up. One of my men, who had been there, pushed in between Pelang and the boy.

"Let me tell you, Mr. Duprès," he said, putting his hand on Pelang's arm and trying to lead him away from Jean. I could see him thinking that there was no need to harrow up Jean with a rehearsal of what had happened. But Pelang threw him off.

"Tell me? Tell me what?" he shouted, pushing the man away, to face Jean again. "What happened?"

"We buried her, Daddy," I heard Jean saying quietly. "And afterward we'll send her to Earth—"

"Buried her—" Pelang's face went black with congestion of blood under the skin, and his voice choked him. "She's dead!" He swung on the man who had tried to lead him away. "You let her be killed; and you saved this—this—" He turned and struck out at Jean with a hand already clenched into a fist. Jean made no move to duck the blow, though with the quickness that I had seen in him while coming to the Strongpoint, I am sure he could have. The fist sent him tumbling, and the men beside him tried to grab him.

But I had lost my head when he hit Jean. I am not sorry for it, even now. I drove through the crowd and got Pelang by the collar and shoved him up against the concrete side of the watch-tower and banged his head against it. He was blocky and powerful as a dwarf bull, but I was a little out of my head. We were nose-to-nose there and I could feel the heat of his panting, almost sobbing, breath and see his brown eyes squeezed up between the anguished squinting of the flesh above and below them.

"Your wife is dead," I said to him, between my teeth. "But that boy, that son of yours, Duprès, was there when his *mother* died! And where were you?"

I saw then the fantastic glitter of the bright tears in his brown squeezed-up eyes. Suddenly he went limp on me, against the wall, and his head wobbled on his thick, sunburned neck.

"I worked hard—" he choked suddenly. "No one worked harder than me, Pelang. For them both—and they . . ." He turned around and sobbed against the watchtower wall. I stood back from him. But Jean pushed through the men surrounding us and came up to his father. He patted his father's broad back under its white glass thick shirt and then put his arms around the man's thick waist and leaned his head against his father's side. But Pelang ignored him and continued to weep uncontrollably. Slowly, the other men turned away and left the two of them alone.

There was no question about the man to send to contact the half company at the unfinished Strong-point west of us. It had to be the most jungle-experienced of us; and that meant me. I left the fort under the command of the factor, a man named Strudenmeyer. I would rather have left it under command of one of my two remaining enlisted men, but the factor was technically an officer in his own Strongpoint and ranked them, as well as being known personally to the local planters holed up there. He was the natural commander. But he was a big-bellied man with a booming voice and very noticeable whites to his eyes; and I suspected him of a lack of guts.

I told him to be sure to plant sentinels in the observation posts, nearly two hundred feet off the ground in treetops on four sides of the Strongpoint and a hundred meters out. And I told him to pick men who could stay there indefinitely. Also, he was to save his men and ammunition until the Klahari actually tried to take the Strongpoint by assault.

". . . You'll be all right," I told him, and the other men, just before I went out the gate. "Remember, no Strongpoint has ever been taken as long as the ammunition held out and there were men to use it."

Then I left.

The forest was alive with Klahari, but they were traveling, not hunting, under the impression all humans still alive were holed up in one place or another. It took me three days to make the unfinished Strongpoint, and when I got there I found the sergeant and his men had been wiped out, the Strongpoint itself gutted. I was surprised by two seniors there, but managed to kill them both fairly quietly and get away. I headed back for Strongpoint Hundred Fourteen.

It was harder going back; and I took eight days.

I made most of the distance on my belly and at night. At that, I would never have gotten as far as I did, except for luck and the fact that the Klahari were not looking for humans in the undergrowth. Their attention was all directed to the assault building up against Strongpoint Hundred Fourteen.

The closer I got to the Strongpoint, the thicker they were. And more were coming in all the time. They squatted in the jungle, waiting and growing in numbers. I saw that I would never make it back to the Strongpoint itself, so I headed for the tree holding the north sentinel post hidden in its top (the Klahari did not normally climb trees or even look up) to join the sentinel there.

I made the base of the tree on the eighth night, an hour before dawn—and I was well up the trunk and hidden when the light came. I hung there in the crotch all day while the Klahari passed silently below. They have a body odor something like the smell of crushed grass; you can't smell it unless you get very close. Or if there are a lot of them together. There were now and their odor was a sharp pungency in the air, mingled with the unpleasant smell of their breath, reminiscent, to a human nose, of garbage. I stayed in that tree crotch all day and climbed the rest of the way when it got dark. When I reached the platform, it was dark and empty. The stores of equipment kept there by general order had never been touched. Strudenmeyer had never sent out his men.

When morning came, I saw how serious that fault had been. I had set up the dew catchers to funnel drinking water off the big leaves in the crown of the tree above me, and done a few other simple things I could manage quietly in the dark. With dawn the next day I set up the post's equipment, particularly the communication equipment with the Strongpoint and the other sentinel posts. As I had suspected, the other posts were empty—

and Strudenmeyer had not even set a watch in the communications room at the Strongpoint. The room when I looked into it was empty, and the door closed. No one came to the sound of the call buzzer.

I could see most of the rooms of the Strongpoint's interior. I could see outside the buildings, all around the inside of the walls and the court separating them from the buildings and the watchtower in the center. The scanners set in walls and ceilings there were working perfectly. But I could not tell Strudenmeyer and the rest I was there. Just as I could get radio reception from the station at Regional Installation, but I could not call R.I. because my call had to be routed through the communications room in the Strongpoint, where there was nobody on duty.

A hundred and eighty feet below me, and all around the four walls that made the Strongpoint what it was, the Klahari were swarming as thickly as bees on their way to a new hive. And more were coming in hourly. It was not to be wondered at. With the group to the west wiped out, we were the forward point held by humans in the jungle. Everything beyond us had been taken already and laid waste. The Klahari post-seniors leading the horde could have bypassed us and gone on—but that was not their nature.

And Strudenmeyer was down there with twenty men and a boy—no, seventeen men. I could count three wounded under an awning in the west yard. Evidently there had already been assaults on his walls. There was no real discipline to the young Klahari, even now, and if a group got impatient they would simply go ahead and attack, even if the leaders were patient enough to wait and build up their forces.

So either there had been premature assaults on the walls, or Strudenmeyer was even more of a bad commander than I had thought, and had been putting men up on the walls to be shot at, instead of using rifles through the gunports on automatic and remote control. Even as I thought this, I was putting it out of my mind. I think that at that time I didn't want to believe that the factor could be that poor a leader, because I had the responsibility for him, having put him in charge of the Strongpoint. Just at that moment, however, something else happened to help shove it out of my mind, for I discovered a new wrinkle to this treetop post that they hadn't had back when I was learning about sentinel duty.

In addition to the wall scanners that gave me an interior view of the Strongpoint, I found there were eight phone connections inside its walls from which the commander there could check with the sentinels. All he had to do was pick up the phone and ask whatever questions he had in mind. But the damn things were one-way!

I could activate the receiver at my end. In other words, I could hear what anyone was saying in the immediate vicinity of the phone. But I couldn't make myself heard by them until someone lifted down the phone at that end. And there was no bell or signal with which I could call them to lift a phone down. I jammed the receivers all open, of course, and several different conversations around the fort came filtering into my post to match up with the images on some of the scanners before me. But nobody was talking about trying a phone to one of the sentinel posts. Why should they? As far as they knew they were unmanned.

I lay there, protected by the shade of the crown leaves, as Achernar climbed up into the sky over the jungle and the Strongpoint, and more Klahari filtered in every moment below me. I was safe, comfortable, and absolutely helpless. I had food for half a year, the dew catchers supplied me with more pure water than I could drink, and around me on my pleasantly breezy perch were all modern conveniences, including solar cookers to heat my food, or water for shaving if it came to that. I lay there like an invisible deity, seeing and hearing most of what went on below in the Strongpoint and entirely unsuspected by those I was watching. A commander without a command, spectator to what, it soon became plain, was a command without a commander.

You might think the men who would delay longest before pulling back in the face of a threat like the Klahari would be the bravest and the best of the planters. But it was not so. These men were the stubbornest of the planters, the most stupid, the most greedy; the hardheads and unbelievers. All this came out now before me on the scanners, and over the open phones, now that they were completely cut off and for the first time they fully saw the consequences of their delaying.

And Strudenmeyer was their natural leader.

There was nothing the factor had done that he ought to have done, and there was nothing he had left undone that he had ought not to have done. He had failed to send out men to the sentinel posts, because they objected to going. He had omitted to take advantage of the military knowledge and experience of the two enlisted men I had brought to the Strongpoint with me. Instead he had been siding with the majority—the combat-ignorant planters—against the military minority of two when questions of defending the Strongpoint came up. He had put men on the walls—inviting premature assaults from the Klahari that could not have taken the Strongpoint in any case, but that could whittle down his fighting strength. As they already had by wounding three of his able men, including Pelang Duprès. And, most foolish of all in a way, he had robbed himself of his best rifle and his most knowledgeable expert of the Klahari, by reducing Jean

Duprès from the status of fighting man to that of seven-year-old child.

He had done this because Pelang, lying under the awning, groaning with self-pity at the loss of his wife, and a lance-thrust through his shoulder, and abusing his son who was restricted to the single duty of waiting on the wounded, treated the boy with nothing but contempt. Jean's only defenders were my two enlisted men, who had seen him in action in the jungle. But these two were discounted and outcast anyway in the eyes of the planters, who would have liked to have found reason to blame them, and the military in general, for the whole situation.

So—fools listen to fools and ignore the wise, as I think I read sometime, somewhere. The booming-voiced, white-eyed factor, his big belly even larger with fear and self-importance, listened to the shortsighted, bitter and suffering father who knew nothing but his fields—and ignored the quiet, self-contained boy who could have told him, day by day, hour by hour, and minute by minute, what the Klahari response would be to any action he might take inside the Strongpoint. The afternoon of the first day I was in the sentinel post, there was another premature assault on the walls of the Strongpoint, and another planter, a man named Barker, was badly wounded by a crossbow bolt in the chest. He died less than an hour later.

Just before the sun went down, there was a calling from the jungle. A single, high-pitched Klahari voice repeating itself over and over. I studied the scanners that gave me an outside view of the Strongpoint and the jungle surrounding, but could not locate the caller. In fact, from what my scanners showed, the scene was peaceful. Most of the Klahari were out of sight under the jungle greenery, and the Strong-point seemed to swelter almost deserted in its small cleared area, its thirty-foot-

high concrete walls surrounding the interior buildings dominated by the watchtower which rose from
them like a square column of concrete some fifty
feet into the air. Strudenmeyer had a man on duty
up there, in the air-conditioned bubble under the
sunshade, but he had been napping when the calling started.

Then the sound of Jean's voice from a scanner
screen drew me back to the bank of them showing
the inside of the Strongpoint. I saw him, halfway
between the awning-covered woundeds' area and
the west wall. Strudenmeyer had caught his arm
and was holding him from going further.

". . . what for?" Strudenmeyer was saying, as I
came up to the scanner screen.

"It's me they're calling," said Jean.

"You? How do they know *you're* here?" the factor
stared uncertainly down at him.

Jean merely stared back, the blank stare of the
young when explanation is hopeless. To him—and
to me, watching—it was so obvious why the Klahari
should know not only that he was there, but that
everyone else in the fort who was there, was there,
that words were a waste of time. But Strudenmeyer
had never risen to the point of giving the Klahari
credit for even simple intelligence. He ignored the
cities and the schools from which these ornamented
young natives came, and thought of them as
savages, if not near-animals.

"Come back here. We'll talk to your father," said
the factor, after a moment. They went back to
Pelang, who listened to Strudenmeyer's report of
the situation and cursed both the factor and his
son.

"You must be mistaken, Jean. You don't understand Klahari that well," decided Strudenmeyer,
finally. "Now, stay away from that wall. Your father needs you and I don't want you getting hurt.

That wall's a place for men and you're just a little boy. Now, mind what I say!''

Jean obeyed. He did not even argue. It is something—inconceivable—the adaptability of children; and it has to be seen to be testified to. Jean *knew* what he was; but he *believed* what his father and the other adults told him he was. If they told him he did not understand Klahari and he did not belong on the wall of the Strongpoint, then it must be so, even if it was against all the facts. He went back to fetching and carrying cold drinks to the wounded, and after a while the voice from the jungle ceased and the sun went down.

The Klahari do not as individuals try to kill each other at night. So, automatically, they did not try to storm the Strongpoint under cover of darkness, when their chances of taking it would have been best. But the next morning at dawn, two thousand of them threw themselves at the walls from the outside.

They were not secretive about it; and that alone saved the Strongpoint, where the single sentry on the watchtower was sleeping as soundly as the rest below. The whole men in the fort manned the walls and began firing, not only the guns under their hands, but a rifle apiece to either side of them on automatic remote control. I ought to say instead, that about three quarters of them began firing, because the rest froze at the sight of the waves of dark seven-foot bodies swarming up to the base of the wall and trying to lean tree trunks against it, up which they could clamber. But the remaining three quarters of able men, multiplied three times by the automatic control rifles, literally hosed the attackers from the wall with rifle slugs until the assault was suddenly broken and the Klahari ran.

Suddenly, under the morning sun, the jungle was silent, and an incredible carpet of dead and dying Klahari covered the open space surrounding the Strongpoint on four sides. Inside, the fighters—and the non-fighters—counted one man dead and five wounded in varying degrees, only one badly enough to be removed to the hospital ward under the awning.

The fallen Klahari lay scattered, singly and in piles, like poisoned grasshoppers after their swarming advance has been met by the low-flying plane spraying insecticide. The others in the jungle around them dragged a few of the wounded to cover under the ferns, but they had no medicines or surgical techniques and soon there was a steady sound from the wounded natives outside the wall and the wounded humans within. While shortly, as the sun rose, unseen but felt, the heat climbed; and soon the stink of death began to rise around the Strongpoint, like a second, invisible outer wall.

I am sorry to make a point of this, but it was this way. It is this way such things have always been and I want you to know how it was for Jean Duprès. He was seven years old, his mother was dead, he was surrounded by death and facing it himself—and he had lived through all that had happened to the men around him so far. Now he was to see many of those within the Strongpoint with him recovering their birthright as men before his eyes.

For most did recover it. This too always happens. The full assault of the Klahari on the Strongpoint had been like a flail, striking the grain from the plant and chaff. When it had passed, Strudenmeyer was no longer in command; and several among the wounded like Pelang Duprès were up and carrying a gun again. Strudenmeyer had been one of those who had not fired a weapon during the attack. He and one other were never to fire a gun right up to their deaths, a few days later. But where the Strongpoint had been manned by civilians two hours before, now it was manned by veterans. Of my two enlisted men, one had been the man to die in the assault and the other was badly wounded and dying. But a planter named Dakeham was now in charge and he had posted a man on the watchtower immediately after the attack was over and had gone himself to the communications room to call Regional Installation Military Headquarters, for advice, if not for rescue.

But he found he could not make the radio work. Helpless, watching from my sentinel post through the scanner in the room wall, I raged against his ignorance, unable to make him hear me, so that I could tell him what was wrong. What *was* wrong, was that Strudenmeyer, like many operators living off by themselves, had fallen into careless individual ways of handling and maintaining his set. The main power switch had worn out, and Strudenmeyer had never put himself to the trouble of replacing it. Instead he had jury-rigged a couple of bare wires that could be twisted together, to make power available to the set. The wires lay before the control board, right in plain sight. But Dakeham, like most modern people, knew less than nothing about radio—and Strudenmeyer, when they hauled him into the communications room, was pallid-faced, unresisting, and too deep in psychological shock to tell them anything.

Dakeham gave up, went out, and closed the door of the communications room of the Strongpoint behind him. To the best of my recollection, it was never opened again.

That evening, the Klahari hit the walls again in another assault. It was not as determined as the first, and it met a more determined resistance. It was beaten off, with only two men slightly wounded. But that was just the first day of full-scale attack.

Twice and sometimes three times a day after

that, the Klahari attacked the Strongpoint. The odor of death grew so strong about the fort that it even got into my dreams, high up in my treetop; and I would dream I was wandering through fields of dead of the past and forgotten wars I had read about as a student in school. The Klahari lost unbelievably with every assault—but always there were more coming in through the jungle to increase their numbers. This one Strongpoint was holding up all the Klahari advance, for psychologically they could not break off a contest once it was begun, though they could retreat temporarily to rest. But inside the Strongpoint, its defenders were being whittled down in number. It was almost unbearable to watch. A dozen times I found my gun at my shoulder, my finger on the trigger. But I didn't pull it. My small help would not change the outcome of the battle—and it would be suicide on my part. They would come up after me, in the dark, watching me, waiting for me to sleep. When I dozed I would be dead. I knew this, but it did not help the feeling of helplessness that overwhelmed me while I watched them die, one by one.

Daily, though neither the besieging Klahari nor the humans in the Strongpoint could see or hear it, a reconnaissance plane circled high up out of sight over the area, to send back pictures and reports of the sight there to Regional Installation. Daily, swaying in my treetop sentinel post, I heard over my voice receiver, the steady clear tones of the newscaster from Regional Installation, informing the rest of the humans on Utword.

"... the thirty-seventh attack on the Strongpoint was evidently delivered shortly after dawn today. The reconnaissance plane saw fresh native casualties lying in the clearing around all four walls. Numbers of Klahari in the surrounding jungle are estimated to have risen to nearly forty thousand individuals, only a fraction of whom, it is obvious, can take part in an attack at any one time. With the Strongpoint, pictures indicate that its defenders there seem to be taking the situation with calmness . . ."

And I would turn to my scanners and my phones showing me the inside of the Strongpoint and hear the sounds of the wounded, the dying, and those who were face-to-face with death . . .

". . . They've got to quite sometime," I heard Bert Kaja, one of the planters, saying on my fifteenth day in the tree. He was squatting with the wounded, and Dakeham, under the awning.

"Maybe," said Dakeham, noncommittally. He was a tall, lean, dark individual with a slightly pouting face but hard eyes.

"They can't keep this up forever. They'll run out of food," said Kaja, seated swarthy and crosslegged on the ground. "The jungle must be stripped of food all around here by this time."

"Maybe," said Dakeham.

They discussed the subject in the impersonal voices with which people back home discuss the stock market. Jean Duprès was less than eight feet from them, and possibly he could have answered their questions, but he was still in the occupation to which Strudenmeyer had assigned him—caring for the wounded.

Right now he was washing the lance wound, the original wound in his father's shoulder. Pelang watched him scowling, not saying anything until the other two men rose and left. Then he swore—abruptly, as Jean tightened a new bandage around the shoulder.

"—be careful, can't you?"

"You . . ." Pelang scowled worse than ever, watching the boy's face, tilted downward to watch his working hands. "You and she wanted to go back . . . to Earth, eh?" Jean looked up, surprised. "You said she wanted to be buried back home?

You told me that!" said Pelang. Still staring at his
father, Jean nodded.

"And you, too? Eh? You wanted to go back, too,
and leave me here?"

Jean shook his head.

"Don't lie to me."

"I'm not!" Jean's voice was injured.

"Ah, you lie . . . you lie!" snarled Pelang, unhappily. "You don't lie to me with words, but you lie
anyway, all the time!" He reached up with his
good hand and caught the boy by the shoulder.
"Listen, I tell you this is a terrible place, but me,
your daddy, worked hard at it to make you rich
someday. Now, answer me!" He shook the boy.
"It's a terrible place, this jungle, here! Isn't it?"

"No," said the boy, looking as if he was going to
cry.

"You . . ." Pelang let go of Jean's shoulder and
clenched his fist as if he were going to strike his
son. But instead his face twisted up as if he were
going to cry himself. He got to his feet and lum-
bered away, toward the walls, out of range of my
immediate scanner. Jean sat still, looking miserable for a moment, then his face smoothed out and
he got to his feet and went off about some business
of his own to do with the wounded.

In that evening's assault they lost two more men
to the attacking Klahari, one of them Dakeham. It
was the fifteenth day of full-scale assaults and
they were down to eight men able to man the
walls, each one of them handling half a wall of
rifles on automatic remote, instead of one rifle
direct and the rest on automatic. They had found
that it was point-blank massed firepower that beat
back the attacks; and that what was to be feared
were not the Klahari rushing the walls, but the
one or two natives who by freak chance got to the
top of these barriers and inside the Strongpoint. A

Klahari inside the walls could usually kill or wound at least one man before he was shot down.

The one who killed Dakeham did so before any of the others noticed it and went on to the wounded under the awning before he could be stopped. There, Jean killed him, with a rifle one of the wounded had kept by him—but by that time the wounded were all dead.

But there were fresh wounded. Pelang had been lanced again—this time in the side, and he bled through his bandage there, if he overexerted himself. Kaja had been chosen to command in Dakeham's place. Under the lights, once night had fallen, he went from man to man, slapping them carefully on unwounded back or shoulder.

"Brace up!" he said to them. "Brace up! The Klahari'll be quitting any day now. They must be out of food for miles around. Just a matter of hours! Any day now!"

No one answered him. A few, like Pelang, swore at him. Jean looked at him gently, but said nothing. And, voiceless as far as they were concerned, up in my sentinel's post, I understood what Jean's look meant. It was true that the Klahari were out of food for kilometers about the Strongpoint, but that made no difference. They were able, just like humans, to go several days without food if it was worth it to them—and in this case it was worth it. Going hungry was just the price of being in on the party. After several days the hungriest would break off, travel away in search of fruit and roots and when they were full again, come back.

". . . the season's not more than a week from being over!" said Kaja. "With the end of the season, they always move to a new place."

That was truer. It was a real hope. But two weeks was a long way off in a Strongpoint under two or three assaults a day. The evening radio news broadcast came on to emphasize this.

". . . this small jungle outpost holds all the Klahari young men at bay," recited the announcer calmly. "The native advance has been frustrated . . ."

I dozed off in the rocking treetop.

Sometime in the next two days, Jean finally returned to the walls. I did not remember, and I think no one in the Strongpoint remembered when it happened exactly. He must have taken over a bank of rifles on automatic fire when the man handling them was killed by a Klahari who had gotten over the wall. At any rate, he was once more fighting with the men. And the men were now down to three able to fight and two dying under the awning, so no one objected.

They did not lose a man for two days. Jean not only manned his section of the walls, but shot the three Klahari that got over the walls, in that time. It was as if he had eyes in the back of his head. Then, suddenly, in one morning assault, they lost two men and Pelang went down from loss of blood—the wound in his side having reopened and bled during the fighting. Later on that day, the two wounded died. At the evening assault, Pelang lay useless, half-dozing under the awning, while Jean and the remaining planter in fighting shape stood back-to-back in the open middle of the Strongpoint, scanners set up in front of them, each handling two adjacent walls of guns on automatic remote fire.

Half a dozen Klahari made it over the walls and into the Strongpoint. Jean and the planter—whose name I do not remember—grabbed up hand weapons and shot them down. By what amounted to a wild stroke of luck, the man and the boy were able to get them all killed without being wounded themselves.

Night fell, and brought an end to the day's fighting. But later on, about the middle of the night, there was the single, sharp report of a handgun that woke me in my treetop. I turned to the scanners, lifting their hoods one by one, and located Jean standing in the open space before the awning, half in shadow above something lying in an interior angle of the walls. As I looked, he turned, crossed under the lights and came back underneath the awning. I had a scanner there, as I may have mentioned, but the night contrast between the shadow and the interior lights was such that I could barely make out the darkly upright shape of Jean and the recumbent shape of a man, who would be Pelang. Pelang had been half-unconscious earlier, but now his voice came weakly to the phone connection nearby.

"—what is it?"

"He's shot," answered Jean; and I saw the upright shape of him fold itself down beside the larger darkness of his father.

"Who . . . ?" Pelang barely whispered.

"He shot himself."

"Ah . . ." It was a sigh from the man's lips, but whether one of despair or just of weariness or exhaustion, I could not tell. Pelang lay still and silent, and Jean stayed sitting or crouching beside his father . . . and I almost dozed off again, watching the screen. I was roused by the whispering sound of Pelang's voice. He had begun to talk again, half to himself, just when, I was not sure.

". . . I am a man . . . I can go anywhere. Back home . . . look at the stars. I told myself, Elmire and me . . . Nobody farms better than me, Pelang. Nobody works harder. This is a terrible place, but it don't stop me. Elmire, your mama, she wanted to go back home; but we got earth here you can't match on them stony old fields, *bord la rive* Mistassibi. Man don't let himself be pushed from his crops—no, they don't get away with that, you hear?" He was becoming louder-voiced and excited.

I saw the shadow of him heave up and the shape of Jean bowing above him.

"Lie down, Papa . . ." it was the boy's whisper. "Lie down . . ."

"This terrible place, but I make my boy rich . . . you'll be rich someday, Jean. They'll say—'Hey, Jean, how come you're so rich?' then you say—'My daddy, *mon père* Pelang, he made me so.' Then you go back home, take your mama, also; you let them see you way up beyond Lac St. John. 'My daddy, Pelang,' you say, 'he don't never back down for no one, never quits. He's a man, my daddy, Pelang . . ."

His voice lowered until I could not make out the words and he rambled on. After a while I dozed; and a little later on I slept deeply.

I woke suddenly. It was day. The sun was up above the leaves over me—and there was a strange silence, all around.

Then I heard a voice, calling.

It was a calling I recognized. I had heard it once before, outside the walls of the Strongpoint, the first day I had been in the treetop sentinel post. It was the calling of the Klahari, that Jean had told Strudenmeyer was for him, days before.

I rolled to the scanners and flipped up all their hoods. Jean was still where I had seen his indistinct form in the darkness, above the shape of his father, under the awning. But now Pelang was covered with a blanket—even his face—and unutterably still. Jean sat crosslegged, facing the body under the blanket—not so much in the posture of a mourner, as of a guard above the dead. At first as I watched; it seemed to me that he did not even hear the calling beyond the walls.

But, after a while, as the calling kept up in the high-pitched Klahari voice, he got slowly to his feet and picked up the issue rifle beside him. Carrying it, he went slowly across the open space, climbed to the catwalk behind the west wall and climbed from that on to the two-foot width of the wall, in plain sight of the Klahari hidden in the jungle. He sat down there, crosslegged, laying the rifle across his knees and stared out into the jungle.

The calling ceased. There came after that a sound I can't describe, a sort of rustling and sighing, like the sound of a vast audience, after a single, breath-held moment of uncertainty, settling itself to witness some occasion. I switched to binoculars, looking directly down into the clearing before the west wall. Several tall Klaharis came out of the jungle and began clearing the dead bodies from a space about twenty feet square before the west wall. When they had gotten down to the macerated earth below the bodies they brought out clean leaves of fern and covered the ground there.

Then they backed off, and three Klahari, feathered and ornamented as none I had ever seen before, came out of the jungle and sat down themselves on the ferns, cross-legged in their fashion—which Jean had imitated on the wall above. Once they were seated, Klahari began to emerge from the jungle and fill in the space behind them, standing and watching.

When as many were into the open space as could get there without getting between the seated three and their view of Jean, another silence fell. It lasted for a few seconds, and then the Klahari on the end got to his feet and began to talk to Jean.

In the Rangers we are taught a few Klahari phrases—"you must disperse—" "lay down your weapons"—and the like. A few of us learn to say them well enough to make the Klahari understand, but few of us learn to understand more than half a dozen of the simplest of Klahari statements. It is not only that the native voice is different—they talk high and toward the back of a different-shaped throat than ours; but the way they think is different.

For example, we call this planet "Utword," which

is a try at using the native term for it. The Klahari word—sound rather—is actually something like "Ut," said high and cut off sharp, toward the back of your mouth. But the point is, no Klahari would ever refer to his planet as simply "Ut." He would always call it "the world of Ut"; because to the Klahari, bound up in this one planet there are four worlds, all equally important. There is the world yet to be, the world of time to come. There is a sort of Klahari hell—the world populated by the dead who died in failure; and whose souls will therefore never be reincarnated in Klahari yet to be born. And there is the world of the physical present—the world of *Ut*. So "Utword" is "*Ut*"-tied onto the human word "world" minus the l-sound the Klahari can't pronounce.

Therefore I understood nothing of what was said by the Klahari who was speaking. From his gestures to the Strongpoint walls and the jungle behind him, I assumed he was talking about the conflict here. And from the way Jean sat listening, I guessed that Jean understood, where I did not. After the speaker was finished, he sat down; and there was a long silence that went on and on. It was plain even to me that they were waiting for some answer from Jean, but he simply sat there. And then the middle Klahari stood up to speak.

His gestures were more sharp and abrupt, more demanding. But aside from that he was as incomprehensible to me as the first, except that something about the gestures and the talk gave me the impression that a lot of what he said was repeating what the first speaker had said. At last he sat down, and again there was the silence and the waiting for Jean to speak.

This time Jean did speak. Without standing up, he said one short phrase and then sat still again, leaving me with the tantalizing feeling that I had almost understood him, because of the simpleness of his statement and the fact that it was made by a human mouth, throat and tongue.

But the response was another rustling sigh from the audience, and when it died, the third and tallest Klahari got slowly to his feet and began to talk. I do not know if the few words from Jean had sharpened my wits, or whether the last speaker was himself more understandable, but without being able to translate a single word, I felt myself understanding much more.

It seemed to me that he was asking Jean for something—almost pleading with the boy for it. He was advancing reasons why Jean should agree. The reasons were possibly reasons the first two to speak had advanced—but this speaker seemed to take them with a deeper seriousness. His gestures were at arms' length, slow and emphatic. His voice rose and fell with what seemed to me to be a greater range of tone than the voices of the others. When at last he sat down, there seemed to be a deeper, more expecting silence, holding all the listening jungle and the silent Strongpoint.

Jean sat still. For a moment I thought he was not going to move or answer. And then he said that phrase again, and this time I understood why I had almost felt I could translate it. The first sounds in it were "*K'ahari . . .*" the native name with the throat-catch in the beginning of it that we replace with a more humanly pronounceable "l," to get the word "Klahari." I had almost had the whole phrase understood with that identification, it seemed to me.

But Jean had risen to his feet and was finally beginning to talk, his high-pitched child's voice matching the pitch of the native vocal apparatus.

He spoke impassionedly—or maybe it was because he was as human as I was that I could see the passion in him, where I hadn't been able to see it in the Klahari. He gestured as they had, but he gestured in one direction that they had not gestured, and that was back the way they had come to the Strongpoint, back toward the now overrun fields of his family farm, the deep jungle and the desert beyond. Twice more, I caught in his speech the phrase he had used to answer the second and third native speakers—and finally it stuck in my head:

"K'ahari tomagna, manoi . . ." —or that at least was what it sounded like to my human ear. I sat back, staring at him through my binoculars, for his face was as white as if all the blood had drained out of it; and suddenly, without warning, tears began to brim out of his eyes and roll down his cheeks—silent tears that did not interfere with the violence of his words but continued to roll as if he were being secretly tortured all the while he was speaking. The words poured out of him to the listening natives below—and suddenly I was understanding him perfectly.

For a second I thought it was some kind of miracle. But it was no miracle. He had simply broken into English, without apparently realizing it. It was English geared to the rhythm of the Klahari speech:

". . . I am a man. This is a terrible place and my mama did not want to stay here. My daddy did not like it here, but he was making me rich. Nobody works harder than my daddy, Pelang. I don't want to stay here. I will go home and be rich with the old people above Lac St. John; and never see any more K'ahari and the jungle. And the K'ahari will go back to the jungle because a man don't let himself be pushed from his crops. No, you don't get away with that, and you don't come into this Strongpoint, because I am a man and I don't let the K'ahari in. . . ."

He went back into their tongue, and I lost him. He went on standing there with the tears rolling down his face, no doubt telling them over and over again in Klahari that he would not surrender the fort to them. He wound up at last with the same phrase I had heard before; and finally, this time, I understood it, because it was so simple and because of what he had said.

"K'ahari tomagna, manoi!"—"I am no brother to the Klahari, but a man!"

He turned with that and jumped down off the top of the wall to the catwalk inside and crouched there, immediately. But no crossbow bolts or lances came over the wall. He went crouched over to the steps at the point where the walls made a corner and went down the steps to back before the awning. There, he pulled the scanners showing the outside views of all four walls into a battery facing him, and sat down on a camp chair with his rifle over his knees, looking at them.

On his scanners as on mine, the Klahari were fading back into the jungle. After they had all gone, there was silence, and after a little he wiped his eyes, laid down his rifle, and went to get himself some food. As if he knew that since they had not attacked immediately, they would not attack again for some little time. I sat back in my treetop with my head spinning.

I remembered now how I had seen the boy walking his own plowed fields as a Klahari walks. I remembered how his reaction to being under possible attack alone at the place, and even his reaction to the killing of his mother, had baffled me. I understood him better now. The jungle with its Klahari was something he took for granted, because it was the only world he had ever known. Not Earth, the place he had only heard about, but this all around him was the real world. Its rules were not human rules, but Klahari rules. Its normal shape was not the grass and sun of home, but the searing white light and fern and macerated earth of Utword. He believed his father and the rest of us when we talked about how alien Utword, and its people were—but they were not alien to him and it was the only world he had.

Now the Klahari had come calling on him as a brother to take up his birthright, by joining them and opening the Strongpoint to them. So that they could destroy it and move on against the rest of the human outposts. He had refused to do so, and now he was down there, alone. The thought of his aloneness abruptly was like a hard shock all through me. Alone—down there with the body of his father and the other men, and the Klahari outside, ready to attack again. I told myself that I had to get him out of there, whether I got myself killed trying or not.

The only reason I did not start down the tree trunk right then in broad daylight was that I wanted some kind of a plan that had at least a faint chance of success. I was not concerned about saving myself, but I did not want to waste myself—for Jean's sake. I got up and paced my comfortable, safe perch, two paces each way, swing, and back again . . . thinking hard.

I was still at it, when the Klahari assault came. An explosion of yells and noise almost right under me. I jumped for the scanners.

Jean was standing with his back to the west wall of the watchtower, his own bank of scanners before him, handling all the rifles in all the walls on remote automatic. If the rifles had not been self-loading, as they were, not a half-dozen years before, he never could have done it. But as it was, he stood holding the Strongpoint alone, a faint frown of concentration on his face, like a boy back home running a model train around its track at speeds which come close to making it fly off on the curves. Two of the attackers made it over the wall hidden from him by the watchtower at his back;

but still it seemed as if he had eyes in the back of his head, because he abandoned his scanners, turned and crouched with a rifle in his hands, just as they came together around the side of the watchtower after him. The lance of the second one he shot thudded against the wall of the watchtower just above his head before the native fell dead. But Jean's face did not change.

The assault failed. The natives drew off, and Jean abandoned his scanners to go to the heavy task of dragging the two dead Klahari back around the corner of the tower out of his way. He could not have dragged grown men that way, but the Klahari are lighter-boned and -bodied than we, and by struggling, he got them cleared away.

There was another, lighter assault just before sundown that evening, but none of the natives got over the walls. Then darkness covered us—and still I had worked out no plan for getting the boy out of there.

My general idea was to get him away, and then leave the gates of the Strongpoint open. The Klahari would enter, ravage the interior and move on—to points better equipped than we to continue the fight with them. Perhaps, with the Strongpoint taken, they would not look around for Jean—or me.

But I was helpless. I raged in my treetop. Up here and unnoticed, I was safe as I would have been at home on Earth. But let me descend the tree trunk, even under cover of darkness and I would not live thirty seconds. It would be like coming down a rope into an arena jammed with several thousand lions. Dawn came ... and I had thought of nothing.

With it, came the post-dawn attack. Once more, Jean fought them off—almost more successfully than he had the attack of the evening before. It was as if his skill at anticipating their actions had been sharpened by the pressure on him to defend the Strongpoint alone. He even walked away from his automatic rifle controls in the heat of the battle to shoot a Klahari just coming over the north wall.

There was a noon attack that day. And an evening one. Jean beat all of them off.

But that night I heard him crying in the darkness. He had crawled back under the awning, not far from the body of his father, and in the gloom next to the ground there, I could not pick out where he lay. But I could hear him. It was not loud crying, but like the steady, hopeless keening of an abandoned child.

When dawn came I saw his face seemed to have thinned and pinched up overnight. His eyes were round and staring, and dusted underneath with the darkness of fatigue. But he fought off the dawn attack.

A midday attack was beaten back as well. But I had not seen him eat all day, and he looked shadow-thin. He moved awkwardly, as if it hurt him; and after the midday attack was beaten off, he simply sat, motionless, staring at and through the scanners before him.

Just as the afternoon was turning toward evening, the Klahari calling from the jungle came again. He answered with a burst of automatic fire from the wall facing toward the location of the voice in the jungle. The voice ceased as abruptly as if its possessor had been hit—which he could not have been.

The evening attack came. A full eight Klahari made it over the walls this time, and although Jean seemed to be aware of their coming in plenty of time to face them, he moved so slowly that two of them almost had him.

Finally, this last and hardest assault of the day ended, with the dropping of the sun and the fading of the light. The lights inside the Strongpoint came on automatically, and Jean abandoned his scanners and controls to crawl under the awning. As with the night before, I heard him crying, but after a while the sounds ceased, and I knew that he had gone to sleep at last.

Alone, safe in my treetop, still without any plan to save the boy, I drifted off to sleep myself.

I woke suddenly to the sounds of the dawn assault. I sat up, rubbed my eyes—and threw myself at the scanners. For on the screen of the one with its view under the awning. I could see Jean, still stretched in exhaustion-drugged slumber.

Already, the Klahari were at the walls and clambering over them. They poured into the open area before the watchtower as Jean woke at last and jerked upright, snatching up his rifle. He looked out into the semicircle of dark, staring faces, halted and caught in astonishment to find him unready for them. For a second they stood staring at each other—the Klahari and the boy.

Then Jean struggled to his feet, jerked his rifle to his shoulder and began firing at them. And a screaming wave of dark bodies rolled down on him and bore him under . . .

Behind them, more Klahari warriors all the time were swarming over the walls. The gates of the Strongpoint were torn open, and a dark, feathered and bejeweled river of tossing limbs and weapons poured into the open area. Soon, smoke began to rise from the buildings and the flood of attackers began to ebb, leaving behind it the torn and tattered refuse of their going.

Only in one area was the ground relatively clear. This was in a small circle around the foot of the watchtower where Jean had gone down. Among the last of the Klahari to leave was a tall, ornamented native who looked to me a little like the third of those who had spoken to Jean before the wall. He came to the foot of the watchtower and looked down for a moment.

Then he stooped and wet his finger in the blood of Jean, and straightened up and wrote with it on the white, smooth concrete of the watchtower wall in native symbols. I could not speak Klahari, but I could read it; and what he had written, in a script something like that of Arabic, was this:

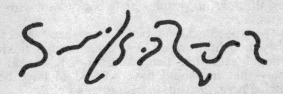

—which means: *"This was one of the Men."*

After which he turned and left the Strongpoint. As they all left the Strongpoint and went back to their jungles. For Jean's last two days of defending the place had held them just long enough for the season to end and the year to change. At which moment, for the Klahari, all unsuccessful old ventures are to be abandoned and new ones begun. And so the threat that had been posed against all of us humans on Utword was ended.

But all ends are only beginnings, as with the Klahari years and seasons. In a few weeks, the planters began to return to their fields; and the burned and shattered Strongpoint that had been besieged by forty thousand Klahari was rebuilt. Soon after, a commission arrived from Earth that sat for long talks with the mature Klahari of the cities and determined that no new planters would be allowed on Utword. But those that were there could remain, and they with their families would be taboo, and therefore safe from attacks by young Klahari attempting to prove their jungle manhood.

Meanwhile, there being no other heirs on Utword, the Duprès property was sold at auction and the price was enough to pay for the shipping of the bodies of Pelang and Elmire home for burial, in the small Quebec community from which they had emigrated. While for Jean, a fund was raised by good people, who had been safe in the Regional Installations, to ship his body back along with his parents'.

These people did not believe me when I objected. They thought it was all I had been through, talking, when I said that Jean would not have wanted that—that he would have wanted to have been buried here, instead, in his father's fields.

> *"The perisht kernell springeth with increase*
> *The lopped tree doth best & soonest growe."*
> —Robert Southwell

BREAKTHROUGH GANG

Breakthrough Gangship No. Four hung in interstellar space, one and a half light years 'down'—i.e., toward Galactic Center—from the Kinsu solar system. She was one and a half light years away from the situation now developing, as the Driver Gangships, with forty unmanned mech dreadnaughts on slave circuits apiece, engaged the mass of manned Kinsu warships and drove them back into the Kinsu home solar system.

Breakthrough Gangship Four, with her own twenty-four mech ships, was on bolthole duty. She was holding a steady position with regard to the Kinsu system, a single shift of eight crew members on duty at her instruments in Main Room and Instrument Room—the other three shifts on standby. There was no reason to expect any unusual trouble.

"—Hold it!" snapped **Dave Larson**, her Tactician, without warning. *"All hold!"*

The three other shift members on duty in the main room of the ship reacted automatically, damping all channels of mechanical and human transmission from the ship. But then they spun about in the swivel chairs before their instrument boards to stare at Dave.

"What is it?" demanded Hallie Suboda, tightly.

It was the question in all their minds. But it was Hallie's right to ask it first. For Hallie, despite her pert face under its dark helmet of hair that made her look more like a schoolgirl than a Mech shipmember, was currently in command of the vessel. Not merely because she was the leading 'sensitive' aboard—they were all sensitives of one order or importance or another—but because her sensitivity was momentarily of most value to the ship. Hallie was Contact member of this shift. In this moment when the Gangship was out of the battle and waiting, she was the only one fully engaged with the minds of the enemy. If anyone should have been likely to have signalled an emergency situation, it should have been she.

Of course, the signal was possible to others in the Main Room as well. Jafe Williams, as Coordinator of the shift, could have discovered an internal ship's problem requiring a hold. Marge Lacey, occuping the Alien Sociologist's chair, might have uncovered some potentially dangerous factor in the Kinsu retreat. These were possible, barely possible.

But Dave was Tactician—and Breakthrough Gangship Four was not even yet potentially in conflict with the Kinsu forces. All Dave was supposed to be doing at the moment was keeping track of the tactical shape of the distant battle as it developed, figuring ahead into the possibilities, for possible troubles or advantages.

"Blank spot," said Dave now, tersely. He had not been idle since he had spoken and he was not idle now. His fingers were flying over the board in front of him, correlating the physically-received data on the Kinsu situation with the shaping pattern of the insight in his mind.

"Blank spot . . . ?" began Hallie. "But how can there be a blank spot?"

"Blind spot, then! Shut up, will you?" snapped Dave. He had a lean pleasant, ordinarily cheerful face with a crown of whitish-blond hair—but now his features were unexpectedly savage. Hallie fell silent and, with the other two in the Main Room of the Gangship, sat watching him as his fingers continued to fly and his face to stare fixedly at his instruments.

Finally, his fingers slowed. He sat back from his board, staring at it, then slowly seemed to become conscious of the rest of them in the room. He swung his chair around to face the rest of them who were all now sitting with their backs to their damped boards, watching him.

"Oh—sorry, Hallie," he said, like someone coming out of a nightmare to realize that he had been fighting his awakener.

"That's all right," said Hallie, frowning. Mental Privacy was a rigid rule aboard the Gangships; but Hallie was a Contact, and more than that, she was in love with Dave. Certain overtones from his thoughts and emotions leaked through to her, regardless—and these had already warned her that it was no small thing that had made him call a hold.

"I don't know what it is . . ." said Dave grimly. "There's an influencing factor on this tactical situation that goes outside."

"Outside?" said Jafe, the Coordinator. "How far out?"

"I . . ." Dave stumbled. "I don't know.—All the way."

"All the way!" echoed Marge Lacey from her

Alien Sociologist's chair. "Dave! What's that supposed to mean? It's like saying 'out to the end of infinity' or 'right to the end of up'!"

"I can't help it," said Dave, his mouth line thinning stubbornly. "I tell you it's a tactical factor stretching out beyond my perceptive limits, and I get the feeling it goes all the way to . . . whatever."

"Does it go far enough back to involve itself with the internal tactical pattern of Earth—I mean the pattern of logical interaction of the people back home?" asked Hallie, sensibly.

"Yes," said Dave, reluctantly. He hesitated again. "It goes further."

"Further!" said Jafe. His dark sharp-featured face stared almost suspiciously at Dave. "Do you feel all right?"

"Of course I feel all right!" snapped Dave. He started to put a hand to his head before he realized what he was doing, then he jerked the hand down. "I'm in full possession of all my faculties and perceptions! It's just that—if it's hard for you to believe this, what do you think it's hitting me like? I tell you . . ."

"Just a minute," interrupted Jafe. With an internal problem now occupying the ship, he was now in command rather than Hallie. "Hallie, we can't drift like this without Contact while we hold a debating session. Break your hold and put us in touch while we catch up with the battle situation." He glanced back at Dave. "That means you, too."

"Right," said Dave.

They all swung back to their boards. For a moment Hallie reestablished Contact, and for perhaps thirty seconds, they were all very busy, bringing their particular areas up to the moment in information.

"All right," said Jafe. The Kinsu warships were still retreating and had perhaps an eighth of a light year to go before they would have to break, one way or another. "Back to Dave then." They all swung their chairs around and Dave faced them across the center of the small room. "Now, Dave," said Jafe, "you've got to give us some idea of why you called this hold."

"All right," said Dave. "Take a look for yourself!"

It was an indication of the seriousness of the situation that he should invite them into his mind. They hesitated, then stepped in. There was a long moment of silence in the room and then Hallie, herself, shook her head.

"It's no good," she said.

With Hallie's admission of defeat, Jafe and Marge sat back, shaking their heads. If Hallie, who was not only their best Contact, but had an emotional bond with Dave, could not make sense out of what was in his mind, there was little hope that they could. The difficulty was, of course, that none of them were Tacticians. They could 'read' the situation as Dave's mind saw and showed it to them, but they could not understand what they 'read' —any more than a man can understand a highly technical explanation of a situation in a field to which he has been neither trained nor educated.

"Get another Tactician up here," suggested Hallie.

"Of course!" Jafe snapped his fingers angrily at not thinking of this himself. He jabbed a stud on the instrument board before him. Less than sixty seconds later, a tall, brown-faced individual stuck his head into the Main Room.

"You wanted a Tactician?" he asked Jafe.

"Right, Billy," said Jafe. "Check with Dave, here, will you? He's got something he can't explain to us."

Billy Horgens nodded and looked over at Dave. Their eyes met and held while a slow minute more went by. Then their gazes broke apart, and Billy shook his head, turning to Jafe.

"No go," he said.

"What do you mean, no go?" demanded Jafe. He interrupted himself, swinging around to face Hallie. "What's going on with the Kinsu?"

Hallie hooded her eyes with the dark lashes of her eyelids. For a moment the more-than-a-light-year distant ships filled with squat, yellow-furred forms became more clear around her than the Gangship itself. Then, she opened her eyes fully and turned back to Jafe.

"Still pulling back to their own solar system," she said. "They don't believe they're completely trapped, yet."

"How soon until they do?" asked Jafe, swinging on Dave, who had immediately integrated this latest information with his picture of the situation, as had everyone else in the room.

"Seven minutes—maybe less, maybe a little more. They'll be trying a breakthrough in eight minutes max," said Dave.

"All right." Jafe reached up to set the stop clock on his board. "We've got five minutes then, to get to the bottom of this hold of yours. If the Kinsu break toward some other Gangship, maybe it won't matter if we solve it or not. But if they come this way, I don't want us worrying about some unknown —or unexplained—" he looked at Dave, "factor."

He swung back to face Billy.

"Now, just what do you mean? No go?"

"Just that," answered Billy, laconically. "Sorry, Jafe. But you know that Dave's the most powerful Tactician aboard. That's why he's on your first shift, instead of being on one of the other shifts with the rest of us. You're taking a problem that your best man can't give you an answer on, and handing it to your Number Two boy for solution. Well, I can't do it. If I could, I'd be on the first shift, and Dave'd be on the second."

"Can you see what he says is there?" snapped Jafe.

"I can see . . . something, now that Dave's pointed it out to me," said Billy. "But what it is, whether I really see it or whether Dave's pointing it out has made me imagine it, I don't know."

"Would you be able to tell us what you do see?" put in Hallie, gently. Billy threw her a grateful glance.

"All right," he said. "It's a massive decisive factor, running back beyond this battle with the Kinsu, beyond the Earth situation behind it. And," Billy hesitated, "unless I'm wrong, back behind that into time, back out of sight."

"Back out of sight in time!" Jafe jerked his head up as if to glare Billy out of countenance. "But that's impossible. We only decided to fight the Kinsu a year and a half ago. We only knew about them fifteen years ago!"

"That's it," said Billy unhappily.

"Twenty years ago," put in Marg, "we didn't even know there were any intelligent aliens within two hundred light years of Earth, let alone that they were hostile, let alone that they'd attack us on sight."

"Sorry," said Billy. "I can't explain it, I'm just telling you what I read."

"Dave—" Jafe turned back to him. "If Billy can tell us that much, you can tell us more!"

"Yes. But . . ." Dave wet his lips and glanced unhappily, almost apologetically at Hallie. "I don't know if I should—on my own."

"Don't know if you should!" Jafe's eyes were like brown stones. "In less than ten minutes the Kinsu may be breaking through right on top of us; and if there's an unknown tactical factor it could cost us the lives of everyone on board here—or the whole war with the Kinsu, itself. And you say you don't know—"

"I mean it!" said Dave, doggedly. "I think . . . maybe we ought to contact Headquarters."

"Headquarters? Back on Earth. What for?"

"For . . ." Dave hesitated. "A general hold—until we know about this."

"A general hold? In the middle of a battle. Are you insane?"

"No," said Dave. He added bleakly, "That's what's scaring me, Jafe. I know you Coordinators can get through to HQ if you want to."

"Not," said Jafe, harshly, "until I know what this is all about."

"I don't know if I can tell you . . ." Dave's eyes flickered to the sweep-second hand of the stop clock over Jafe's head, the clock Jafe had set on five minutes to place a time limit on their solution of this problem. Fully two of those minutes were already gone. Three remained. And, in a tight crescent formation, less than one and a half light years distant, now, the human mech forces were pounding the Kinsu warships back toward the planets of their own alien system. Soon, the Kinsu would see that there was no hope of stopping the human advance, and their commanders would try to break through and away, saving as many of their war-ships as possible to fight again some other day. It would be then that Gangship Four with its forty automated mech dreadnaughts would be all that stood between the manned Kinsu vessels and escape, if they broke this way. Once free, the aliens could carry on the war for years yet. Or even try to hit Earth itself in retaliation.

None of this must happen. It was the mission of Breakthrough Gangship Four, in that eventuality, to block the Kinsu escape like a lone tackler between the enemy runner and the goal line. It would be their duty to hold the superior numbers of the escaping ships until help came to contain them. For only if the Kinsu ships were completely englobed, completely defeated, would the arrogant Kinsu character be broken sufficiently to permit them to surrender unconditionally, rather than fighting to the last alien.

The outcome of the whole battle might depend on this one Gangship. It might all hang on his own refusal or inability to make clear this vital tactical factor to his fellow crew members. It was a time for clear, sharp decision. And yet . . . Dave shivered, visualizing the massive, far-reaching enigma of the factor he visualized—

"Try!" Jafe was snapping. "Do I have to make it an order, Dave?"

"No. I'll try," said Dave, unhappily. He examined the overall network of the tactical situation and the massive factor that was troubling him, striving to resolve it somehow into words. It could not really go into words, of course, any more than a situation in multidimensional mathematics could be reduced to words.

"Look," he said, after a long second of thought, "I want you all to think.—Consider something. Maybe a hundred thousand years ago we were stone-age men, just finding out how to make fire. A little less than three thousand years ago, about eight hundred B.C., the Egyptians were cracking through to make iron. Three hundred and some years ago, we were getting steam engines to work for us. A hundred and fifty years ago, we came up with the airplane. Seventy-five years ago, we put a man on the moon. . . . Anybody see what I'm driving at?"

He looked around the room, at the three seated there and at the standing Billy. But even Billy's eyes showed no light of understanding.

"I'll go on," said Dave grimly. "Fifty years ago, we made it to Alpha Centauri and back. Thirty years ago we had outposts on planets nearly a hundred light years from home. Fifteen years ago we encountered the Kinsu, who'd been in space since about the time our ancestors were knocking two rocks together for the first time and noticing that the pretty sparks started a fire. A year and a half ago we decided to give up trying to make peaceful contact with them, and decided to wage our first interstellar, spatial war. Three ship-days ago, we met their front line warships beyond the Pleiades, with a completely revolutionary new concept of space warfare.—Twenty to forty sensitive and highly trained individuals to each Gang of twenty to forty automated fighting vessels, as a base combat unit. A battle plan aimed not at destruction of the enemy forces but at breaking the emotional strength of character of our enemy. And a system of tactics built upon the purely human psionic abilities that our opponent did not possess."

Dave paused and looked around. They were all watching intently, and listening, but he saw no sudden kindling of comprehension in their eyes.

"Look what's happened," Dave went on desperately. "The Kinsu have been retreating from the first moment. Half an hour from now we ought to have this race of intelligent aliens who overran other worlds beside their own while our ancestors were still scratching in the dirt with a pointed stick—we'll have them not just conquered, but *broken*, and subjected by weapons of the human mind they can't match because they're not human." He glanced desperately at the clock which now showed less than a minute left of the five Jafe had set it for.

"Don't any of you see what I'm driving at?" Dave pleaded.

"You mean," said Billy slowly, frowning, "that it's too much weight of odds to be accumulated on one point of tactic. But—"

"No, you mean it's too good to be true, don't you?" interrupted Hallie, swiftly. "You mean things have gone too well and too fast for us, from the stone age to now—so that things have been too perfect and now we have to pay the price? Is that what you mean?"

"No. I—" burst out Dave. "I don't know—I can't explain what I mean." He looked stubbornly, grimly at Jafe. "I want to talk to Headquarters!"

"What can you tell Headquarters, you can't tell us?" demanded Jafe.

"I don't know! Maybe they know something about this factor already!"

Jafe sat for a second, just looking at him.

"Suppose I call Headquarters," he said, finally. "—just suppose it. I'm not saying I will. But suppose I did and told them what you've just told us— that the human race seems to have developed too fast to its present state of strength. And that this seems to you to create a massive, dangerous tactical factor involved in the present situation.—What do you suppose they'd say? 'Put your man on right away, this sounds vital!'—or—'Sounds like your number one Tactician's had a nervous breakdown, better replace him with number two!'?"

"You could try it," said Dave stubbornly.

"I think you're holding something back," said Jafe. His face twisted unhappily as he said it, for the words came out like an accusation. But it was the only way he knew to run things, he told himself desperately. He was aware that he did not have Dave's instinctive likeableness, just as he was aware that Dave was—with the possible exception of Hallie—the most powerful sensitive aboard the ship. "Tell me one thing," Jafe wound up, almost pleadingly, "tell me what this factor of yours can do to us in this battle, if the Kinsu try to break through in our area, here!"

Dave opened his mouth and then shut it again.

Jafe turned to the Number Two Tactician.

"Billy?" he demanded.

Billy looked unhappy. He glanced at Dave.

"Sorry, Dave," he said. He turned to Jafe again.

"According to what Dave showed me—what's bothering him can't hurt the battle with the Kinsu. It . . ." he hesitated in his turn. "It might very well help us with the Kinsu from what I read of it."

Jafe swung back to face Dave.

"I can't contact Headquarters on that," he said. "Dave, do you want to be relieved by Billy, here?"

"What good would that do? Do you think what I read'll go away, just because I'm not on duty—?"

"If it's not a factor," snapped Jafe, "that can keep us from winning over the Kinsu, then it can wait until we've won and got back to Earth and Headquarters in person. I'll go over personally with you, then—"

"But that's just it!" Dave half-shouted. "It *can't* wait until then. If we wait until after we beat the Kinsu, it may be too late—"

"*Breakthrough!*" cried Hallie, the high notes of her voice cutting like a razor slash through the deeper-toned male argument. "Breakthrough, our sector. Stations! All stations manned! All stations manned!"

She was once more in command, and her mind as well as her voice was broadcasting her orders to all corners of the ship. There was no delay in answering. The crew, forseeing a breakthrough in Gangship Four's direction, were all awake and alert, and waiting. Immediately, the four on duty in the main room were swinging around to their instrument boards. At the same time the walls of the room itself were folding outward like the petals of a flower, to reveal a larger, surrounding chamber ringed with twenty-eight other seats and instrument boards—each one linking whoever would operate it with one of the twenty-four first-line automated ships controlled by Gangship Four.

All twenty-four off duty members of the Gangship crew were now pouring into these seats—their sensitivities now, and for the duration of the conflict with the escaping Kinsu warships, directed to the job of fighting one of the automated ships through linkage with the mech brain of the ship. It would be a cruder job than a shift at one of the four chairs in the Main Room or one of the four in the Instrument room aft, but a more dangerous and demanding one. Identification with the mech ships was almost as complete as identification with the parts of their own living human bodies. And destruction to the ship they controlled could bring severe, possibly fatal, psychic shock to the operator.

The outer ring of seats was almost filled. The four on duty in the Main area were still at their original duties.

"Four minutes to estimated collision area!" chanted Hallie. "Four minutes. Enemy force, a hundred and thirty-one fully armed vessels. Sixty-even, dreadnaught class. Thirty-nine, cruiser class. Twenty-five lesser classes. Kinsu Command ordering breakthrough at any cost. At any cost!"

By this time mech control seats of the outer ring were all filled, and the crew members in them had their own picture of the oncoming Kinsu through instruments and their own sensitivities. The Kinsu on their part were aware of Breakthrough Gangship Four with its twenty-four fighting mech vessels; and the aliens were approaching this small picket in space with the same formation from which they had just fled in the shapes of the human Main Battle Fleet. That formation was the crescent line of attack, most practical for a superior force approaching conflict with an inferior force which could be first encircled, then englobed.

"Three and a half minutes to collision area . . ." Hallie's voice was dominating the rest of the listening, ready crew. "Prepare for timal discontinuity. Prepare timal discontinuity, all vessels including Gangship."

It was the order to use the weapon that was the

newest of those in the human arsenal. So new, that it was as yet no real weapon, but a device for attacking enemy morale. It had been held in reserve for just this moment of attempted breakthrough by the survivors of the defeated Kinsu forces, who for centuries had been so used to thinking of their power and numbers as overwhelming that they could not consciously entertain thoughts of the situation possibly being otherwise.

—Such rote-confidence, the new 'sensitive' sociologists of the human race had said, must invariably imply an area of psychological blindness that could be used to destroy the race that possessed it. The belief in an unquestionable superiority would be like some small object, held ever closer to the organ of vision as time went on, that would progressively block out the perceptual area. His efforts, hidden in that blocked-out area, an opponent could prepare unseen until the time came to smash the long-held belief with overwhelming evidence of its falsity.

Once smashed in that fashion, the Kinsu murderous-suicidal arrogance would be completely destroyed. He would have no psychological strength for anything but surrender.

The crew now swung into action at Hallie's words—when there was an unbelievable interruption.

"Hold!" they heard the voice of Dave, shouting. "Hallie, you're in command, now. Call Headquarters.—I know you don't know how to route the call the way Jafe does. But call anyway. They'll have to answer!"

The crew, caught in the midst of vital activity, checked only for a second, then went on. They could not spare the time to stop, or look at Dave, or do anything but listen with half an ear. But an emotional shock wave went through the expanded room at his words.

"No, Dave," said Hallie, without raising her voice or without turning around. "—Time discontinuity, preparation, report!"

"Ready! Ready! Ready . . ." the answers came back from the larger circle of crew, as each one of them keyed in the necessary equipment aboard his mech ship.

"Hallie!" Dave's voice climbed a note. "Can't you listen to me? I can read it even clearer now! Stop what you're doing and call Headquarters! We mustn't stop the Kinsu breakthrough. We mustn't win, now! Do you hear—"

"Billy," said Hallie, without turning her head, "replace Dave in the Tactic chair. That's an order, Billy—"

Behind her there was the sudden scurry of feet across the Main Room floor and a sudden clatter and cry from Jafe. Hallie swung around, to see Jafe sprawling on the floor and Dave standing over him, holding the pistol that the duty Coordinator was required to keep in the drawer under his instrument board.

"Stand back—everybody!" said Dave. "Hallie, tell them to stop. No more action!"

Her eyes met his, and he saw they were glistening with tears, but her voice was steady.

"Ready!" she said, as if he had never spoken, "Time discontinuity, in effect—*now!*"

All around the circle, crew members depressed a purely instrumental switch. The time discontinuity apparatus required no mental involvement in its workings, although it had grown out of psionic researches into the nature of time. Suddenly, to the perceptions of the Kinsu instruments, the space around the forty-one ships of Breakthrough Gangship Four was filled with a crescent formation of hundreds of other ships identical in shape and size—it was as if the whole human space navy that had harried them to the boundaries of their home system, had suddenly contrived to reappear from the scene of the main battle, where a rearguard action was still going on, and confront the escaping warships.

But that was impossible. And equally impossible was the fact that the suddenly appearing ships were some sort of fake or illusion. Kinsu instrument readings reported them not only as having mass and weight, but as containing the emanations of living, intelligent creatures of human size and shape.

Therefore all that was possible, incredible as even this seemed, (for the Kinsu knew Occam's Razor by another name) was that the humans had owned not merely one fleet vastly superior in size and numbers to the Kinsu warships, but two fleets. And this second fleet had somehow guessed or known where the Kinsu breakout would take place, so that they could appear in the crucial moment to frustrate it.

It was the end. The Kinsu command had been prepared to accept any losses to get even one or two ships free to strike some suicidal, if face-saving blow at the home human world. But in the face of such superiority, no alien ship could possibly escape; and the deaths of all of the remaining ships and their crews would be for nothing.

It was the last straw to the crumbling Kinsu rote-confidence in their own innate superiority over all other living creatures. The order to halt flashed out from the command ship, and the whole Kinsu breaking-out force checked their drive on Gangship Four.

"It worked!" breathed Hallie, momentarily diverted even from the fact of Dave, pistol in hand. And indeed, the timal discontinuity had worked. With a mechanical application of linear timal theory, the Gangship and each mech ship had evoked a dozen pre-images of itself in the position it had occupied at time intervals of a few minutes up to an hour previously. What the Kinsu had seen was the Gangship and its forty mechs in twelve different previous moments of time, simultaneously.

—And so, the Kinsu had halted. It was well they had—not because the pre-images were any less real than the Gangship and mechs of the present moment, but because the pre-images belonged to earlier moments in which they were merely cruising peacefully through vacuum, and were merely going through the motions they had already established. The pre-images could be shown to the Kinsu, but they could not be made to fight the enemy.

"—*Headquarters!*" Dave was now saying, out loud, while holding Jafe and everyone else at bay with the pistol. "*Headquarters, this is Number One Tactician of Breakthrough Gangship Four. Headquarters, if you hear me, come in! This is Tactician BG Four. Do not accept the Kinsu surrender. I repeat, do not accept the Kinsu surrender. . . .*"

He was sending blindly in the direction of the main battle human forces, and of Earth. It was a desperate, almost certainly futile, effort. Powerful as Dave's sensitivity was, it was like all such talents, geared to his individual personality. And his personality had shaped it into a tool directed—not outward as was Hallie's, in the way that made her fitted for Contact work even with alien minds over great distances—but inward, to the work of subjective insight on tactical problems. In trying to call Earth from their present position in deep space, he was like a champion weight-lifter trying to compete in an Olympic javelin-throw.

"*. . . Come in, Headquarters!*" he was pleading now, while even at the same time, elements from the main battle were driving swiftly toward the Kinsu break out ships, to accept their surrender. "*Come in, Battle Command, then—*" he broke off, suddenly white faced. "I can't get through! —Hallie, try it." Her eyes met his, pityingly. "No!" He shouted at her suddenly. "Don't you understand? Even I ought to be able to reach, intership, to our Battle Command. But I *can't get through!*" Hallie's eyes abruptly widened. Those aboard the ship felt her drive a sudden call outward, toward the approaching Battle Command. "—*Battle Command, this is Gangship Four. Are you in Contact with me? Are you in Contact—*"

She broke off, herself. Her eyes locked with Dave's.

"*I'm* not getting through!—Dave!" It was very nearly a cry of pure pain from her lips. Since Hallie had first become aware of her powers of Contact, she had never known any impediment or crippling of them other than that imposed by social custom or her own good taste. As a practical matter, it was impossible for her to be so far distant from her receiver that her call would be lost among attempts at Contact by nearer calling minds. But theoretically, the call itself went on forever, or until it reached its goal. Never before this had she felt failure.

"You see—" Dave was beginning.

"But I'm doing it to myself!" cried Hallie. Except in her own field, she had instantly identified what Dave had simply assumed was a failure of his lesser ability at Contact to penetrate some barrier. "Don't you feel it, Dave? It's as if I was under a post-hypnotic command not to make Contact! Jafe—you try!"

The Gangship, drifting in space while the Driver Gangs of the main human command drove in to accept the Kinsu surrender, was caught in sudden, strange silence. Jafe, crouched to spring on Dave, straightened up. His eyes went hooded, then widened.

"No!" he said. "Hallie, you're right. It's as if we've been conditioned, somehow!" He swung toward Dave. The whole crew was watching Dave, now. "Dave," said Jafe, almost fiercely, "maybe you were right. I . . . what's going to happen, now?"

"I don't know," said Dave. The now-useless pistol was hanging in his hand. He let it drop with a soft thud to the floor at his feet.

"You wanted Headquarters not to win. You wanted Battle Command not to accept the Kinsu surrender, Dave," said Hallie, white-faced. "Why? Do you know more about this factor you talked about now, than you did before?"

"Only . . ." Dave looked at her, and hesitated. He looked around at the other thirty crew faces watching him. "I think . . . we may have been through all this before."

For a moment there was a wash of silence so profound in the room, following his words, that they could all hear the roaring of the blood in their ears the way it is heard in a seashell held to the ear. Like the roaring of the seashell, this roaring seemed to tell them of a sea that rolled on through distances of time and space too great to be imagined.

"You don't mean just this war with the Kinsu, before!" said Hallie, suddenly. "You mean, things like this, that the human race has been through, and somehow forgotten, and. . . ." her voice dwindled and was swallowed in a sudden yawn . . . "You mean . . . Dave . . ."

A faint, sodden note of fright sounded in her abruptly sleepy voice. She struggled up out of her chair and made a faltering step toward Dave.

"Hal . . ." began Dave, stepping toward her as she went down. He made one more step and his knees were abruptly strengthless. But he stumbled one more step before they betrayed him and he fell. On hands and knees fighting the internal command that ordered him to stop, to slumber, he wrenched himself toward Hallie, reaching out as he collapsed, to finally catch hold of her fingertips. Then the room about him spun away into darkness.

Less than half an hour later, a strange, oblate spaceship coated with a surface that bent around itself nearly all radiation and signals, including those of the human mind, nosed like a fuzzy ghost up to the airlock of Gangship Four and opened its lock from the outside. Two fuzzy, moving clouds that would have baffled any eye that might have been there to see them, and speaking a tongue no human would have recognized, came through the lock into the ship, and into the central, expanded room where the crew slumbered. Small, perfectly visible, mechanicals scuttled after the moving clouds, and on orders from the fuzzy clouds began to collect the slumbering humans and carry them off to the other ship.

"Have you got the destructor?" one of the clouds asked the other. A stumpy, elephant skinned gray grasping pad brought a black, metallic object out of the other cloud into visibility. "Put it in the center of the floor, here. We want it to look like the ship got a direct hit."

The gasping pad placed the metallic object and withdrew into fuzziness of the second cloud.

"This one," said the second cloud, protruding a footlike appendage, gray and elephant-skinned to nudge the silent form of Dave, "it was this one who almost understood what was happening. Look—how it almost made it to this female here before the command carried down the generations in its genes put it to sleep. See, how they're touching each other?"

"You sound almost sentimental," said the first cloud. "They'll have plenty of time for touching when they wake—if they still know each other."

"Sentimental? Certainly not!" said the second. "With my choice of fifteen beautiful, endearing or useful pet races to be sentimental about, do you think I'd pick a pair of these wolves?" There was a pause. "Besides, as you say, they've got a long, happy life before them on some new world—provided they don't get eaten or have some accident."

"—Or fall sick. That's the largest cause of death among replants," said the first. "But these are fine, strong specimens. If the other stock crews do half as well as we have here ... By the way, does it seem to you they're healthier each time we replant them?"

"Yes—I've noticed that," said the second. "They thrive on this, apparently. And in spite of the genetics people saying that there can't be any knowledge leakage, they evolve a space going culture faster each time. Yes, and they civilize faster and come up with better weapons. Look at this 'sensitive' business the current crop here's come up with. I never heard of anything like that before. Did you?"

"No, can't say I have," said the other, turning to direct the mechanicals. The last of the crew at the mech control boards had been carried out, and the first cloud now directed the mechanicals to the four unconscious humans in the inner Main Room area.

"And that timal gap business—there's another brand new field they've come up with," went on the second, thoughtfully. "To say nothing of this new theory of conquest that finds the blind spot in another race's character and works within it. They're bursting with new tricks."

"Well, they'll have forgotten all about them, by the time they wake up where we're planting them," said the first. "They'll be stone age savages all over again—these breeding stock ones anyway. The ones we don't replant will fail in their productive cycle during their next three generations and painlessly eliminate themselves. You can't say we aren't humane."

"Oh, I know it's humane."

"Then, cheer up! In just a handful of centuries, their time, we'll have a fine new set of worlds to use with all the humans gone and the local predators, these Kinsu, nicely broken and tamed."

"—While these breeding stock ones begin the climb up to civilization again, on some new world salted with a fake of their own pre-history," said the second. "I know, But it bothers me."

"And you insisted you weren't sentimental!" The first turned to indicate Dave, the last of the humans to be transported, to a mechanical, who carefully lifted and carried off the lax, human figure.

"I'm not. I'm ... possibly a little ... well, concerned," said the second. "What if the geneticists are wrong and something of the learning process does leak over, and accumulate? What if a hundred thousand years from now, or less, our breeding stock have got to the point that this last individual here was almost at, where they begin to realize someone like us is using them to clear out other savage, animal races from desirable territory? Stop and think. They could be a nasty handful to deal with, even the way they are now, if they got to be aware of our existence."

"Let's go," said the other, turning and leading off back to their own ship. "—A nasty handful, maybe, but that's all. Anyway, it's a hundred thousand years or so off, human standard. Our next generation can worry about it."

"Maybe. But *they* might still surprise our children." Following the first out of the ship, the second stopped for a second and faced the other, who also stopped. "Did you notice that conquest theory of theirs depends on working inside another race's blind spot? What if we have a blind spot—like these Kinsu thinking that they didn't have to worry about any question to their superiority?"

The first was moved by, what passed in their race, for laughter.

"I don't see the humor of it!" said the second.

"All right," said the first. "What if the worst was true and you were right. Suppose we had such a blind spot. You're overlooking one point that makes the whole question academic."

"What?"

"Why, just that we actually are superior to all other races. And the sixteen others we've domesticated prove it."

There was a moment's pause while the answer sunk in, and then the second also was moved to laughter-response, a little shame-facedly.

"Of course!" he said. "You're right, as usual. You must think this business of human replantation is finally getting to me. Let's go!"

"Right. Back to our own ship and forget it!"

Reassured and quite refreshed by the fact that the doubt could now be put completely out of his mind, the second followed the first back out of the Gangship, that in a few seconds now would be destroyed completely. Lesser empires fail, thought the second to himself poetically—for he was something of a poet after the manner of his race—but ours endures forever. . . .

ETERNITY

MACK REYNOLDS
═WITH═
DEAN ING

Picture yourself in the arms
of a beautiful woman.
Suddenly you realize you
have made love to her
before. But that was
twenty years ago
and she hasn't
aged a day

256 pp   S2 95